C000203231

SHILLINGSTONE
STATION

Published by Honeybee Books
Broadoak, Dorset
www.honeybeebooks.co.uk

Copyright © Brent Shore 2015
Cover Illustration © Charlie Sutton

The right of Brent Shore to be identified as the author of
this work has been asserted by him in accordance with the
Copyright, Designs and Patents Act 1988.

No part of this book may be reproduced in any form or by any
electronic or mechanical means including information storage
and retrieval systems without permission in writing from the
author.

Printed in the UK using paper from sustainable sources

ISBN: 978-1-910616-36-9

SHILLINGSTONE
STATION

A Novel

Brent Shore

For my girls

PART ONE

EVENTS IN THE LIFE OF
EDWARD FLEET

1960

1

As the train lurched away with a muscular jolt from the dimly lit station, two raggedy figures barely managed to stop themselves falling into the compartment, propelled through the narrow doorway as if by a passing rugby forward.

"Watch where you're steppin', Tommy!" said the woman, turning back to glare from under a soft hat at the companion who had caught her heels. He was wearing a similar coat to hers, a dirty green waxed jacket, hanging open, and his balding head shone with perspiration.

"Sorry, my lover," he answered, peering from behind her bulky frame into the space occupied by a single passenger, a young gentleman in a dark suit sitting by the window with an open book in his hand.

"This'll do, Jessie," he went on, ushering her towards a middle seat opposite the fellow. "Put your basket up there in the rack and I'll get myself comfy here by you."

Very gradually the train picked up speed, thick clouds of smoke pushed high into the night sky above the locomotive, its steel wheels rolling ponderously over the rail-tracks heading south. Within seconds the couple had filled the space with the fetid smells of stale animal fat and cheap perfume.

Wiping a crumpled handkerchief over his brow and addressing the man who had only briefly looked up from his book to acknowledge their inelegant entry, the sweating man coughed and then spoke.

"Evenin', sir. Sorry to disturb you like that, I'm sure. Don't you worry, sir, you'll have some peace and quiet again very soon, if that's what you're after. The wife and me won't be on for very long, will we, Jessie? Next stop, that's ours. We'll leave you in peace at Stur."

"Don't worry, that's quite alright," replied the younger man curtly, his accent noticeably more refined than the unpolished Dorsetshire burr of the old couple. Edward Fleet was not averse to company, a short to and fro of conversation was welcome enough as a rule. In fact he had shared a pleasant dialogue with a rather plain but amiable and well-proportioned woman only a little older than himself, not to mention her bar of milk chocolate, during half an hour of her company shortly after changing trains to join the Somerset & Dorset line at Bath Green Park. At this stage of his long journey from Bristol on a rickety, draughty stopping train, however, the truth was that he was no longer in the mood to be gregarious. It was late October, it had been a gloomy sort of day from the start, and the afternoon light was already fading as his taxi had swung on to the forecourt at Temple Meads what now seemed an age ago; he simply wanted to reach his destination, to untie his shoes, loosen his tie and lie on his hotel bed with a large glass of Scotch.

There was a fragile moment of unease, the space between them filled with uncertainty. Edward sensed in the man an itch to communicate, yet for his part he could feel himself already losing interest. He tried to remember where he had left off his reading. Theatrically lifting his book, he smiled at the countryman and then looked away, back to his own reflection in the carriage window, the soft yellow glow of the electric lamps lending his face a surreal sheen. He swept his thick dark fringe back across his forehead and studied again how his left-sided parting looked oddly right-sided in the glass.

"We've been over to see the daughter and her fella."

The man, Tommy, was speaking to him again.

"And the new grandchild," chirped in his wife, who, having unbuttoned her raincoat, was now leaning back into her seat and kicking off her shoes with the ease of someone relaxing in front of the fire in her own parlour.

Basic politeness dictated that the least Edward should do was re-engage eye contact.

"That's nice," he said.

The woman returned a slightly crooked smile.

"They've got a nice little cottage by the market square in Stalbridge, they have. Since just a month ago gone. Rented elsewhere for a year or two afore that, didn't they, Tommy? You know the village, sir?"

"No. No, I don't," answered Edward with a patient smile. "I'm not from the area, as a matter of fact."

The woman's blank look seemed to demand some addendum.

"I'm a tourist, I suppose," he said.

"On your holidays, then?"

"I suppose so, yes."

"You'd like a smoke, wouldn't you, sir?" The man had pulled out a squashed packet of cigarettes from inside his coat and was offering a protruding one across the gap between the seats. It was a Woodbine, one of the foul gaspers that Edward had had the misfortune to inhale with some of the squaddies once on a training course.

"No, thank you. Very kind, I'm sure, but really, I don't."

I don't smoke shit like that, he wanted to say. *I'm a Rothmans man, filtered, naturally,* he wanted to say. *And smoke yours out there in the corridor,* he wanted to say, *with the window wide open, if you don't mind.*

Tommy struck a match, lit up his cigarette and sat back to enjoy it.

3

"Mild for the time o' year," he offered, exhaling harsh tobacco smoke towards the carriage ceiling. "For late October, I'd say."

Edward pretended not to hear.

"The boy's our first." It was suddenly the wife speaking again, looking up from a bunion beneath her sock.

"Is he?" enquired Edward passively after a deliberate hesitation.

"Little Joseph. Our first grandchild. Lovely little lad. Sweet-natured. Not a cryer at all. Just like his mother, ain't that right, Tommy? Just like Lucy was. No bother. No trouble, as a baby, was she, Tommy? You remember how very sweet-natured she was back along?"

The husband nodded and flicked a little ash on to the floor.

"Little Joseph's just the same. You got any family?" she prodded, looking straight into Edward's vacant eyes.

"Sorry?"

"Do you have little uns? At home somewhere?"

"Yes. Yes, I do. I have a small son."

"That's nice. A little boy, eh? Just a nipper, then? How old?"

Edward sighed without disguise and slowly opened his palm to indicate five.

"That's a nice age, isn't it, though?" she said. "I'm bettin' you spoil him, don't you? I can tell you're a proper family man, you're readin' a story there called *Mother*. Am I right?"

"Yes. In translation, sadly. It's about the Russian Revolution."

The woman looked puzzled.

"Oh," she said, with a blank smile.

Edward had never been averse to playing the intellectual superiority card. He could have added: *One of the Realists I never quite managed to finish when I was up at Cambridge*, but he had already achieved the desired effect.

"Leave the fella alone, Jessie," the husband said with a mock glare to his wife and a wink to Edward. "I'm sorry. My wife is a nosy beggar, and that's the truth. Give the fella a bit o' peace, love."

The woman, unnecessarily reprimanded in public, straightened in her seat and assumed a sulky expression. Edward was unconvinced that it wasn't an act. Ten more minutes under her interrogation and he would have found himself obliged to tell her his entire life story, never mind explaining what he was doing on the late train to Bournemouth West, holidaying alone, out of season.

*

The only son of a retired Tory MP from one of the more prosperous of the English shires, Edward Fleet was a professional undercover operative, he could have told her, working on behalf of Her Majesty's Government. He had never planned on becoming a spy, he could have added, but when his ambitions to join the Royal Navy Officer corps after Cambridge reached the antennae of the watchers, and when his philosophy tutor, the heroic Arundel (*Cooperman* to his acolytes), took him to one side, bought him a pint of Guinness in the snug in the Red Lion and whispered in his ear, the idea took root. When the special visitors to the Academy praised him for his fierce intelligence, his resourcefulness, his supreme clear-sightedness under pressure, and when he was made to understand his value to the Crown as both a ranking naval officer *and* a secret agent, then flattery and his own pride blended with a sense of duty made the decision as easy as it was inevitable.

The younger Edward Fleet, the slim, twinkly-eyed, loquacious student from Marlborough, had breezed into Trinity College with breathtaking confidence, a conscientious learner, a voracious reader of German then later Russian, and yet a chap with an eye always open for the pretty girl. With a couple of good-looking pals whose company he found amusing, he became one of the *flâneurs* of the streets around Newnham and Girton, and it took him very little time to earn a reputation as what was politely termed a *ladies' man*. Though he had been a decent athlete at school, he eschewed the sweaty, competitive masculinity of college sports and for a time developed the persona of an aesthete, *der junge Philosoph*. To attract attention he would play his favourite role as the devil's advocate. *Stalin in his time must be considered to be far less of a threat to Western civilization, whatever that might be, than Bonaparte ever was in his,* he liked to say, with the flourish of a sneer, to stir up a room. *There was more musicality in the works of Gershwin, Porter and Rodgers than anything in the entire Mozart oeuvre.* Or, flippantly, *One day the Japanese will thank the Americans for dropping an atom bomb on Hiroshima.* With some friends he joined a theatrical set, just for fun, happy to be led along by the drama students and play the joker in front of the dazzling young women.

It was in the January of his second year, at the very start of 1950, that the two émigré girls arrived, smuggled out of Soviet Latvia to be placed, at the financial cost to unknown benefactors, in the bosom of the English educational elite. Two strikingly blond sisters, Katarina and Erika, one year between them, both blisteringly intelligent, appeared together at a party for Newnham girls one frosty evening and Edward was determined within minutes of meeting them to have one, either, even both before the term was out. Katarina, the elder, was perhaps the more classically beautiful: eyes of sapphire, skin of silk, sharp symmetrical features below an angelic brow. Her English was superior too, and throughout the late winter months they became great friends, a golden couple. Separate college lives could not keep them apart for long; they walked, went together to pubs and concerts, recitals and galleries and parties, and there was nothing at all to stop them becoming furtive lovers. But Katarina had been too easy for Edward. In the summer term he ditched her for her sister as carelessly as he abandoned his winter coat and scarf.

Erika was more abrasive, elusive, not quite such a romantic cliché. She had hot sparks deep in her soul where Katarina had only sugared strawberries and custard. She affected a taste for little café-crème cigars, which he found amusing. She liked to provoke an argument with him, a sparky bout of verbal swordplay, which he found arousing. She despised Tchaikovsky as much as he revered him, she adored Beethoven with a passion equal to his conviction that the German's music was predictable and therefore drab in its composition. She was a follower of contemporary American cinema whereas he found it low-brow. He tried to convince her of the value of Italian renaissance art but she had little time for Catholicism in any guise. And so it went on. What brought them together, he supposed, was a shared sense of the absurd, a mutual physical attraction and a love of all things English. To him, Cambridge was the apogee of the civilised English way; to Erika, a Latvian girl with a mind full of questions, fleeing the locked society imposed by diktat from Moscow, England, with its freedoms and opportunities, with its fresh green lawns, with its tea and crumpets and its effortless good manners, with its cultured, dignified architecture seemingly bathed in permanent sunshine, this slice of England was to her simply the promised land.

Edward found that sex with Erika, a more defiant, wilful creature, was more rewarding, more intense. And it was the younger sister that, to no-one's surprise, he married in 1954, and although Katarina had since moved on, for she had men hovering over her like bees around summer lavender, her relations with her new brother-in-law were not quite so cordial ever again.

Edward Fleet's double life, working both for Her Majesty's Navy and quietly but rather more frequently these days for an indistinct section of the SIS, was no secret to his wife. Following his officer training he had served three months in the Mediterranean and then briefly on a patrol of the Red Sea and the Persian Gulf before they found him a small office in the Admiralty and an even smaller one in a draughty prefab in Portsmouth's naval dockyard. Exceptionally for a recruit of his age he was allowed on to the margins of strategic planning. From time to time he was absorbed into the secret world and became a ghost. He reported for training camps in Scotland, on the Suffolk coast, in the port city of Copenhagen. His instructions came predominantly from a quietly spoken intellectual of a man called Johnston, a fleshy Scot, dressed like a badly made bed but with eyes of ice and an intensity of stare to stop a clock. Edward listened to Johnston's wisdom with respect - he was indeed a man of substance who deserved it - but part of him guessed that although the Scot spoke the lines, they had been written for him in Cambridge by Cooper Arundel. Sometimes as he watched his lips move and the spittle fly from his mouth he heard only the soft West Country accented words of his mentor, and in his imagination, the Trinity clock-tower bell peeling in the background.

And what had been overwhelming at first, memorising lists of addresses, alphabetically ordered names, catalogues of codes (the absolute minimum to be ever written down), routes to safe houses, numbers of left luggage lockers, all was now second nature. He had his methods of communication, his tradecraft, his hiding places, his escape routes, his hardware, his protection, his instincts honed. He had been taught how to observe, how to act when being observed, how to draw attention and how to be inconspicuous, how to listen and how to make people listen to him. Johnston had issued him with ammunition and two firearms: a lightweight Browning for operations and an old army stock Webley Mark IV as an emergency back-up, which he had decided to grease up liberally, wrap in tight rolls of thick plastic tape and bury under the roots of a beech tree which shaded the headstone of his mother's grave in a quiet corner of Highgate cemetery.

Erika had been cleared by a security vetting team shortly before their marriage, his mission to undermine Soviet intelligence chiming perfectly with her unforgiving hatred of Russia. Whereas Katarina had suppressed her bitter memories of Latvia, a woman greedily breathing in the sweet air of the west in denial of her pain, Erika never let the fire burn itself out, her desire for revenge in check, cloaked, controlled but never extinct. Her father, Andris, the owner of a fish processing plant in Riga which had functioned satisfactorily throughout the war, even during the Nazi Occupation, had been forced to hand over operations in 1947 to a Soviet management committee. He had no option but to cooperate, but, fatally for him as it turned out, he was persuaded to join a secret resistance movement. Thousands of like-minded men and women were rounded up in the spring of 1949 and put on to goods trains bound for Siberia. Erika had never seen her father since the morning of his arrest when he had been ripped from his bed-sheets before sunrise. Her mother remained in Riga, a broken woman, aging visibly from one day to the next until she became shrunken and hollow and snowy-haired years before her time.

With regard to her new husband's role Erika was afforded only the broadest of brushstrokes with absolutely no fine detail, which suited everybody concerned. Post-war life in London was hard but she knew how lucky she was to be there. Although Edward's Russian was functional she helped him from time to time with technical papers. She did a little private teaching, bits and pieces of writing, mostly polemics on Baltic affairs for the émigré community, but ever since the first day of February 1955, Edward understood that the true centre of her life was a son. Andris Henry Fleet, born three weeks prematurely shortly after midnight at Charing Cross Hospital, Agar Street, WC1, was her focus, her flame, her very heart from that day on.

*

Edward Fleet allowed himself a smile of self-satisfaction. As far as he could tell his wife had everything that she needed. The boy was five years old and still seemed to take all of her attention. A second child had not been seriously considered. The woman could not share her love of their son with another. Not yet, anyway. She had little enough left for her husband as it was. Edward had seen this before in marriages: colleagues, friends of his whose wedding-day passions faded to the stale bread of drudgery when a child arrived. He still loved Erika, though their arguments, once a source of energy, a friction to light a spark, were becoming more surly and left only sullen, cold silences. No matter. He had made plans, he knew plenty of people who could introduce him to beautiful women, and his time in Denmark hadn't been taken up entirely with matters operational. He still knew how to set a girl's heart aflutter. He still kept a full address book out of sight, but not out of service.

The train had crossed the dark flat water of a river and was gradually coming to a rickety halt. The couple opposite, mercifully quiet for the past five minutes, were already standing to fasten their coats. Edward watched their reflected movements in the window, ostensibly peering into the darkness as the sparse street lights of the town began to give definition to houses, a garage, the shadows of a goods yard, a squat brick signal box. Sturminster Newton, he managed to read. The wife straightened her hat and fiddled with the strands of grey hair that protruded from beneath it while the husband lifted down the wicker basket from the rack. The contents were covered with a red and white gingham teacloth: fruit and vegetables, a cake perhaps, or something more sinister, Edward wondered in amusement.

"Goodbye," said the woman, refreshing the crooked smile. "You be havin' a nice holiday, won't you."

"This is our stop," added the man redundantly.

"Well, goodbye to both of you," offered Edward, turning his head towards them and adding a little half salute.

"Good evenin', sir," said the man, edging towards the compartment's outer door, placing his large leathery hand on the handle in anticipation. "Enjoy the rest o' your journey, now, won't you. Safe landin's."

*

The train sat at the platform for two or three minutes, its engine hissing like an ill-tempered cobra, doors being slammed shut, whistles being blown, several passengers coming and going. Edward Fleet had opened the compartment window as far down as it would go for a moment to let the cool air drift into the fug. Outside hung the smell of burning coal. He had watched the grandparents waddle off into the distance until they were out of sight, and he had studied the figures waiting to board. He could hear a group laughing loudly, settling into the compartment behind his: two young couples, he had noticed them skylarking on the platform, as if they had been drinking. Outside in the corridor nobody passed by, nobody appeared at his door to disturb him; he had the impression that the next compartment up ahead was empty. There was another shrill whistle from outside, he raised the window, another door banged shut somewhere down the line, and the tired beast once again flexed its muscles to haul the coaches, reluctantly it seemed, out of the station's patchy yellow light and onwards into the night.

Relieved to be sitting alone, Edward considered his features reflected in the window once again: he really did have the most perfectly noble nose. He straightened his tie and slipped the novel into a slim black attaché case half concealed between his body and the wall panel of the carriage. He had had enough of reading for the moment. The lighting in the compartment was poor and his eyes had grown weary from the strain. He rubbed them with his smooth, bent knuckles.

Suddenly the door from the corridor slid open with a harsh clack.

"Hello there. These seats aren't reserved or anything, are they?"

Edward refocused his eyes to take in a tall man in a dark grey business suit, about his own age, facing him from inside the door, an inquisitive smile on his thin, angular face.

"No. No, be my guest."

Where had this chap come from? He was smartly dressed, had short fair hair, an athletic gait, and Edward had seen nobody like him on the platform at the previous station. Had he decided to change seats, change compartments part way through his journey?

"I don't believe there are any reserved seats at all on this train," he added.

"Righto. Thanks," said the man, stepping briskly into the space between the banquettes. He was carrying a small matt black leather suitcase which, before taking the seat across from Edward that the countrywoman had vacated, he placed in the luggage rack above Edward's head, adjacent to his fellow traveller's caramel-coloured ELF-monogrammed valise.

"You're a businessman, like me, I suppose?" asked the man abruptly. Edward wanted a conversation with the newcomer no more than he had desired engagement with the grandparents.

"Yes, I am," he answered curtly, taking in the man's clothes and shoes in the same parabolic glance.

"Livingstone," said the man. "Fine china and glassware. Pleased to meet you."

He offered his hand across the diagonal divide. Edward coughed to clear his throat.

"Likewise, I'm sure. Fitzgerald," he lied. "Edwin Fitzgerald. Insurance."

The men shook, and having shaken, settled back into their seats and withdrew to their own thoughts.

The train was picking up a little speed, the land outside looked flat, as far as Edward could tell: dark empty meadows or arable tracts, distant lines of trees smudgily highlighted by a fleeting dabble of weak moonlight. He was not by nature a suspicious man but he had always been cautious and had been schooled by Johnston to notice inconsistencies in appearances. The man had pulled out a folded newspaper (he couldn't tell which, maybe a local evening edition) and now appeared to be engrossed in an article. To start with, he wondered why Livingstone hadn't placed his suitcase on the rack on his own side of the compartment, over his own head, instead of so close to Edward's. He had spoken in a modified northern accent: Yorkshire? Lancashire? Was there actually a difference? His suit was fashionable: slim lapels, two buttons on the jacket, good quality fabric. He had no coat. He appeared well groomed although was in need of a shave; was he one of those Neanderthal types that needed to use the razor twice a day? More of a puzzle were the man's shoes. Edward lived or died in classic brogues: black, chestnut or oxblood, they finished off a suit perfectly, nothing else would do, nothing else came close. This chap Livingstone was wearing what looked like black combat boots, brilliantly polished, granted, but who could tell how high above the ankle they were laced? Amusing, really. Was it a mark of bad breeding or deliberately inappropriate? Did it actually matter? He was losing interest and growing more and more impatient with the inability of the train to accelerate beyond a stately chug. An engine whistle hooted out into the night air.

Edward peered out of the window once more; they were crossing a river again, this time by a dark mill. The same river as before? In the reflection he noticed that Livingstone was looking over his newspaper up at the luggage rack bearing the pair of suitcases. Edward glanced wordlessly towards the other, who acknowledged the look with a resigned smile as though to share the burden of travelling long distances on local service railways. Edward looked away and began to daydream again.

A moment later Livingstone abandoned the newspaper and stood to reach up to the luggage rack above Edward's head. He seemed to be fiddling with the latches on his case. Edward raised his eyes to watch and then, not wishing to appear to pry, turned them back out towards the blurred dark shapes beyond the window. He sighed. He was hungry and bored.

Livingstone had dropped on to him before he knew it, the brute weight of the man pinning Edward's arms to his body.

"What the hell?" spat out the seated man, vainly trying to

sprawl free. He was nobody's pushover but the shock had winded him and the other man's left hand was rammed hard into his mouth just as he was forcing his knees up into his attacker's back. The fist rammed hard again. The harsh engine whistle pierced the air once more. He tasted blood and felt a tooth snap. Then a sharp pinprick as the man's right hand arced over and jabbed something pointed deep into his neck. A rush of smoke drifted past the window. Edward was choking, he felt his throat expand, heard the man's gasps and grunts, smelt his sweat in his bleeding nostrils, and as his limbs spasmed, as his heart stopped and his sight failed, the very last thing he heard, over the fading background of wheels on rails, was the sound of muffled laughter coming from the next compartment.

*

The instant Livingstone feels the life drain from his victim he springs back and closes the blinds on the compartment corridor windows and locks the door. He has very little time, as he knew he would: the whole operation depended on minute-lead action. By now the train is running across the farmland he had traced on the map he'd been given, entering the shallow cutting. Yes, he can see the moving lights of the carriages flickering over the contours of the grassy bank outside. Next comes the quarter mile of ditches where the line is raised, depressions in the ground covered in weeds, partially lined by bushes and trees. Praying that the group of friends in the next compartment are preoccupied in their inebriated amusement, he twists the handle on the outer carriage door and grips the frame to stop himself toppling out. The door catches the train's draught and bangs hard against the coachwork, the rush of air suddenly sweeps by the open space, the violent clattering of the wheels is magnified, and the smell of soot and the taste of smoke invade the compartment. With his feet wide apart for balance, Livingstone drags the limp body out off the seat and, before it slumps to the floor under its own weight, he manages to direct it to the doorway, and with a hefty grunt forcibly pushes it out into the void. He hears it catch the side of the carriage with a glancing bump and roll down the bank into the ditch like a huge rag-doll.

The ground will level out soon. Another engine whistle; with the door swinging open the note cuts through the darkness like a blade slicing a wound. Livingstone reaches up to the luggage rack, grasps the smooth handle of Fleet's case and hurls it into the darkness; it is caught by the draught and flies like a paper aeroplane. Until now he hadn't spotted the man's overcoat, a light woollen Crombie neatly folded beneath the case. He rolls it into a tight bundle and throws it as far as he can. The train clatters over a road crossing and on into a wood.

The final effort to lean into the wind and tug back the door takes all his strength. Fortunately the train is slowing down and the resistance drops fractionally. He pulls it to with as gentle a bang as he can, fastens the catch and falls back into his seat gasping for air, filling his lungs for a full thirty seconds, listening for sounds outside. The laughter in the next compartment has subsided; in its place he can hear the intonations of a more sober conversation. He reopens the blinds, unlocks the door and tries to compose himself. He notices that the tiny syringe has rolled on to the floor. He picks it up carefully and lays it in a small plastic case which he snaps shut and puts back into his jacket pocket. Also from the floor he retrieves a fragment of tooth and wraps it in a handkerchief, wiping a smear of blood from his knuckle with the cotton. The wrinkled, anonymous newspaper remains on the seat, announcing something unimportant about Mr Macmillan; it can stay there.

The train is rattling over a viaduct, braking now as it pulls in towards the little station at Shillingstone. He straightens his hair, smoothes down his jacket and stands to collect his own suitcase. No-one else is in the compartment with him. No-one else ever was. Fleet was not here. He never sat in that corner. There are no traces of the man.

Until Livingstone notices an attaché case which is now half-buried, wedged down the side of the seat by the force of their struggle. He cannot leave it on the train; someone would find it and raise the alarm. Nor can he be seen leaving the train carrying it. Stepping once again to the outer door he forces the window open to its limit and flings the flat leather case out across the fields. He knows there is a river out there running pretty much parallel to the track. If it hasn't reached the water it will land in the long grass. It's the best that he can do. Before he stops trying to imagine its trajectory, the train is already crawling along the narrow platform, tamely lit by sporadic paraffin lamps.

In his trouser pocket he hurriedly finds a black shapeless woollen hat which he pulls on to his head to cover his hair, his ears and his forehead right down to his eyebrows. Grabbing his suitcase, he has opened the door and is stepping off the train before it comes to its squealing halt. He is already running back along the platform, with neither time nor inclination to look at the faces in the window of the next compartment, a man and a woman observing him until he disappears from view. Other passengers are alighting here but not many. The station master watches him skip past, his double chin quivering like a soggy doughnut.

"What's the hurry, son?" he calls, directing the other travellers towards the footbridge to cross the track for the station exit. Livingstone knows that the way out is by the ticket office on the northern platform, but he has no time for such formalities. He also knows that the man in the tight S & D uniform is far too stout to start chasing after him.

"You can't get out that way!" he is shouting. "It's through the other side! Hey, come back here, damn you, I need to see your ticket!"

But sweeping well beyond the footbridge, beyond the furthest lantern, Livingstone is swallowed up in the gloom, and, where the platform has ended in a steep gravel slope, he climbs over the railings and, still gripping the suitcase, rolls down a long, greasy embankment, landing as if blind-folded in clumps of soft damp grass and thick nettles. He is at the edge of a dark, muddy field and has earned himself a moment to catch his breath. His hands are stinging, his heart is pounding like a landed eel, but, as far as anyone else is concerned, he is suddenly invisible.

2

Mary Abbott, the farm manager's daughter, loved this spot at Lamb House Bridge, under the heavy brick railway arch, hooded by its curved, crusted ceiling; especially in the dark, away from the village centre, sheltered from the rain, out of the wind, always a corner to dart behind if the headlights of a vehicle approached. It was where she brought many a young man, who had nowhere warmer or more comfortable to suggest, to spend an hour of mutual sensual exploration when they had got a step or two beyond holding hands in the pub. It was where she had allowed herself to be taken for the first time, a few years ago as a plump sixteen-year-old, by a man she thought she was in love with, a man long since departed from the village if not the country, a man she could never have denied, so magnetic, so insistent, so physical and yet so reassuring had he been.

Mary still remembered that night: the warm, fragrant darkness of July, the smell of his sweat, his hair oil, his cigarette, and the faint rumble of the train approaching the viaduct, the hiss of steam, the pale glow of lights in the blackness above them, the clackety-clack ringing ever louder, the rhythmic beat of the great metallic beast galloping towards them, the thunder as it careered relentlessly across the tracks directly over their heads, carriage after carriage after carriage booming, sound echoing off the walls, clouds of smoke billowing above, his groin thrusting in spasm into hers, pinning her hard against the dusty brickwork, her eyes agog, staring wildly into his own pleading gaze, her one hand now rocking his head like a baby's, her other pressed against the warm flesh of his muscular buttocks, his breathy gasps of release swallowed by the sudden desperate squeal of brakes as the engine decelerated like a spent firework on its arrival at Shillingstone Station less than half a mile beyond their tender embrace.

These days she came here alone almost as happily, timing her walks from the farm to be in position for the even louder trains, the expresses that didn't stop, shooting southwards to the coast, full of families from distant northern cities come to spend a summer week away from their gritty, grimy lives. Or the slower, lumbering goods trains, taking an aching age to clatter and choke over her arch, carrying coal and crops and cattle and cloth to and from the ports.

Ronnie Parr was still a boy, really. A sweet young boy, a mechanic's apprentice who had been lusting after Mary Abbott for months. Not the sort who only wanted a fumble and would claim the right to brag about it to his mates for weeks afterwards, like some lads did. She would take him under her wing, teach him how to make love to her, tell him how to take it slowly, not to be in such a rush. Ronnie, however, was in more of a hurry tonight, servile to his young male instincts, exhausted of conversation and in thrall to Mary's curves.

It was a dark, breezy night, the moon peeping briefly, shyly, from behind heavy storm-clouds, but the air was mild, oppressive, unseasonably so for the end of October. The harvests were gathered in for the most part and the faint tang of rotting stalks and damp, ripped earth came and went on the draughts. She had let him kiss her on the lips: a warm, dry kiss. He had mumbled that he thought her to be very beautiful, which made her smile, perhaps a little patronisingly.

Mary knew she was getting a reputation for being an easy shag, but that was unfair, she felt. She enjoyed sex; wasn't a modern woman supposed to? Was she expected to lie back and let the man have all the fun? Mary loved the power it gave her, however briefly, over men. It gave her an insight into their shallow selfishness, their short-termism, their need for instant gratification, their fatal weakness (slaves to their dicks) and, she had concluded, their plain inferiority to women. She knew she was attractive, sexually alluring without even having to try, for not only men complimented on her thick auburn hair, her dazzling hazel eyes, her full, love-heart lips. In her wickedest moments, or when she looked longingly at a fancy embroidered camisole she might find in a magazine photograph, she had contemplated making money out of her assets: she would leave the village, rent a cheap flat in Bournemouth, buy make-up and some flimsy dresses and for at least the next ten years could make a fortune from the grockles. But she had no real intention of joining what she had heard an aunt once call *the oldest profession*. She was far too proud, had too much self-esteem to sell her body, and in any case she had her heart set on a career in wood. If it was good enough for Our Lord it was good enough for her.

Her father was no carpenter but he was a useful handyman who knew his way around a box of sharp tools. As a girl Mary had watched him produce a shelf for the kitchen wall, a rough box for an ornamental bush, a wobbly rack for wet boots to dry out on. She had copied his skills in balsa wood, creating tiny versions of shelves, tables, even a little rocking chair for her doll's house. Latterly she had designed a full-sized bookcase and, together with her father, had finally created the piece, measured out and crafted with borrowed tools over weeks and weeks from planks of seasoned oak. It was a pipe dream, of course, an actual career in carpentry. For a start being a joiner was a man's job. She had had no proper training, no school had ever honed her skills (she'd heard there were actually colleges of design in places like London) and, ever the pragmatist, she was already resigned to a life in the village as a shop-girl like her sister or a farmer's wife like her mother.

"Here comes the train," she said suddenly.

Ronnie looked up into her eyes.

"What train? I can't hear nothin'."

"You'll hear it in a minute, you will. It's the vibrations I can feel. I know the signs, Ronnie. I can feel the ground vibratin'. Just a tiny little bit. Stand still. There. There!"

"You're mad, you are. I can't feel nothin'," he said, smiling. "I just wanna feel you, Mary. Let me hold you, come on."

They embraced again and she let him loosen a pair of buttons on her blouse and slip a hand awkwardly past her little silver crucifix, over and then inside her ample cotton bra. His head was beside hers but she could picture his face. She let her arms slide down his sides, her hands met at the base of his spine and she pulled his waist gently up towards her belly. Now she could hear the train's soft, purposeful breath in the distance, whistling through the veil of darkness, heading southeast in their direction.

Ronnie had fallen silent, his right hand tenderly cupping her breast like he might stroke the warm head of a newborn lamb, uncertain of what his next move might be and how then he should even attempt to make it. As if by some unspoken accord, he was relying on the woman for guidance before the animal deep within him was allowed to run free. And yet as for Mary, she was going no further this evening. Ronnie was a nice lad, well-mannered and clean (his hair smelled of soap and she knew how difficult it could be to remove engine oil from under fingernails) and she could already feel that he had plenty down his pants, but she really wasn't in the mood tonight. If truth be told, she had brought him to the arch in time for the train crossing not for him to experience the full adrenalin-fuelled collision of a knee trembler with an overhead assault on the senses but in fact so that she would have an excuse to uncouple.

"Listen, Ronnie," she ordered. "The train's comin'."

Before he had time to respond he had already been politely pushed away. Mary was fixing up her clothes and was stepping out from under the archway into the dark lane up towards the river.

"What you doin'?"

"Come on," she said, laughing. "Let's run into the field and watch it pass over the bridge!"

"I have seen a train at night before, Mary," he said, a look of disappointment still on his face.

"Not this close, I'll bet. Come on, hurry!"

"It'll be as muddy as fuck down that there embankment," he protested, but she was already striding through a gap in the hedge and on into the shadows, her skirt swishing against the long grass.

"Come on," she shouted. "Don't be such a soft girl!"

And suddenly he could hardly see her at all in the blackness, and he ran to catch her up while he still had a broken view of her dancing figure, anxious not to lose sight of her altogether.

"Wait for me, Mary! Where you to, you daft mare? Wait there, I'm comin'."

The locomotive was already in sight, its bright headlights filling the space ahead of it with a lurching yellow luminescence. Within seconds it was thundering over the brick arch, a trail of smoke and steam high in its wake, followed by its line of dark, clattering carriages with their blurs of lamplight in the flashing sequence of windows, piercing the night like a string of racing glow-worms. Twenty yards away, faces shining in the flickering light, stood Mary and Ronnie, out of breath, hand in hand, up to their knees in grass and reed, their boots covered in mud, smiling, laughing, eyes following the monster as it galloped on, now perceptibly slowing, braking with a smooth steely violence. Neither said a word. Mary had never lost her sense of awe at the sight of these colossal railway machines.

"Look!" cried Ronnie all of a sudden. "What's that?"

"What?"

"That, in the sky," he shouted, pointing at a dark object arcing out towards them, projected, apparently, from one of the train's carriages.

Mary saw it at once: a flat black shape spinning through the night sky. They both heard it land with a heavy thud as it crashed through the cropped corn-stalks in the field about fifty yards to the left of where they were standing.

Moments later, like an exhausted stallion at the end of a steeplechase, the engine came to a controlled halt, hissing and steaming and panting and clanking, its lights still shimmering in the distance through the black outline of trees and fencing lining the southbound platform of the station.

"Come on, Ronnie!" whispered Mary, pulling his hand. "Let's go and look for it, whatever it be. How are your night eyes, lover boy?"

3

The man whose head is covered by a stretched woollen hat, the man who has so spectacularly failed to show a railway ticket to the S & D collector at Shillingstone Station, this willowy man has already crawled twenty feet into the shadows cast by a scruffy knot of prickly bushes. Some hundred yards behind him, high up the dark bank, the Bournemouth train is still standing at the platform, the engine panting gently, its thin clanking and the distant shards of human voices barely reaching his ears. If he turns his head he can make out the tiny yellow squares of light from the carriage windows peeping through the darkness of the foliage. There is some sort of commotion going on, obviously; the train should have pulled away by now. One of the passengers must have reported hearing a scuffle, someone else has heard the body, or the luggage, strike the side of the carriage. Was there damage to the paintwork? Are they inspecting the panels? Is somebody searching his compartment for evidence of a fight?

Several more minutes pass and the man remains huddled in the dark with his little suitcase, and his anxiety. From time to time a torchlight sweeps over the fields, then a second, brighter one casts out its beam towards the river. The man is invisible to them but he dare not move. Now he can hear snatches of more voices, different, insistent voices from the platform. Still no closer to him than the platform, he reckons. But how much longer before some station lackey is sent over the fence and down the embankment to search? Or even a constable, and a few brazen volunteers from the village? The torchlights swoop away to the right and then disappear again. He has to act.

Apart from the nettle stings burning his hands he has recovered from the fall. He is breathing normally, his limbs are steady. He takes off his jacket, briskly removes his tie and flicks open the clasp of the case. Inside it there is nothing but a folded black jumper and, held in place by elasticated pockets, a torch and a small pistol. He empties out the contents, placing the firearm inside his belt, and pulls the jumper on over his head, replacing it in the case with the jacket and tie. Another bright arc of torchlight suddenly lengthens the shadows of his hiding place. Silently closing the case, he then fumbles at its side for a pair of retractable canvas straps which he stretches out and clips on to two metal retainers hidden on the opposite side. Slipping his arms one by one between the straps he manoeuvres the case on to his shoulders like a *de facto* rucksack. Hands free, he straightens his headgear, picks up the torch, gives a quick look back towards the station (the train has not advanced an inch) and moves stealthily out of his hiding place and down towards the river's edge. He will not use the torch, of course - it's for an emergency only; far safer to let his eyes, now accustomed to the darkness, guide him naturally across the rough ground.

If anyone is still peering out from the southbound platform towards the Stour, towards the faint, fragmented glow of the village of Child Okeford a mile away in the night, if eyes are scanning the distant horizon with its high dark humpback of Hambledon Hill, at this very moment when the clouds briefly split apart and the three-quarter moon casts its soft blue wash across the valley, then they might very well catch sight of a tiny indistinct figure scampering away over a narrow, poached field bordering the river.

Through wet, long grasses and over muddy, rutted earth, Livingstone - and that is no more the man's name than is Father Christmas - bounds on, in and out of shadow, finally ducking down the slippery bank where reeds and ripples mark the water's edge, currents shimmering like silver snakes caught in the moonbeams. Up on the tracks, now further away, the train is still a motionless line of twinkling lights. Once again someone flashes a feeble torch-beam uselessly out towards the river. Just as the moon disappears behind a curtain of cloud he scoops his hands into the silt and smears clag over his face to hide his pallor.

Then the man is already skirting northwards, splashing his boots in the shallows; he disturbs something soft and skittish like a water rat, and now he is scampering up the bank and into the undergrowth, fringing an open field, forced this way and that by the unlit, uneven topography. He feels energised, high on adrenalin, strangely at peace at the height of action; this is what he loves, this is what he is good at. The fugitive is sometimes known as Macduff, his standard operational alias, and under this name he was hired, for this mission as for many more before it. Tonight Macduff is once again the name he will answer to.

There is a suspicion of rain in the air. He keeps moving.

Following a bend in the Stour he sees the wide outline of the road bridge a little way ahead: Hayward Bridge, he recalls, having memorised not only the geographical features but also the names of the landmarks on the map he had been given. He will stay in the shadows and pass by the bridge on this side of the river (it is too exposed) and instead will take a small footbridge he had spotted on the map which crosses the flow half a mile further north.

He has emerged into an open space that had latterly been a cornfield and he can smell the vegetable sourness of rotting husks and roughly chopped stalks. Suddenly, at the other end of the field (not far from its edge where the lane runs along it, he is guessing) flickers a tiny but bright yellow light, making the space all around it ever darker. Macduff crawls into the brambly undergrowth and on his hands and knees lies motionless, his breathing shallow, his eyes hypnotised by the distant flame. At that moment he hears a faint hoot and then the soft hiss and grunts of the train chugging away at last from Shillingstone. Meanwhile the fire (what is it, a match-stick burning? a cigarette lighter?), the fire produces against its fragile glow the black outline of a crouching figure. Next he notices a second figure, previously hidden by the silhouette of the first. And then the flame goes out. He can hear quiet voices, indistinguishable mutterings in the night.

The flame reignites. They seem to be on their knees, this pair, praying, or digging, engrossed in something between them in the damp, flinty earth. Are they poachers, farm-lads up to no good? Then all at once one of the figures, too far away to tell even the sex, stands up and walks off in the direction of the lane. The flame disappears once again, but the second someone is still in the field, squatting in the dark, in the sudden silence, not much more than fifty yards away. Macduff is about to take a chance to make a furtive move when he hears a shrill voice call out: *Wait!*

It's a woman's voice, he would swear, and she is standing. From his prone position in the bushes he listens to the second figure rustling through the corn-stalks, clumsily following in the footsteps of the first.

4

Although Mary had crashed into the field a minute or two ahead of her hesitant boyfriend, it was Ronnie who stepped on the object by accident. Neither had seen the projectile land and they spent a while floundering in the pitch darkness, treading over the gluey earth, tripping over sharp cornstalks, waiting for the moon to reappear.

"This is bloody stupid!" complained the boy.

"Don't be so feeble, Ronnie!" she called back. "Concentrate on lookin'. You go on over that way."

"I can't even see you properly no more. Where you to?"

"I'm over here, I am. Follow my voice."

"I've got my lighter."

"No, don't use that."

"Why not?"

"It'll make everythin' else more darker."

"How's that, then?"

"I dunno. Just will. Just does. It's science."

"Science? What you know 'bout science, Mary?"

"More than you do, that's for sure."

"Well, I can see fuck all anyway. Apart from them lights over there," he said, pointing vaguely towards the station.

"Peculiar the train hasn't moved off," said Mary.

"So what?"

"So it's still there. They've kept it from leavin'. Somethin's up, I'll bet."

"My shoes are gettin' filthy."

"They'll clean."

"My mother'll kill me if I come home covered in shit."

"No she won't. Go over that way and look harder. Do as you're told, then, go on."

Suddenly Ronnie tripped over and fell into a dip in the ground, catching himself on several sharp corn-stalks.

"Fuck, what were that?"

Like a spotlight at the theatre the moon shone on cue over the prostrate youth, a sleeve of his jacket torn, his hand beginning to bleed, a sorry victim of the night starting to moan in pain.

"Where you to? Ronnie? Oh, there you are. You alright, Ronnie?"

Striding over to where he was lying, Mary caught sight of a flat, rectangular object, and suddenly her concern for the boy's injuries was abandoned.

"Hey, Ronnie, you daft donkey, you found it. You only went and trod on it!"

"On what?"

He was sitting up already, dishevelled, out of breath, looking like he'd lost a fight with a yearling bull.

"On this," she said, lifting the treasure up in the air. "It's a bag. Like one of them leather briefcase bags. You know what I mean. Come here, look. Can you stand? Come here. Can you crouch down?"

Ronnie picked himself up, decided he was better off sitting, and rubbed his ankle.

"Slide over here," Mary went on. "Now you *can* get your lighter out. I want to see what we've found."

"*We've* found?"

"Alright, smart arse, *you've* found."

As the clouds drew across the moon, the little flame of Ronnie's cigarette lighter flickered over the attaché case which the kneeling Mary, heart aflutter, was already looking how to open. She found a zip, tugged it harder and harder until it ripped apart, and peered inside.

"Hold it closer," she said.

"It's goin' to run out."

"Hold it closer, you naggerhead. Shield it."

Ronnie meekly obeyed, knelt down beside her in the cornfield, so intrigued by their find that neither noticed the sounds of the train departing.

"It's documents and stuff," Mary said with authority.

"What stuff?"

"I dunno. Papers. There's a book. And some envelopes, I think."

"Not very interestin', then," decided the boy, closing down his lighter.

"What you doin'? Put it back on, you lump!"

In the darkness as she blindly fingered a card folder, a sheaf of loose foolscap papers, several waxed pages, she felt at the bottom of the case a thick pliable envelope neatly packed with paper. She knew instinctively that she was holding money: banknotes, lots of banknotes, a wad a good inch thick.

The flame reignited, catching the blaze in her eyes.

"Lower down, Ronnie."

She took the folder of documents and opened it up on the ground. They looked like business papers, fluttering in the breaths of wind, official papers, government papers, she thought. She fanned out a few pages and noticed that some were not in English, not even in her own alphabet.

"Look at these here," she said quietly.

"That's Chinese, that is," said Ronnie.

"No. No, it's not. It's Russian. It's the Russian way of writin'. I've seen it before."

"Where in Shill you seen Russian?" he laughed. "Where you seen writin' like that round here then, Mary?"

31

"I've seen it on telly."

"On telly? Have you?"

"Yeah, I have. I saw a programme about outer space with my dad. You know them Russians have sent rockets up into space?"

"Yeah."

"Next thing is, they're goin' to send a man up in one."

"Yeah?"

"Yeah."

"Sounds like Dan Dare."

"It's the truth. Can you believe it? Anyway, I saw some writin' like this here."

"I wish we had a telly. You're lucky, Mary. Can I come watch it at yours somewhen?"

"Course you can. But look, Ronnie, on these papers here, it's in Russian or Siberian or somethin' like that, anyway."

"Borin'," declared Ronnie, shutting the lighter and limping away.

"Come back!" Mary called.

"I've had enough, I have. My ankle is killin' me, I've got wet feet and it's startin' to rain."

"Come back!"

But the boy wasn't coming back. Mary put the documents back in the attaché case, zipped it up, wiped a patch of soft mud off one of its corners and stood up. She would take it home, show her father, they would have a good look at the contents between them, then they would take it to the police first thing in the morning.

"Hey, wait!" she shouted after the lad. His silhouette was already merging with the dark shapes of the hedges as he plodded through the field towards the lane, back towards the shelter of the railway arch, back to where the evening had seemed so full of promise less than half an hour ago.

5

"I'm sorry, I'm not convinced," he had said dismissively. "It seems to me to be a very risky mission. There are just too many imponderables."

Macduff remembers expressing his concerns some weeks ago in a sparsely furnished office in central London where he was given the outline plan, dates, times, coordinates, and presented with a detailed, small-scale map of a certain unfamiliar section of the Stour valley.

"All the pondering has been done for you," his controller had replied without a moment's hesitation. "We have assessed the risks. And we believe it to be a good fit, if not a perfect fit. A very good fit. We expressly want *you* to perform the task. And if you do have to abort, for whatever reason, be assured that there is a fall-back."

"A fall-back?"

"Yes, of course. You can withdraw at anytime, even until the final moment, and still remain *virgo intacta*. The target will be hit in Bournemouth instead by a standby. It won't be so neat, but the job will be done one way or another. But, Mr Macduff, we have complete faith in you. You have a track record of high efficiency. You are reliable. And you are lucky."

A lucky man. He had been called that many times before, it was true. And, operationally at least, he knew it to be a fact.

He knew it when his sergeant major took a shine to him on his very first day as a recruit. He knew it with the military police in Cyprus in '56, when, on foot patrol in a market with a young lance corporal, two shots rang out from a EOKA sniper's rifle. The first bullet hit a Cypriot schoolgirl less than a yard away from him, and the second caught the soldier, his partner, Mickey Butler from Derby (he would never forget the boy's name) full in the neck. A crowd quickly formed around the fallen. Both died before help arrived and Macduff, in spite of his training, could do little more than sit in the dust in shock, trembling at the sight of so much fresh blood and with the wailing of bystanders ringing in his ears. By 1959 he had been co-opted into the intelligence services and he was given another reminder that he was a lucky bastard during a shortened stint in Northern Ireland. He had been tasked with the infiltration of what was thought to be an IRA safe house. The very day before the operation he fell in a horse-riding accident and dislocated his shoulder: not so fortunate. His place was taken at short notice by a female agent, name withheld, by all accounts as skilful an operator as he was; the woman lost her sight and half of her face when a booby-trapped bomb exploded as she stepped on a loose floorboard in the dark.

But Macduff considered himself lucky in more ways than simply in what he called his *active* life. He was lucky to have been born too late for D-Day; part of him, now fully trained, fully formed, would love to have served in France, but it was no glory rush, far from it. Shooting matches across ploughed fields in Normandy were no picnic: the German army, even more ruthless in retreat than they had been in advance, fought hard and rough and Allied casualties were huge.

He was lucky to have grown up as a boy in the beautiful Peak District, he was lucky to have two loving, supportive parents, to have made good friends. And even during the long, miserable years of rationing he never went short of food: he was lucky that his grandfather ran a grocery business in Buxton. He was lucky that his family could afford to send him to the grammar school, where he could be educated past the age of fourteen, where he was challenged and encouraged and nurtured while the boys he'd been with at the village school were already starting their long years in the fields, in the quarries, in the mills. He was even lucky in love. He was blessed with the fair-faced good looks and imposing physique that few women had so far chosen to ignore.

The risks of tonight's mission had been assessed, most certainly, but Macduff was correct to be sceptical nevertheless. He had followed Fleet from Bristol, had kept in the shadows at the railway station in Bath, watching his quarry choose a compartment and then selecting his own seat in the following carriage. So far, so textbook. It was imperative that he made his move as the train travelled between the stations of Sturminster and Shillingstone: a ten-minute window. If Fleet were not alone at that time then the job was off. Similarly if other passengers were coming and going up and down the corridor, there would be suspicions raised by him closing the compartment blinds. *It's a late evening train. The route has been well observed*, he had been assured. *It will not be busy.* But what if Fleet were restless after the long journey, if he wanted to stretch his legs, stand up, leave the compartment even, visit the WC? Macduff had considered delaying the attack if necessary, beyond Shillingstone to some later instance when the coast might be clear, but the problem of an escape then became complicated (too many factors unknown) and the convenience of the Sturcote exit route would be sacrificed. Better to alight on schedule and leave Fleet to the back-up. But once entrusted with a job, his pride dictated that he accomplish it, and, yes, so far, luck had been on his side once again tonight.

*

He has crossed the wooden footbridge and has followed a path running by a copse of trees which hides the lights and shapes of the nearby village of Child Okeford. He has no need to refer to the map, still folded in his shirt pocket; he has studied this land and has committed to memory every track, every stream, every last contour. Sturcote House is not far away now, a mile at the most, fifteen minutes by this most circuitous route.

The moon has been fitfully concealed by banks of heavy cloud, but his eyes remain sharp: he advances by differentiating shades of grey, intensities of black, by sensing danger and evading it. The wind has dropped, and the temperature along with it, and it is starting to drizzle again. He can smell wood-smoke drifting from the chimneys out over the tree-tops. He knows to avoid tracking too close to the village lest he be spotted by a dog-walker out late even on this inclement night.

He heads out across a tussocky field of long grass and weeds, and presently rejoins the sunken river bank, paddling through the boggy shallows half-hidden from view. In places the shoreline is impassable and he has to drag himself through reeds and hedges of hawthorn and wild, tangled bramble. He climbs over a wooden stile and comes to the corner of another open field, planted with a crop he doesn't recognise, and follows the hedge-line in the general direction northwards, the distant cottages and outbuildings on his right as before. All at once from the bushes on the other side of the field a fox emerges, freezes for a second, before bobbing back under cover, its snow-tip of tail, dimmed in the grainy light, the last of it to silently disappear. He hasn't seen another human for half an hour at least, since the figures by the flame in the cornfield.

He is breathing easy. He is safe now. He is on the home stretch. He checks his watch: twenty minutes past ten.

At the end of the field he finds another stile, slippery and unsteady, and beyond it lies the entrance to a small wood of dripping sycamore and beech and oak, through which he follows an uneven path, littered with sodden fallen leaves. Once out of the wood he recognises from his map the neat fencing which arcs around the perimeter of a paddock, enclosing stable buildings and a yard. A little further along is the brick-walled garden and between the high trees he finally sees the silhouetted roofline of Sturcote House. He dashes past the paddock, silent and empty in the misty gloom, notices lights in the stables, hears the soft, gaspy whinny of an animal, and already he can taste in the cold air the sweet smell of horses, their coats, their sweat, their muck. The painted wooden door at the northern corner of the garden wall is exactly where he had been told it would be. And as expected it is secured from the outside by a heavy padlock. From a deep trouser pocket he produces a key and, now with the aid of his torch, he turns the lock and releases the bolt.

The moment Macduff pushes the door open, a harsh light is beaming into his face; so white, so dazzling that his pupils dilate in pain. Instinctively he shields his eyes with his forearm. Everything else around the light has become a void, out of which, over a rustle of movement, roughly spoken, comes a single word:

"Speak!"

"I have no words," Macduff intones. "My voice is in my sword."

And the light is lowered, its brilliant beam cast to the path and the corner of a vast lawn.

"Very well. Come in. You are expected."

It's an old man's voice, slow and broad. There is no apology for the blinding. After a moment's confusion Macduff is able to focus on the shape of a small, slight figure in working clothes who is already turning towards the house. His torch is now pointing ahead of them over the garden, illuminating a narrow path of flagstones. In his other hand the imp carries a long pitchfork (his weapon of choice?), which gives him the look of a conscript from one or other of the sides in the English Civil War.

"Follow me across to the back steps," he grumbles. "Mind how you go. Some o' these pavin's are not so steady as they ought to be."

Even from the rear the house is imposing. It looks like a Georgian manor, built in stone, of whose tall oblong windows three are lit: two on the ground floor, one on the floor above. As the old man leads him up the steps towards a double door, half-paned, the rain begins to fall with a new intensity. An hour of this downpour and the boot-prints he has left behind him will be all but obliterated; the good fortune of Macduff continues to hold.

Somewhere in this house, then, the final stages of the operation are about to take place: the debrief, a hot bath, a change of clothes, a light meal. And, if his demands have been met to the letter, he will have access to a helmet, goggles, a set of leathers and a serviced BSA with enough fuel in the tank to get him to the outskirts of London before daybreak.

PART TWO

THE AWAKENING
OF ANDRIS FLEET

1990

1

Whenever people talk about lone-parent families, am I right in thinking that the sympathetic shakes of the head tend to be directed squarely towards the lone parent, be it a single mother (usually) or a single father (rarer), rather than towards the family? Am I being oversensitive in my belief that the child, or indeed the group of children, is very often lumped in with all the other stuff that the lone parent has to juggle? A job (imperative), the housework (sporadic), a budget (reduced), outside interests (variable), a sex life (complicated), sanity (fragile) and, yes, childcare. Childcare is just one of those coloured balls in the air, just one of those plates to be kept spinning.

I do not believe my mother was ever a great juggler, and even before my father died I cannot imagine that looking after me was ever more important than any other of the demands on her time. At a very young age I had the impression that I was little more than an inconvenience, a bit of grit in her shoe causing an impediment, an irritant. This might be quite unfair to the woman, but I cannot, with any accuracy, coat my childhood with a sugary gloss. And, knowing no better, I would have liked to give her the benefit of the doubt. I was only five years old when I was sat down at the breakfast table (in my foggy memory it was the old wobbly white-painted breakfast table) and she told me that Daddy had gone, darling, and would not be coming back. Ever. *No, Andris, he really wouldn't.* Is it paranoia to claim that that morning was probably the last time, at least in reference to something important, that she told me a genuine truth?

That short, probably tearful conversation, is not my earliest memory. I do have a vague picture of my father in my mind: I see him as a tall, handsome figure (there are a few photographs to help with this), chasing me around a garden, hiding behind a tree and suddenly appearing, sweeping me off my feet and lifting me high up to the sky, gripping me with two firm hands like the FA Cup. And his voice? Not really. Not addressed to me at any rate. I remember hearing him rowing with my mother downstairs when I was supposed to be fast asleep. I have no idea what that was all about.

I don't even properly remember the incident on the swing, the sorry result of which has probably shaped my whole life to some degree. I don't think we ever had a swing in our little garden, so it must have happened in a park somewhere. We were living in north London at the time, apparently, in some avenue in Harrow. I had been left on a swing one afternoon by Erika, my mother, and she must have wandered off to buy an ice cream, to stroke a dog, to flirt with someone, I don't know why. The story goes that some older children arrived on the scene and started pushing my swing faster and faster, higher and higher. Of course I lost my grip, flew off, landed awkwardly and must have wept noisily with the pain. I imagine I was told not to make such a fuss and Erika would have me limping home with nothing more than lollipop stains on my chin and a damp handkerchief around my knee. According to my grandfather, long since deceased but in those days a regular substitute for my father who was often abroad, I was hobbling around, bravely disguising the torment for over a week before my mother deemed it serious enough of an injury to take me to see a doctor. There was bone and ligament damage, repairable after a fashion but I was too young at the time for remedial surgery; that came later, in my early teens, and was a partial success. I recall the grey, intense face of the surgeon as he told me what a brave young chap I had been. Nevertheless, I have walked with a slight limp ever since.

Nobody spoke much about my grandmother, my English one, that is. I know that she was killed in the London Blitz, working as a volunteer first aider in the East End. She must have been very young, in her forties, maybe. The memory of her death was too painful for conversation, I suppose, and too upsetting to burden a child with. As for my Latvian grandparents, I never met them. And they too were barely mentioned, never without a tear from Erika. For me it was almost as if they had never lived. One day when I was older she spoke a little about the Russian Communists and what they had done to dissenters in Riga, but it was only a sentence or two and she would answer no questions. I had to use my imagination instead, and for a moment I would feel desperately sorry for her.

*

Following the death of my father, Erika wasted no time in moving on; the grieving widow was not a role she had any intention of playing for very long. She was a good-looking woman, though it still seems strange for me to describe her like that. It must have been just over a year later that she married Adrian Plummer, a wealthy London lawyer from a dynasty of wealthy London lawyers. So, really, am I making too much of a fuss about being in a lone- parent family? We moved to his fancy house in Richmond-upon-Thames and

I had to leave behind the small group of half-friends I had made, not to mention my ailing but doting grandfather who felt obliged, I think, to become more and more peripheral. In the course of the next two years the happy couple produced two daughters, Tiffany and Patricia (or Tiffy and Trixie as they affectionately came to be called). And so Erika the part-time political activist (she sometimes described herself in this way although I didn't understand what she meant) took on the mantel of suburban mother and housewife, and I was promptly sent off to a prep school a hundred miles away. From being in a one-parent family I had suddenly become part of a no-parent family in a corner of the country I knew nothing about.

Brydmouth Hall was, and probably still is, a prestigious boarding school on the south coast whose unique feature, apart from the architectural elegance of the eighteenth century manor which housed much of the body of the school, was its position on a wide estuary and its own sailing academy. There must have been a long-established link with Royal Navy families, and I was led to believe that my funding was supported by a services bursary in recognition of my father's curtailed career. Everything was in place there for the confident children of the English upper-middle class, particularly for those who were academically brilliant or simply naturals in a dinghy. I tried, of course I did, but I was neither of the above: a timid boy of moderate intelligence with a constantly sore knee and, on my arrival at least, a head of long sandy curls that my mother adored but which made me look like a girl.

And so under blue skies, in this idyllic coastal setting, in a most magnificent mansion surrounded by sloping lawns and winding floral beds and mighty trees, here, from the very first day, the bullying began. Sadly I had neither the confidence nor the wit to fight back. Once the matron had given me a more acceptable haircut they started on my uneven gait: name-calling as before, nothing physical but just as painful. An older boy with greasy skin called me Hopalong, the name of a television cowboy I had never heard of, which stuck for months and was often accompanied by spiteful laughter. A little later in my time at Brydmouth the name changed to Cossack; there was a rumour spreading that my father was a Russian. Knowing this to be nonsense I insisted that he had been as English as anyone else's father and not only that, he had served in the Royal Navy.

"That's as maybe," another boy would scoff, "but my father said your old man was a Russian spy. What a louse!"

I had nowhere to go beyond a denial, a denial repeated and repeated until the words meant nothing.

The next stage was for someone to ask me: *Do Cossacks float?* as we were lining up in our trunks to be checked for verrucas before a weekly swimming lesson in the huge, draughty hangar of an indoor pool. I had no idea what he meant until two brutes, in the same year as me but much larger, pounced on me at the end of the session when the teacher's back was turned. I was pulled into the centre of the pool, way out of my depth, and wrestled under the surface. It was a five-minute free play and my gurgled shouts were lost in the echoey noise of twenty others. I was held under, inhaling more water with each futile cough, my limbs pinned by the bastards until bubbles stopped coming from my mouth, my nose, and whether I kept my eyes open or closed it made no difference to the watery veil of grey then black which engulfed me. I felt a tingling in my fingers and toes, and my limbs go limp like tissue paper. Then I was suddenly forced up and out of the water, instinctively gulping for air, flailing like a fighting drunk. I heard a commotion of claims and counter-claims, the teacher chiding the boys who in turn were arguing that they had been trying to rescue me from drowning. All the voices were identical: boy, master, another boy, then matron, then more boys, like the muffled humming of a monotone spoken at the far end of a telephone line in somewhere like Siberia.

*

During a holiday I found a moment to speak to my mother. She had asked me if I were happy at school, a throwaway question which she imagined would be answered both briefly and positively.

"Well, that's alright then, darling."

She hadn't been listening.

"Mummy, the boys at school call me Cossack," I repeated for her.

"Cossack? That's a funny nickname. Do you mind?"

"Well, yes. I do."

"Do you?"

"I hate it."

"Hate is a very strong word, Andris."

"Well, I do hate it. They say Daddy was a Cossack too. A Russian."

"That's absolute nonsense, darling."

"I told them it was."

"Well, then."

"But they say one of the boys' parents knows all about him."

"They're just making up stories to tease you."

"They say Daddy was a Russian spy."

"A spy?"

"You know, like a secret agent."

"Such nonsense!"

She came closer to me, crouched and gently cupped my warm face in her hands.

"Working for Russia, they said." I went on. "Are they our enemy, Mummy?"

"Well, I suppose they are in a manner of speaking," she said softly. "It's very complicated, Andris. There's no war or anything horrible going on. There's nothing for you to worry about, and these chums of yours are just having a little joke at your expense."

"Daddy *was* in the Navy, wasn't he?"

"Of course, darling. The *Royal* Navy."

"Did he drown at sea?"

She stood up and moved back to her coffee cup.

"No, darling, he didn't drown."

"So how...?"

"Your father was a hero, and you can tell your pals at school with your head held high. You can tell them that, yes, he *was* a spy. Edward Fleet *was* a secret agent."

"Really?"

"He was. I haven't told you this before, Andris. You were too young to understand. But you're old enough now, you're getting to be a big boy."

I remember feeling my heart swelling in my chest.

"He died in Germany. You know about the wall they built in Berlin a year or two ago?"

"I've seen photographs."

"Well, it was built by the Russians to keep their people and the German people living there, in the eastern districts, to keep them prisoners, prisoners in their own city. Can you imagine that, darling? Can you imagine a city like London being divided, and no movement between the divisions?"

"Like, what, like you couldn't get from Richmond to Tower Bridge?"

"Yes, something like that. Before they built the wall it was just wire at first, barbed wire, lookout posts, soldiers and dogs and so on, but people could get out, they got smuggled out. Your father worked in Berlin at that time, Andris. He helped to get people out to the western sectors. Good people, people who just wanted to be free. And he was shot for his troubles. By the Russians."

She paused, offered me a sad smile and a moment to digest her story.

"But he got many, many people out to freedom before they shot him. That's the truth, my son. Never forget it. And don't let those boys say otherwise."

I remember feeling immensely proud of my father at that moment, the picture of him in his uniform, long since packed up in the attic, suddenly reappeared in my mind's eye: his solemn face winked at me and broke into a warm grin. Erika gave me a cursory hug, tousled my hair and said:

"And if anyone ever says your mother is a Russian, you know what to say, don't you?"

"That you're a Latvian."

"That I'm a Latvian. Exactly. Never was a Russian and never will be. We're Latvians, you and I." And looking down at me and touching my hair again, "I liked you with longer hair, Andris. I suppose short hair is the modern style for lads like you. Never mind. Come on, let's go outside. Come and look at what Adrian has bought for the girls."

Nobody at school really believed me when I told them that my father had been a secret agent and had been killed in action in East Berlin. Nevertheless, Cossack was dropped pretty soon, but in place of name-calling came the psychological bullying: I was sidelined, pointedly ignored, spoken to in the third person even when I was amongst them in the dorm. There was little respite, little warmth in that endless, pitiless gloom.

On my tenth birthday, in the darkest dead of winter, my mother forgot to send me a card.

*

I have only miserable memories of prep school, and to her credit Erika did listen to me when I begged to be taken out at eleven to start at a new school rather than stay on till thirteen like everybody else. A dwindling bursary might have been a consideration, but she agreed that I should start the new term as a first-former at a local grammar school whose entrance examination I mercifully passed.

Living at home again was unnerving. The new grouping of Erika, Adrian and the girls had become an entity in itself, a closed circle, self-absorbed, self-congratulatory, and I felt like I couldn't even speak their language. My new stepfather seemed like a vaguely decent man but he had little time for me. I was something appended to his wife like her collection of knee-high leather boots or her lattice-work bookcase. When he was not absorbed in his work *in chambers* (his italics), his world spun around rugby, fine wine, right-wing politics and, of course, his very special daughters: little common ground with me, fair enough, but what irritated me about him was his hypocrisy, his faux-concern for my welfare.

"How are we doing, fella?" he might ask. "We'll have to invite some of your new pals over to the house for a barbecue one of these evenings, eh?"

He hadn't spotted that I had no new pals, and even if I *had* had a friend round he would have made sure he was out, otherwise occupied, preparing a really, really important case.

All I remember of those years, from 1966 to 1968, were hours spent in my bedroom grappling unsuccessfully with Latin homework and endlessly, repeatedly, listening to my treasured copy of *Sergeant Pepper's Lonely Hearts Club Band* and studying its wonderful gatefold sleeve. And tuning in to secret midnight music on an undercover transistor radio which was becoming a greater source of comfort than diminishing maternal affection. Oh, and getting regularly beaten up in the schoolyard. At the state grammar school, the cleverest boys in the area, carefully selected for their uncommon intelligence, preferred physical bullying over the psychological. And plenty of it. Much of the grisly evidence I hid from my mother, explaining away bruises and gashes as sports injuries. My weak knee entitled me to be excused outdoor games but the PE master we had at the time insisted that I took part (*Don't be such a bloody pansy, Fleet!*) and stuck me in goal where I would often stand shivering in the rain while waiting to be attacked by clumsy oafs with only one eye on the football. On one occasion when I received a black eye *and* a split lip, Erika was angry enough to promise to go in to school and have it out with the Head of Games, but, well, she never seemed to get around to it.

By the age of thirteen I had moved school again, a permanent refugee, this time back to the independent sector, to a small private school with little prestige to speak of in a quiet valley in the middle of Dorset. I have no idea who paid the fees; was it the Navy, or did Adrian feel a little guilty having recently paid enormous deposits, years in advance, to secure places at Roedean for Tiffy and Trixie?

For a little while things looked up. I was placed in a house where there seemed to be fewer than the average number of unsavoury characters. The housemaster, a kind, soft-hearted Cornishman called Hussey, took a shine to me and his study became for me on many occasions a haven of compassion and good sense. He allowed me to express myself, to unload some of my unease, to talk without fear of denigration. I trusted him. He was a great believer in honesty, in encouraging boys to get things off their chest, to make a clean slate of things. On his desk amidst the piles of marking and opened books (he was Head of the Religious Studies Department) was an embroidered quotation in a frame: *Lies are the religion of slaves and masters. Truth is the god of the free man. Maxim Gorky.* I once asked him who Maxim Gorky was.

"Maxim Gorky, born 1868, died 1936," he said with a flourish, looking at me with a smile on his face that allowed me to smile back and acknowledge the fact that he was showing off, "was a Russian writer, Mr Fleet. One of the wisest of all the very wise Russians."

The darling Mrs Hussey was a legend in the house, a pink-cheeked, chubby mother hen who baked scones daily and dispensed them to wobbly boys along with large helpings of love, empathy and wisdom. I was by no means her only visitor, I must say. I had pretended that my tears, induced by threats or taunts, were the symptoms of homesickness, but in many cases it was a fact: some fourteen-year-old boys in boarding schools do still miss their mothers, you know. Mrs Hussey was the first person ever to call me Andy, which I decided I liked. My stepsisters also steered away from my full given name, preferring instead, as soon as they were capable of clear pronunciation, to call me Dris, which I liked a good deal less; at the time it sounded to me like the name of an alien character lurking behind the cardboard props in *Dr Who*.

Meanwhile Erika excelled herself during the February half-term break. I made my way home as usual on the bus to London that the school arranged, then took a taxi from Victoria to Richmond, only to find the house empty. A neighbour rescued me from the frosty doorstep and contacted my step-father's chambers. The four of them were in Chamonix for a skiing holiday. My mother later explained that she had muddled up the half-term dates: she had been convinced that the girls' dates were a week earlier than mine.

I was mortified when the Husseys left at the end of my Fourth Form. He'd got a job as a deputy head at some place in Devon, I think. Meanwhile, I was left in limbo and my O Level year turned into a disaster. I was no more than a mediocre pupil, as I have probably said already. I was particularly hopeless at French, which appalled my mother, who was fluent in Latvian, Russian and, of course, English, and who picked up bits and pieces of other languages as easily as a bee collecting nectar. Not to mention my father's degree. Not only was I frustrated by my academic limitations, I was lame in one leg, suffered weeks of raging acne (hidden as much as possible by a long, swooping fringe) and had a queue of enemies ready at any opportunity to stick the silent boot in. I often took shelter in the Art department (the rooms were open when most of the other classrooms were locked) and in the kitchens where the staff were happy for me to help peel vegetables and stack away cutlery. It was in the days before Health & Safety in the workplace.

Fifth Form socials were a special chore. Dances (excuses to smoke, drink and feel up schoolgirls) were arranged and attendance was compulsory. How many times did I have to endure the repartee of one random pair of classmates after another trying to make a group of girls laugh?

Bastard One: This is Fleet, ladies, but don't get too close.
Bastard Two: He's got a limp, don't you know? Haven't you, Fleet?
Bastard One: A limp? A limp what?
Bastard Two: Boom boom!
Bastard One: A limp wrist?
Bastard Two: Oo-er! No, just a limp dick!

In August I was rewarded with four O Level passes: art, woodwork, English and, most surprisingly, mathematics. Four out of nine: adequate but sadly not enough for me to move seamlessly into the Sixth Form. Erika was adamant that she would convince the school to relent. She pleaded with the Headmaster, an elderly man with a face like a mole's whose name I have forgotten, but I think it was actually a rather half-hearted appeal. For one thing the money for the fees was no longer guaranteed and it seems that the wealthy Adrian was reluctant to open his chequebook on my account. And for another thing, *half-hearted* was generally a good description of her whole approach to my upbringing.

Instead I had a year in the local FE college studying design and catering: an unusual combination which meant that I spent more hours on the premises than most other students. It was at this time that my interest in music became more pronounced, specifically in that branch of the modern idiom known as progressive rock. I bought only LPs (singles were for plebs), collecting a dozen or so by such groups as Yes, early years Genesis, ELP and my absolute favourites, Pink Floyd. In the privacy of my bedroom I drank in the lyrics, soared with the striking melodies, plucked air-guitar, fast-fingered air-mellotron, played air-everything incredibly well and lost myself in the artwork on the sleeves, daydreaming of becoming the next Roger Dean, of landing a top job in the design room at Hipgnosis.

In 1973, while I was still at college, I was offered a part-time position in a large hotel in the West End as a kitchen porter. The day after I finished with studying I started there full-time as a waiter in one of their restaurants. I had been promised a job as a trainee chef but was let down by a two-faced under-manager. By this stage in my life, and in spite of having little truck with triumph, I had already learned to treat Kipling's two imposters just the same. A year later a friend from college called into the hotel with a generous offer: he could get hold of a ticket for a Floyd concert at the Empire Pool if I fancied it. Did I fancy it! As far as I knew all their London dates were sold out and, according to the NME, the performances would be a showcase for nothing less than *Dark Side of the Moon*, my favourite album of the past twelve months (and still to this day, to tell the truth). He duly turned up a few days later with the ticket. I paid him £5, over the odds I thought, but I could afford it, and spent the next week or so staring at the square of stiff paper as if it were the key to the Kingdom of Heaven. Sadly, when I came to present it, I was told it was counterfeit, a forgery, a fake. I was refused entry at Wembley, of course, and I remember sitting on the pavement outside surrounded by noisy punters, angry, frustrated, humiliated.

Hanging on in quiet desperation may or may not be quite the English way, but never had the lines from *Time* meant quite so much to me. Reading the ecstatic concert reviews in the music press only made me more depressed. Naturally enough I never saw again the friend who cheated me. Even at the time, and more so from this distance, it wasn't the theft of a fiver that poisoned my soul so much as the big lie. Another fucking lie.

I've been called a nerd and a pussy, a toff, a snitch, a cripple and a queer, but never in my life have I been called a liar.

*

Having spent most of my life to that point in the midst of boys, the perfidy of the young females I was now meeting went some way to explaining the behaviour of my mother. Actually that is an unfair generalisation which I am already ashamed of making. Although we had nothing in common other than the genetic trait of blue eyes we shared with Erika, I rarely experienced much unpleasantness at the hands or the tongues of Tiffy and Trixie, for example; most of the time they simply chose to ignore me. It is fair to say, however, that relationships with young women was an area of expertise in which I was floundering in the dark. I felt like a caveman might have felt attempting to drive an Aston Martin. Blindfolded. In range of the scent of a floral shampoo I was a classic bumbler: tongue-tied, misjudging signals, letting opportunities slip through my fingers, chancing my arm when it was wiser to keep it firmly on the bar. I had a serious problem differentiating between a tease and a lie, between gentle sarcasm and sheer rudeness.

Nevertheless, by the age of twenty my face was clear of blemishes and I was not a bad-looking lad. I passed my driving test second time round, I spent a decent amount of my earnings on clothes and had started to style my hair into a heavy blond quiff like David Bowie's Young American, which was a talking point if nothing else. *Quite presentable*, as Mrs Hussey used to say, straightening the knot in my tie before Sunday chapel. Dates, as a rule with the odd lost soul working at the bottom of the pile in the hotel industry, revolved around a pint or two and a couple of Babychams, a film (if we could both agree on one), perhaps a shared pizza or a bag of chips. Dancing was out, sadly, as my limp never allowed me to follow a smooth rhythm for long, and I never knew what to do with my eyes in any case, never mind my hands. In that respect, and in that respect only, the advent of punk rock, and with it the pogo dance, was a blessing; I could just about bounce on the spot, lose myself in the driving beat, wander slightly off centre and then fall over on to a sticky dance-floor with the best of them.

One incident will suffice to illustrate how I felt the cards were stacked against me. After one or two false starts, I was getting on beautifully with one of our front-of-house staff, a receptionist called Bella, and a few weeks had passed when she announced that she wanted to take me home to meet her parents. Bella's father, meanwhile, worked in newspapers and he had been doing his homework. When the daughter finally introduced me as Andris Fleet, her boss (which wasn't strictly true), his first question was:

"Andris Fleet. Rings a bell. Aren't you the boy whose dad was a Russian spy? Edward Fleet, the traitor who was murdered, ain't it?"

Any prospect of a future with Bella evaporated in that moment like a desert mirage.

Sally, a laundry manager, my first serious girlfriend, was ten years older than me, and although we lasted for six months I knew after just one that she had been a bad choice. She took things so literally. If I ever mentioned, for example, that a friend had lost his rag over something or that someone had lost their bottle, or even worse, had lost their marbles, I could sense her mind at work, mechanically wondering if there were something she could perhaps do to help in the search. Sally was great on the one level but sometimes she made me feel like Albert Einstein. Nevertheless we made each other laugh, she had the body of a pin-up, and we used to drive off together for weekends of sexual excess in a caravan in Margate. But it couldn't last; I needed to be with someone I could have a proper conversation with. She was still listening to glam-rock and read very little other than the *News of the World* and laundry lists. We were sitting in my car outside her mother's front door when I told her, with a certain firmness in my tone, that I thought we had probably reached the end of the road.

"No, it goes on a bit further," she said. "Round to the left before the dead end in Victoria Close."

I was never quite sure if she was joking.

"But we can still stay friends, can't we, Andris?" she asked a moment or two later, wiping away a tear.

It was a nice idea, Sally, I suppose. Sweet girl. Well, woman, really.

2

It is by no means my intention to elicit sympathy for the particular challenges of my life. I was never really one for self-pity and whoever has it easy anyway? My early years were not as blessed as some, but, for goodness sake, what have I to complain about in the great scheme of things? I was healthy, had all my faculties, was averagely bright and knew my way around one of the world's great cities. I lived far from the breadline, even further from a war zone, and even had my driving licence. I had good teeth, good taste and good manners. I was white, straight, middle class, and English. So no sympathy, please, it's embarrassing. I was doing fine, thanks for asking.

By the spring of 1990, aged thirty-five, I was driving a company car, a newish Cavalier, just ten thousand on the clock, registered to the Cassis Hotel Group UK of Southampton. I found that hotel work suited me. I was industrious, happy enough to embrace the unsocial hours, and came up with the occasional flash of inspiration which kept the bosses sweet. And I learned more and more about people every day.

I had been with Cassis for the best part of ten years, and moved down to Hampshire in 1988 when they relocated their centre of operations outside the capital. This made a good deal of sense as the group was basically a chain of hotels on the south coast; by 1990 we must have had a dozen or so in distinctive locations from Devon to East Sussex. I had worked in our Brighton hotel as an assistant manager, then as manager, and had displayed a flair for design ideas: decor, furniture, colour schemes, unifying themes and the like. Which led to a move off the front line, as it were, and into the heart of the company. As I drove the Cavalier away from the Dorset town of Blandford Forum north towards Shillingstone, the calling cards packed neatly in the pocket of my briefcase were embossed with the legend: *MR ANDRIS FLEET, REQUISITIONS MANAGER* below a shiny purple impression of a small bunch of blackcurrants, the latest configuration of the company logo.

As the lights changed to green I followed the traffic turning left to cross a river bridge and straightened the road map on the empty passenger seat. I was responsible for the supplies of all non-comestibles to the entire range of properties which, as the company boasted, were all quite individual. I supervised the orders of everything from bathroom taps to curtain rails, from carpets to corkscrews. I found business to be not so different from boarding school survival: I had learnt to be cautious, to read a face, to understand body language, when to trust and when to be defensive. I made some mistakes, naturally: there were contractors who were economical with the truth, deliveries that failed to materialise, more than once had I been fobbed off with sub-standard merchandise, razored by sharp practice. But the chiefs in the boardroom liked me, and here I was, still in business, smart suit and shiny black shoes at the ready, on my way to a meeting with another furniture manufacturer. The flaxen fringe was long gone, and the heavy soul-boy quiff too, regrettably; at thirty-five I had a short cut with flecks of silver at the temples, and a neat flat moustache.

Abbott's Furniture was signed at the end of the village, up a right hand lane which lead to a small industrial site with apparently no further exit. As I might have said to Sally if she had been sitting next to me on the seat where the road atlas lay: *We've reached the end of the road.* I found a spot for the car, cut the engine, stepped out and, picking up my briefcase, locked the doors. It was a bright, warm afternoon, the sun hung shyly in a pale blue sky. No need for a coat.

Directly ahead of me was a garage with a collection of second-hand cars for sale outside. A plastic board over the doors with the lettering KP MOTORS served as badge of ownership. Someone was revving an engine hard inside the building and I heard laughter, smelt oil and cigarette smoke, and glimpsed a pair of lads in greasy overalls in the background as I made my way across the yard. To the right stood a prefabricated construction which looked neglected: double doors bolted shut, a line of high windows smeared with old paint and a row of thick weeds running along the crack in the concrete by its outer walls. To the left I saw another flimsy building, with breeze block sides and a roof of corrugated steel. A wide access door was closed so I approached a smaller adjacent door which was ajar. I could hear voices, tinny transistor music and the humming and buzzing of woodworking machinery. By the door, screwed to the wall was a modest wooden board on which the name of the company had been hand-painted in black. I was at the right place.

Once inside the noise was amplified. The scene in the workshop was one of industry, each of the dozen or so machinists, labourers and craftsmen busy at their work, one or two chatting, some mouthing the words along with Michael Jackson on the radio, most absorbed in their tasks. The first man to notice me was working on a lathe near the door, fashioning what looked like table legs. He switched off his machine, lifted his goggles and asked me directly who I was looking for. I was told that the office was in the station building in the far corner of the yard. I thanked him and with a nod he set about resuming his work.

I had no idea that what he had called the station building actually was part of a railway premises long since defunct, but as I approached, the architecture of single-storey brick and the covered walkway with its timbered guttering (leading to a ticket office, I imagined, back in the days of steam), were redolent of old photographs of stations I had seen. The first entrance I came to, a door painted green with the instruction at eye level to *Please Knock*, led me into what I guessed might have been a waiting room at some point in the past. It was now a reception area, and as I pushed open the heavy door, a buxom young secretary stood up from behind a desk by the far wall and greeted me with a smile.

"Mr Fleet, isn't it?" she said. "Hello, how are you? Did you find us without too much fuss then?"

"Hello, yes, Andris Fleet," I answered. "Yes, no problem. The chaps outside, in the workshop, they directed me here. You have unusual premises for offices."

"What? Oh, the old station. Yes, it's a bit different, I do suppose. Have a seat, won't you, Mr Fleet."

The woman's voice, though not dissimilar, was not the same as the one I had spoken to on the phone a week ago, presumably that of a different receptionist. I took a seat, on one of a row of three functional padded chairs, not from the Abbott's catalogue, I noticed.

"One minute, please," said the woman, disappearing through a connecting door into the next room. The walls of the waiting room were decorated on the one side with charts displaying bespoke furniture and on the other with a collection of pictures of vintage steam engines.

When I was shown through to the next room (the station

master's office?), I was surprised to discover that the managing director of the company was a woman. Dressed in a cream-coloured cashmere top and plain navy skirt, she was standing in the middle of a patterned carpet, arms open, and a wide smile on her face as if she were welcoming a long lost friend.

"Mr Fleet, sir," she said, shaking my hand vigorously. "Welcome. Welcome to Abbott's. I'm Mary, Mary White. I run the show here. I'm the boss lady," she added with a grin, "takin' a leaf out of Mrs T's book.".

She spoke with the soft, rounded burr that I recognised from the voices of some of the kitchen staff at my old boarding school.

"Some of the lads, they call you Maggie, don't they, Mother?"

The younger woman was still in the room, hovering by the door.

"Really?" I asked, unsure of my ground with a figure who provoked so much admiration on the one hand and hostility on the other that the country had convulsed into rupture these last few years.

"It's a joke," said Mary. "I don't think I'm ever goin' to be beltin' anyone with my handbag."

"Oh, Mother. You don't know the half of it, Mr Fleet," said the daughter in mock disapproval.

"Go and make us some tea, Annie," said the mother, turning to me. "And don't be rollin' your eyes on your way out."

I watched her leave, guessing her to be around twenty years old, and then glanced around the room. It was a little chintzy, with floral curtains, a large fireplace (filled with coal and rolls of newspaper but as yet unlit), a pair of old-fashioned armchairs, a standard lamp with floral shade, and, like in the first room, photographs of trains and railway artefacts decorated the walls. It was as cosy as someone's sitting room and as unlike any other company office I had ever set foot in before.

"You'll be havin' a cup of tea with me, won't you, Mr Fleet?"

"Yes, with pleasure, Mrs White, thank you."

"Call me Mary. I can't be botherin' with formalities. This is an unfussy, family operation."

"I see."

"And what'll I call you, then?"

"You can call me Andris, I suppose."

"Andris?"

"Yes. Like Andrew. It's a Latvian name. My mother was from Latvia originally."

"Latvia? Now help me, Andris. Where the heck is that? Somewhere in the Middle East? Am I thinkin' of Libya?"

"It's a Baltic country, near Finland, near Russia. You've probably not heard of it as it's been part of the Soviet Union for the past thirty-odd years."

Mary had moved to sit behind a large polished oak desk. It seemed that she had lost interest as soon as the conversation strayed overseas.

"Andrew is my son's name, as a matter of fact, so there's a coincidence. We call him Andy. He's outside somewhere, as far as I know. I'll introduce him later on. Lovely lad, but I would say that now, wouldn't I?"

I smiled back at her. Within just a few minutes I knew that she was as much of an extrovert as I was an introvert, the sort of person who made you smile, who almost insisted that time in her company was fun.

Mary White was plump without being fat, curvaceous but no caricature. She was well-dressed and her dark brown hair was styled into what I think was called at the time a bob. A silver necklace bearing a crucifix was slightly caught up in the fine leather loop around her neck supporting a pair of reading glasses which rested snugly on the soft round slopes of her chest. She had maintained the fresh, ruddy complexion of a milkmaid but I put her in her mid-fifties.

"So," she said abruptly, "you'll be wantin' to buy some furniture, then?"

*

I had been attracted to their unusual range having first come across it at a trade show. Abbott's had fixed up a small corner of the cavernous room with a limited sample of their work, and although the stand was not manned continuously, a pile of catalogues had been available to take way. The pieces were mainly in oak, chestnut, beech and ash, but I had seen examples of inlay or whole sections in walnut and cherry wood which excited me. The designs were fashioned around clean, flowing lines with intricate flourishes, a blend of functionality and embellishment which, in my opinion, worked beautifully. They matched my vision for some of the deluxe rooms in our hotels: a move away from furniture of industrially-produced stained pine designed by robots. The disadvantage, of course, was the price, but I had convinced my immediate boss of the value of marquee pieces and had been given substantial funds. Nevertheless, dealing with a niche company was a challenge, and I had to find a balance between quantities, availability, delivery schedules and the so-called bottom line. To Abbott's, who had been generally content to produce bespoke pieces in small numbers, an order like mine was the fillip the company needed to expand. And plans for expansion, as luck would have it, were already on the cards.

Mary explained that quaint as the station premises were, she had decided that increased sales dictated a move to a larger site with many more employees and a professional marketing department. She had offered eighteen contracts since the start of the year, and that morning had interviewed two young designers a few months away from completing their diplomas. She told me she was of a mind to take them both on. She was in the final stages of signing a lease on a unit on a new industrial park in Poole.

"Apart from anything else," she said, showing me a plan of the current site, "the county council owns the track-bed these days. They're lookin' to use the old railway route as a bypass for the village. All these old buildin's'll be demolished soon enough."

"That's a pity. The way of things, though, I suppose."

"The next time you come to see us, Andris, we'll have moved out of Shill," she added wistfully. "I'll still live here, of course. Have done all my life and there be no reason to move, as far as I can see."

We agreed in principle that the quantities Cassis were considering allowed for a generously discounted price, with the understanding that the whole order could not be completed for at least twelve months. I agreed to take the figures to head office, to confer with an interior design consultant I had been afforded on this project, and explained that I had to consider other companies, but as far as I was concerned my mind was made up.

"You'll be needin' to see the workshop again," said Mary, "and properly this time. Let me take you on a little tour." She came round to my side of the desk, took me by the elbow like a bossy nurse, gave me a wink and led me out into the fresh air.

She guided me first into another large, functional building beyond the workshop, and, flicking on a switch which controlled a dozen hanging lights, she announced that we were standing in the warehouse. Scores of tables, chairs, cabinets and other assorted items were neatly stacked, some bubble-wrapped, and along one side were planks and boards and posts of all lengths and widths, some rough, some smoothed.

"The fella that runs this for me is off today," Mary said. "That's why it's locked up."

A small part of the floor-space was taken up by finished samples which I took a special interest in. The quality of the craftsmanship was high indeed.

"This is what we have as a showroom," she said unnecessarily. "I admit it ain't up to scratch. You'll see, won't you, why the move to Poole is so important?"

In the workshop, I renewed acquaintance with some of the faces I had seen earlier. Under the humming of a series of strip lights, Mary introduced a couple of her senior craftsmen who both shook my hand and apologised for the grease. Most of the others had looked up as we came in, stopping their labours respectfully and waiting to be addressed as if by the Headmistress. I was slightly surprised to see two women amongst the overalls. I found the combination of smells, a mix of animal glue, sawdust, linseed oil and stale armpit slightly sickly and was pleased that we quickly moved on.

Later we visited what Mary called the studio, a small room in the station building where I met a youngish man in heavy spectacles sitting alone at a computer. There was little space in the room but he looked to have all the trappings required of a draughtsman, including a wide table covered with paper of all sizes, pens and pencils and all manner of geometric instruments, pages torn from magazines, a digital camera and good light. He was introduced as Vernon.

"I call him Assistant Product Designer," she said. "Assistant to me, that is. Vernon calls himself Artistic Director. He thinks he's workin' in Hollywood."

Vernon didn't seem to appreciate the joke. He raised his glasses to the matted curls on the top of his head and stretched forward wordlessly to shake my hand.

"He's highly strung," she added, closing the studio door on him. "But has a brilliant eye for detail. Been with me for years, straight from college. Come on, keep up, Andris. Let's go outside."

*

We wandered into the angled sunlight still flooding the old station platform in the late afternoon, the tired wooden canopy with its flaky paintwork offering little shade.

"This was a main line until the 1960s," she was telling me, part of a little speech she gave, I imagined, to all visitors.

"North, that way," she went on, pointing towards the outline of what had once been a signal box, "to Bath and Bristol."

"South, that way," as she indicated the silent, neglected tracks disappearing into a wood (*no coal nor crops nor cattle nor cloth passed this way any more to and from the ports*), "that way towards Bournemouth. It's been closed these past twenty years now, of course, like hundreds of other so called uneconomical lines. I remember the sounds and smells of the trains passin' through here when I was a girl. Goods trains, passenger trains, famous ones like the Pines Express."

Her voice trailed off. She saw that I was looking out over the platforms, beyond the railings, across a wide grassy valley and out to the beached whale of a hill on the horizon.

"Hambledon Hill," she called back, already on her way down the platform. "An Iron Age settlement. Come and meet my Andy."

Andrew was half-hidden in a small patch of garden, a cultivated slope of wild flowers and grasses and little bushes and spring bulbs to the south side of the station house. There were yolk-yellow daffodils growing and clumps of late purple crocus and pale blue hyacinths, and pruned rosebushes waiting naked for the summertime. The boy was working with a wheelbarrow of manure, turning it into the soil with an old spade. He wiped a hand on the seat of his jeans and we shook.

"Andy won't say much, will you, son? He's not one for lots of words. But he loves his gardening, don't you, my love?"

Andrew nodded and said quietly:

"This horse-shit ain't as rich as the stuff we got last year," before wiping his brow with his forearm and continuing his shovelling.

In the midst of a group of clipped rose bushes I noticed a small stone plinth, regular of shape, about two feet high. Screwed neatly to its sloping top to catch the evening sun was what looked like a brass plaque. I leaned over out of curiosity.

"That's the memorial stone," said Mary. "Andy keeps it clean, keeps it polished. It's Purbeck stone; limestone, if you like. It's been there for years, it has. Neglected, it was, until we took over the station and Andy got stuck in to restorin' the garden."

"What's the inscription?" I asked.

"I've forgotten the name. I pay no attention to it. It's to a man who was killed in an accident near here years ago. A railway accident. He was found in a ditch by the track back a mile."

I had to step between the rosebushes and soil my shoes to get a closer look, but something unexplainable, something beyond casual inquisitiveness drew me towards the buffed plate whose words, as I read them, made my blood slowly chill:

IN MEMORY OF EDWARD L FLEET, RN
WHO DIED IN A RAILWAY ACCIDENT
ONE MILE FROM THIS STATION
ON 24TH OCTOBER 1960
LEAVING A LOVING WIFE, A SON AND MANY FRIENDS

I was speechless. I felt faint. Little bubbles of air were floating upwards and a grey veil covering my eyes was turning
black. I must have wobbled backwards.

"Andris? What's the matter?" asked Mary. "You alright
there?"

Andrew stopped digging. I was gasping for breath.

"Hey, take it easy," he said. "Grab my hand. Come and sit
down."

"That was my father's name," I mumbled eventually.
"Edward Fleet."

"Why, that's a strange coincidence!" said Mary.

"It says Edward L Fleet. Even down to the initial."

"There could be other men with that name, I reckon."

"And RN. My father was in the Navy. This is bizarre."

"It ain't your father though, is it?" she asked with a look of
disbelief.

"It can't be."

"Well, it is just a strange coincidence then."

"No, it can't be my father. It can't be. He died in Germany.
About the same time, I think, but I don't know for sure. I was
only five."

"Well, whoever he is, his memorial is well tended. And
Andy will carry on in this garden here whether the business
moves to Poole or not."

I had nothing more to say. I felt drained all of a sudden.
Andrew helped me keep my balance as I limped off the earth
and stepped back on to the platform.

"The boy does it for his own father, you see," Mary went on
presently. "My husband. He was in the Navy too. He died in

the Falklands. His ship was hit by a missile."

"He drowned at sea," Andrew suddenly intoned. "Eight thousand miles from home."

"Andy treats it as his dad's memorial. I don't think that man, that Fleet would mind, do you? There's a memorial over in Portsmouth we could visit but it's a long drive from here just to put a flower in a vase every once in a while."

I sat down on a rusty platform bench. I had lost the wind from my sails and my mind was spinning like a lathe in the workshop I'd just seen. Mary put a maternal hand on my shoulder and asked:

"Listen, you fancy a brandy? I've got a decent bottle in the cupboard."

"Sorry, what?"

"A brandy? "

"No. No, thanks. I just need to clear my head."

"Do you have to leave now? I mean this instant? Why don't you stay and we'll meet up at the pub in the village for a bite of food when I've finished up in the office? I've a few things to do, but you could go for a walk. How's that? Stretch your legs."

It made sense. I was already nodding.

"Take your car over to Child Okeford," she was saying, "it's not far to drive. Walk up over Hambledon. The views'll cheer you up, Andris, I can guarantee, especially on such a bright evenin'. You okay to walk that far, are you now? I notice you was limpin'."

"I'm fine to walk, thanks. It's a good idea."

"Andy will lend you some boots, won't you, love?"

"There's some wellies in the shed," the boy offered, and without another word he strode off down the platform in search of a pair.

3

We had a home-cooked meal at the Old Fox Inn in a rather gloomy dining room which we had to ourselves. A log fire was burning in a dusty grate but by the time we ordered a dessert it had been neglected to the extent that the embers had lost their flame and only a cheerless orange glow lit the hearth. There was a subdued hubbub in the bar, a few regulars were there drinking, smoking, talking in their warm, half-paced way, now a serious lull, now a raucous guffaw.

I had worked up quite an appetite and felt better after a stiff walk on the hills as suggested by my companion. Apart from the solitary dog-walker I met on the summit, I had the clean air and the wide views all to myself. I sensed immediately that Hambledon was a striking, special place. I tried to absorb its significance, the elevated, rippled hillsides, the rough earth once carved into ramparts and ditches, farmed and grassed over thousands of years long past. The sheep I saw grazing had their story there too, their own woolly ancestors in pre-history. Try as I might to imagine pagan burials and ancient, primitive settlements, however, I was still preoccupied by events closer to home. I was drowning in my own tormented thoughts, confused, distressed at seeing my father's name on a tombstone. It was like seeing the death mask of a man slain while my back was turned.

I filled my lungs with the sweet, moist air. I listened for the gentle voices of the past carried to and fro on the wind, and wondered, what languages were spoken here? What sound did they make, those men and women with their calls and their commands, their ringing words of praise, their tender terms of consolation? How were their desires expressed, their promises made, their excuses spilt? What tones shaped their words of anger, of sorrow, of joy? What sweet songs of love were sung, what tales of honour and of shame were told, what childish laughter cascaded down these slopes, what poisoned lies were once cast here?

And who was Edward L Fleet, navy man, not drowned at sea, discovered dead in a ditch, solemnly remembered in a railway yard, with no military honours?

I had wandered aimlessly towards a sloping hollow enclosure, vaguely rectangular, brushed by watery shadows in the failing sunlight: a shallow burial site, a Neolithic pasture, a twentieth-century picnic spot. I felt an ache in my gut, an ache of loss. It was the loss of my self-belief, or at least a part of it, and only ghosts lingered here to fill the void. Was that the relentless refrain of human intercourse I couldn't hear, the silent voices whipped up like ash in a breeze? Were the unstilled souls of centuries long forgotten drifting here over these ancient hillsides, nodding wistfully, perplexed at what man and womankind had become?

I walked slowly back to the village to collect the Cavalier, my limp more pronounced on the downhill, the borrowed boots (one size too tight) adding to my discomfort. I felt unnerved and out of place in this pastoral scene, with cottage curtains closing behind lamp-lit rooms as dusk invaded the lanes, the high-hedged horse-shit littered lanes, and the daffodil-dappled gardens. Deep in the country, yet rootless, and with no real understanding of the place, I felt more like a city boy than ever. By the time I regained my car the daylight had all but faded.

*

Mary White had changed into a coral silk blouse and jeans and she had refreshed my spirits. She was a genial hostess, as I knew she would be, telling tales of life in Shillingstone back in the 1950s when she helped on the farm, skipping school for days on end during harvest time. As usual I was happy to keep myself to myself, but she was the kind of person who has the ability to make a conversation easy. I found myself asking questions of a personal nature which I would normally have steered clear of with a woman, especially a woman I had known for barely five hours.

"There must be a story of how the daughter of a farm-worker came to be the owner of a successful business," I suggested.

"Well, there is, of course," she replied with an guarded look over her spoon. "There's always a story."

"I mean, the capital outlay..."

"You mean, where was I gettin' the start-up, Andris? The money, that ugly word?"

"It's not an ugly word in our world," I said, not wishing to cause offence.

She finished her pudding and licked her lips.

"I was lucky, actually. I came into some money."

"An inheritance?"

She hesitated.

"Well, yes and no."

"I'm sorry, Mary. I didn't mean to pry."

"That's alright. Pry away. The main thing was I could afford to go to college, and then set up a little cottage industry."

"It's more than a cottage industry now."

"Of course it is. I started with what I called the Doll's House range. Twee, I know, but pieces sold, they did. We've done well. But I have been at it for twenty-five years now, I have. I know what I'm doin'."

I too had finished eating. There was a lull. Mary was looking towards the bar, perhaps to see if she could spot somebody she knew. I cast an empty glance at the hunting-related artefacts decorating the dining-room.

"Was your husband involved in the business?" I suddenly heard myself asking. "If you don't mind talking about him. I'm sorry that, you know, you no longer have him around. Actually, I'm sorry for even asking."

She turned to face me again with a smile of resignation.

"Listen, that's fine. He was a brave man. Loved his work. Loved the sea. But he was no businessman. Absolutely no head for numbers, that one. He was no use to me, bless him. No, he was one for followin' orders. We were quite different like that. That's why the firm's still in my name. My maiden name."

"Oh, really? I did wonder."

She paused before asking:

"And you, Andris, are you married? Or are you available?"

I blushed in an instant.

"I'm only muckin' about," she laughed. "Don't run off!"

"I am married, as a matter of fact," I said, coughing, taking a drink and laughing with her. "My wife's name is Jacqueline. We were married five years ago."

"Kiddies?"

"No. And that's a blessing, I suppose. We both wanted them, but it's just as well we couldn't. It was a mistake. The marriage, I mean."

"But you must have loved her."

"Well, of course, we loved each other once upon a time. I don't know, I suppose we were both to blame in the end. We got sick of living in each other's pockets, being a couple, you know, sharing everything. It got very claustrophobic."

I paused to let her in, but she declined, preferring to listen.

"Moving to Southampton was the catalyst," I went on. "Jackie wouldn't come. She was a girl I'd known at school when we were both twelve-year-old kids. Her family lived only a five-minute walk from our house. We both found it hard at school. Jackie was a bit of an outsider, like me, I suppose. We gravitated to each other. Well, until it became embarrassing to be seen with a girl unless you were, you know, going out with her. Then at thirteen I changed schools and we never saw each other much again after that. Then, strangely, as these things can happen, I met her at a concert, years later, in the bar at the interval. An Elvis Costello concert, Hammersmith Odeon."

I smiled to myself at the memory, but, I think, I had just lost my audience.

"She was still living in Richmond, she had a place of her own, and a job as a secretary in one of the university admin buildings. I don't know, it seemed churlish not to give it a try. I'd always liked her, we were both single, and there was still something deep down between us in spite of all the water that had passed under the bridge."

"So, what happened?" said Mary. Was she genuinely interested? It seemed so.

"Oh, it's honestly not that interesting. Looking back, I think we just drifted into a marriage neither of us were really convinced about. We got on great but it just wasn't the romance of the century."

Mary was listening quietly, watching me, studying me like she might a painting, looking for texture and integrity.

"Anyway, Jackie wanted to stay in London. It was for the best, I suppose. So we've lived apart for two years. She moved in with a new boyfriend, somewhere in Putney. I'm happier on my own, to be honest. I don't mind my own company. It's a lot more peaceful in a way."

I had never admitted this to anyone else before.

"Are you fancyin' another drink?" Mary asked after a moment.

"No, thanks. I've got a ninety-minute drive in the dark ahead of me."

"Well, I'm havin' one. What about a coffee?"

"That'll be good."

"Right. You go and order it. I'll have a cognac. Put it on the tab and ask Maureen to bring us the bill with the drinks."

"Yes, boss."

"Sorry, I do tend to give my orders. Please would you be so kind...?"

"I'm going. I'm on my way," I said, trying to smile through a grimace as I stood up; my knee was aching now, the result of the overambitious climb earlier. The pain, as then, sometimes transmitted itself up the leg to my hip. I dragged myself into the bar like a ninety-year-old.

*

When I returned a waitress had cleared the dishes and Mary had placed a flat brown envelope on my side of the table.

"What's that, a contract?" I joked.

"No, that ain't what it is," she said coldly. "Don't open it."

"Why not?"

"I want to tell you somethin' first, Andris."

"Sounds serious."

"Well, it is. You suddenly got very serious yourself this

76

afternoon when you read the plaque there in the station garden."

"I've rationalised it now, Mary, don't worry. Just a very weird coincidence."

"Well, maybe, maybe not. But in any case I saw how much it meant to you. And I might be able to help."

"What do you mean, help?"

She drew herself up a little closer to the table and lowered her voice.

"I was here in 1960, Andris. I was here in the village. And I actually remember that night, I do. The night of the Bournemouth train bein' held up at the station while they examined the carriages, talkin' to all the passengers, and all that. I know they stopped it again in Blandford, the police were involved and everythin'. It got into Bournemouth sometime after midnight, they said, two hours late."

I wanted to interrupt but let her continue.

"They found the body, the body of that man, the one on the memorial, the next morning. A farmer, I suppose it was who found him. He was in a ditch by the track back near Hammoon. I remember readin' about it. Everyone was talkin' about it, you can imagine. But he hadn't just fallen from the train. He'd been pushed out. And not only that, Andris. The fall didn't kill him. They said that he'd already been murdered. Poisoned, I think. I don't know for sure. There was a lot of rumours flyin' around. People just guessin' and gossipin', like they do. Whether it was the truth or not, that part was kept out of the papers."

The landlady arrived with a coffee, a brandy and, folded into a little leatherette wallet, the dinner bill.

"There you go, Mary," she said. "You both enjoyed your meals, did you?"

"Thanks, Maureen," said Mary, dismissively. "Very nice."

The other woman retreated without another word. Mary

picked up the bill, glanced at the total, and placed it back in the wallet.

"My treat, by the way," she said.

"Thanks, that's very kind," I said, stirring sugar into my coffee.

"Where was I?" she wondered aloud, impatiently. "Oh, the poisonin'."

"Did they catch the murderer?" I asked.

"No, they never did. At least as far as I know they didn't. There was police around here for days after, I can remember, but no, he got clean away. Or she did. I expect it was a man, havin' the strength to push him out of the train like that."

Mary paused to lift her glass to her lips. We both needed a sip or two of something.

"Apart from all that," Mary resumed presently, "I found a case, I did. A case belonging to the man, the dead man."

"A case? What do you mean? What kind of case?"

"Like an attaché case."

"What do you mean, you found it? Where?"

"It'd been thrown from the train as it pulled into Shill. I was out that night, I was, in the lane by the bridge, the railway bridge, near the station. I heard it land in the fields. Anyway, the long and short of it, I found it."

"You took it to the police?"

"Yeah, of course I did. I took it home first though, showed my dad. We took it on to the police the next mornin'."

"Did you look inside it?"

"Yeah, it just unzipped easy as you like. I was curious, you can imagine. I didn't know nothin' about a dead man at the time, just that the train was held up at Shill and that a case had landed in a field right by me."

"So what did you find inside it?"

"Documents, mainly, naval registers, stuff in Russian."

"Russian?"

"They said he was a spy, the fella on the train, didn't they? Don't you remember the story? I suppose you'd be too young. There was a bit of a row about havin' a memorial for him here, I remember. Sixty, sixty-one, what'd you be, Andris, still a kid, still in your short pants?"

I didn't answer her question. Again my thoughts raced ahead of me.

Daddy's gone. He's not coming back, Andris, darling.

I missed a part of what the woman had to say next.

"There was a book. A proper book. You know, a hardback. I even remember the title. *Mother*. You heard of that? You ever heard of a book, a proper novel it was, called *Mother*?"

"No. No, I can't say I have, Mary."

"And there was a theatre programme for a show in Bournemouth. A bit odd, don't you think? Anyway, the police was very interested in that, they was. And in the book."

She looked around to check that nobody was snooping, and said in little more than a whisper:

"And then there was that."

"What?"

She was pointing at the envelope by my coffee cup.

"Open it."

I followed her instruction and found myself holding a black and white photograph of a very glamorous woman, the sort of photograph actors have taken of themselves professionally. It was a head and shoulders shot, enhancing the woman's perfect skin, twinkling eyes, lustrous blond curls, her enigmatic smile.

"So, who is she?" I asked.

"Turn it over."

On the reverse was a flourish of faded blue ink: *To my darling Eddie. Much love, P.*

"P?"

"It matched up to one of the actresses in the theatre programme. I'm sorry, I've forgotten it. It's all a very long time ago."

"But you kept it. Or did the police give it back to you?"

"No, I kept it. I didn't give it to the police. I know I should have. I just liked the lace on her dress. It sounds daft now, I know. I wanted to see if I could find some like it in Blandford for myself. I didn't think it would be important. I admit I wasn't really thinkin'. I was only a silly kid myself at the time."

I was still holding the image in my hands: P was smiling at me, teasing me with her unreleasable secret.

"Keep it. Keep it, Andris," she said. "If the man on the memorial be your father then maybe this will help you, you know, find out the truth."

"I don't know what to think," I said, closing my eyes, hiding both women from view. I felt Mary's hands cover mine and opened them again abruptly. I read the concerned look on her face as genuine.

"And don't you worry," she said, calmly maternal. "Whether the name on that plaque be your father's or not, you can be sure that my Andy will keep it nice and tidy, well polished. As I said, he treats it like it's his own daddy's, he does. It's like an unknown soldier. Well, sailor. It represents a sacrifice to him, to us. His loss. Our loss."

I slipped the photograph back into the envelope and then into my jacket pocket.

"Thank you," I said. "It's been a strange day."

"A very positive one, I do hope," she suggested, steering me back to my reason for visiting this place.

"Indeed. And thanks for the dinner. I've really enjoyed it. I've really enjoyed meeting you, Mary."

She smiled to herself.

"You know, if I were twenty years younger," she mused, "I'd be offerin' you bed and breakfast. And anythin' else you fancied in between. And don't you be blushin' up again, Mr Fleet!"

I really didn't know what to say next.

"I don't think it's ever a good idea," I improvised, "to mix business with pleasure." And I immediately regretted saying the word *pleasure* with such unintended warmth. I was more than embarrassed, I was actually rather flattered.

"Instead of bed and breakfast," I tried again, "perhaps you can do me an extra discount on an order of two dozen wardrobes?"

She feigned horror.

"Sorry, young man. I don't do that kind of business after six pm."

She knew she had managed to lighten the mood.

"Just promise me one thing."

"What's that?"

"Get rid of the moustache."

I looked at her with a puzzled expression.

"Sorry. You heard me. Get rid of the moustache."

"Really?"

"Really."

"My wife likes it. Well, liked it."

"Exactly. Your wife don't even like *you* no more."

"Fair point."

"A woman who says she likes kissin' a fella with a moustache," she said, hovering a second over her punchline, "she be nothin' more than a damn liar."

4

I had mixed feelings about living in Southampton. I didn't mind that it wasn't London, or that it felt utterly, unambitiously provincial, or even that I was there alone, my wife preferring to be in Putney with her lover. I had a spacious flat in a house in Upper Shirley, convenient for the office, close to the shops, a stone's throw from the wide, grassy common. It was the perfect spot for a sports fan, not that I ever counted myself as one: a ten minute walk to both the county cricket and the city's football grounds. I avoided the latter, especially on match days when hordes of boisterous young men gathered on street corners looking vexed. I had in fact been to see a cricket match, on one occasion only and that as a guest in some corporate hospitality scenario where most seemed to be ignoring the contest at the wicket in favour of chardonnay and appetisers.

I suppose I found the city a touch drab. There was so little to look at that set the pulse racing. Like all seaports its citizens had a chippiness about them, a fuck-you sense of their worth, a confidence in themselves that I hoped might rub off a little on me. The docks are the heartbeat of the place, a vast, muscular geometry imposed on the metalled shoreline, all the more majestic when the mighty cranes are hauling containers off the lines of hulking cargo vessels, or if the quay is hosting one of those monumental marble-white cruise ships, illuminated at night like a twinkling, floating version of the Ritz. Then, a romantic nostalgia might descend and the misty-eyed can see again, from a distance of so many years, the bunting, the red-white-and-blue, and the flying champagne corks, and hear the brass band and the crowds of well-wishers cheering as they wave *bon voyage* to the ghost of the stately Titanic and other heroes of its lineage.

Away from the water, the city itself appears an afterthought. To my mind it looked like when the plans were drawn up for the buildings to shelter, supply and administer its inhabitants, neither designer nor architect with a shred of ambition was ever invited to the party. In the winter of 1940 the newsreels show the old place taking a pounding from German bombs, but judging from the lack of imagination in the rebuilding projects (there was little money to spare on indulgences, I grant), it is as if an opportunity was somehow sadly missed.

*

During a fitful drive back from north Dorset I had resolved to speak to my mother as soon as possible. It was not until a mid-morning break the following day that I had the chance to make a telephone call.

Erika and Adrian were still rattling around in the spacious family home in Richmond, now just the pair of them getting on each other's nerves and finding refuge in separate rooms a five minute walk apart. I do exaggerate, but the impression I had was not one of marital bliss. The girls had long since flown the nest, both by now self-confident young women in their late twenties. Tiffany, having studied English Literature and Ancient History at Bristol, had married a Welshman and was working as a trainee journalist in Cardiff. Patricia had followed in her father's footsteps to read Law at Oxford and thence to the Inns of Court. I had no idea how often the four of them (five including Rhys) assembled for birthdays, holidays or special occasions of any other kind. I knew that Adrian had developed a portfolio of clients in the Caribbean, of all places, so I imagined he was not in London quite so much anymore. As for me, I kept my distance, quite deliberately, sometimes visiting my mother on her birthday, spending a few Christmases up there too over the years, but as a rule an irregular telephone call was the extent of our contact. Not that relations were sour; it was simply the case that whenever I rang, the conversation usually lasted less than a minute before long, chilly gaps began to take over.

"Hello. Plummers."

It was Trixie's slightly whiny voice, which surprised me as I had expected Erika to pick up.

"Hello, Trixie. It's Andris," I said, in case she had forgotten how my voice sounded over the phone. "How are you? What are you doing home?"

"Oh, hi, Dris. No, I'm fine. I've got a couple of days off, actually. Just down here for a spot of home comforts, you know. Mummy needed a hand with some papers and stuff, Daddy's abroad, and, anyway, how are *you*? We haven't seen you for absolute ages."

"Yeah, I'm well, thanks."

"Still buying toilet roll for hotels?"

"Well, yes. And the rest."

She couldn't resist a little dig.

"And so, are you coming up to London soon? Is that what you're ringing about?"

"No, it's not that. I just wanted a word with Erika. Is she in?"

"Yeah, she's in the kitchen, I think. I'll go and find her for you."

"Thanks, Trixie."

"I'm in the study, so just hang on a sec. I think she's got a phone in the kitchen. Perhaps she hasn't. Hang on."

If my mother were in the kitchen, then study-to-kitchen-to-study, that's a two minute trek, longer if she's got to wash and dry her hands.

Patricia would make a decent barrister, I thought. She was sharp, ultra-confident and had a hard edge. A bit like a machete. Empathetic but definitely not sympathetic. Tiffany was a little more sensitive; she had always been the kinder, the less sarcastic of the two towards me. I was worried she might get eaten alive in journalism if she had ambitions to work in London. Better off staying in Cardiff. One of these days she would make a wonderful mother, would Tiffy. She would provide Erika with the grandchild she yearned for and all would be well in the Plummer constellation. I had met Rhys at their wedding, of course. He seemed very easy-going, rather unconventional, not a suit-and-tie kind of man, which could upset Adrian in the long run. So that would be in his favour, then. I remember he was talking about opening a health-food shop as soon as they got back from their honeymoon on Anglesey.

"Andris? Andris?"

It was my mother's voice. Her tone was one of irritation.

"Hello, mother. You've been busy in the kitchen, Trixie said."

"What do you want, Andris?"

Okay, so we'll dispense with the social niceties.

"I just wanted a word. You can spare five minutes, can't you?"

"What's it about? Why are you being so mysterious?"

"I'm not."

"Five minutes. What do you mean, five minutes?"

"Mother, relax. Can you talk?"

"Yes, I can talk," she relented.

"Sit down and listen, please." I said calmly. "It's important. At least, I think it could be."

"Now you *are* being mysterious."

Talking to my mother was never easy. I had always found her to be a pretty poor listener, at least when she was supposed to be listening to me. As succinctly as I could, I explained that I had spent the previous afternoon in Dorset looking at a furniture showroom.

"In Shillingstone?" she interjected.

"Yes. Have you heard of it?"

"I think I've heard of it," she mumbled.

"Well, either you have or you haven't."

"I'm thinking of Sherborne."

"Sherborne?"

"Yes. That's in Dorset, isn't it? I think so. We drove up there once when we were over at your old school for a parents' meeting. There's an abbey. And a nice tea shop."

Off the top of my head I could not remember a single occasion when she and Adrian had visited the school, for a parents' evening, a speech day, a sports day or any other day.

"Go on, darling. Tell your tale."

I decided to come straight to the point.

"Well, the offices I visited were in an old railway station house. The line closed in the sixties. It's all a bit decrepit now, a bit sad."

"I can imagine."

"All except from on the platform where there's a lovely little garden, very well tended, lovingly in fact. I met the gardener, a young lad, he was preparing the earth around a memorial, a kind of plinth."

"Why are you telling me all this, Andris? Get on with it."

I hesitated, took a long breath.

"The memorial had a plaque inscribed with Daddy's name on it."

"Daddy's? What do you mean? Your father's name?"

"His name exactly. Down to the middle initial. Even including the RN. And the year of his death too. 1960. That was the year, wasn't it?"

There was a silence on the end of the line. After a moment I heard her voice again, matter-of-fact.

"That's a strange coincidence, isn't it, darling?" she said.

"Can it be just a coincidence, mother? Really?"

"Well, it has to be."

"I've been going out of my mind thinking about it. I hardly slept last night."

"It's a coincidence, darling."

"Is it? Tell me it is. Make me believe you."

"Listen, Andris, calm down. Take a deep breath, my love. Your daddy was killed in Berlin. I've told you that before and you can't have forgotten, surely?"

"I haven't forgotten. I believe you, of course I do. But I've never seen any proof. He has no grave, I've seen no death certificate..."

"It's because he was working for the security services, Andris. You know that. His work was largely secret. For MI6. I told you, in Berlin. All the records are restricted. Even I haven't been allowed to see them all. But I did see a death certificate. Daddy died in Berlin, darling. That's where he was killed."

"You are certain?"

"That's where it happened, Andris. By the Wall. Not in Shillingstone, or Sherborne, or wherever it is they sell furniture and have tumbledown railway stations."

I fell quiet, rolling the thoughts around my head like a

student trying to solve a complex maths problem without the aid of a calculator.

"Andris?"

"Yes, mother. I'm still here."

"You'll think no more of it, will you? It's just a very unusual coincidence. Let it rest. You'll do yourself no good worrying. Especially worrying about something like that, something that doesn't mean anything. Do you hear me, Andris?

"Yes. Yes, I do."

"Well, then. I'm fine, by the way, thanks for asking."

She was as adept as ever at sarcasm.

"Sorry."

"I'm back in the old groove, as a matter of fact."

"The old groove?"

"Politically. I've been back in touch with some of the old soldiers from the Baltic movement. Things are moving, Andris. Latvia will be free again, free from the Soviets, and soon. I can feel it. Change has already come to eastern Europe. Since the Wall came down, well, you've seen it with your own eyes, you know that Moscow is in retreat. In Poland, then in Czechoslovakia and Romania last winter. Latvia is close to breaking free too. Gorbachev is a pragmatist; he'll have to back off, he knows it."

"Will he?"

I had not heard everything she had said, but it was clear that news of my discovery had already lost its momentum.

"There have been elections," she rattled on. "Just recently. Two thirds of the seats in the new Supreme Council are held by the Popular Front. I actually know some of those people, Andris. I have been writing again to people in Riga. After all these years. We have meetings of support groups here in London again, just like in the old days. A few of the old faces, and plenty of new ones. It's so exciting, Andris!"

"Mother," I interrupted, "I have a photograph of a young actress."

"I beg your pardon?"

"I was given a photo of a girl. A proper professional portrait of an actress. It belonged to the man called Edward Fleet."

"Andris, we said you'd drop this."

"I'm just asking. Just to be sure. Do you know anything about this?"

"An actress? What actress? What's her name?"

"There is no name."

"No name? What are you asking me this for?"

"Just the initial letter P, in a message on the back."

"P, what, like Patricia?"

"Yes, could be. Does it mean anything to you?"

"No."

"Anything at all?"

"No, darling. Nothing. Nothing at all."

"Are you sure? Mother, it's important."

"How many times do you want me to say it?"

There was a silence as the words dried up.

"Alright," I said at last. "I think we've come to a dead end."

"It sounds very much like you have," she agreed. "So just back up, Andris, and drive away."

"I think I'm going to have to."

"No choice."

"No choice."

"It's for the best."

"Thanks for listening, mother."

"That's what a mother is for, darling. Thank you for ringing. It's always a pleasure to hear your voice."

"I'll ring again soon. You can keep me up to date with the struggle."

"The struggle?"

"In Latvia."

"Right. Of course. I thought you meant..., never mind. I certainly will. There's finally some light at the end of the tunnel. It's been forty years."

"I must go. I've got work."

"Of course you have."

"Give my love to Adrian, won't you?"

"Really? You don't mean that."

"Your words, not mine. Is he in?"

"No, he's abroad again. Barbados this time, for a week. Making money."

"Well, give him a hug from me when he's back."

"As if you ever hugged him, Andris, you tease!"

"Good bye, mother."

"Good bye, darling. Look after yourself, won't you?"

I put the phone down and stood up, desperate to stretch my legs, to wander around the office, to take in the dreary view of rooftops and streets and traffic trapped under the gloomy, grey sky.

*

It was perfectly true that I had nowhere else to go with this.

I had already been officially rebuffed once, many years earlier, a dead end that my mother knew nothing about. 1980 had been a particularly shitty year. By the end of it I was still working in the West End, running a hotel as an assistant manager, taking home half the salary of a scumbag of a manager who was never there. I was still living at home with a family in which I felt an imposter, my love life was an utter embarrassment, my car was off the road after being hit by a dustbin lorry on the Fulham Road, my job was at risk in a new recession just as Britain posted the highest unemployment figures since before the war, Thatcher was growing into her new job and relishing it, my stepfather was blindly cheering her on, and then to cap it all John Lennon was shot dead by some fuckwit in New York City. I still miss John to this day. His star was one that had truly brightened my young life.

Some time just before Christmas, on one of those horrible evenings when Adrian had been at his most pompous, I had retreated to my bedroom wondering why life had dealt me this boorish substitute father, and had penned a letter to Whitehall asking for the chance to be included in the truth about my real one. To my surprise I was granted an appointment and so I had actually turned up at the Foreign and Commonwealth Office, brimming with as much indignation as I could muster, and was afforded the chance to pose a few questions to a minion of absolutely no authority. The underling I spoke to gave me short shrift in the politest possible way:

Mr Edward Fleet's death is subject to the highest level of secrecy for the protection of national security. All records are restricted, as I am sure you understand, with non-sensitive material available only to next of kin, namely Mrs Erika Fleet. Sir, I am sorry to say, you have wasted your time. If you don't mind me saying, I would suggest that you arrange a chat over a cup of tea with your mother.

I had neither the gumption nor the wit to argue with him. He was a shiny-faced man in a pinstriped suit, as I remember, who wore a smile of such insincere concern that I was tempted to reach over and throttle him with his stripy red and yellow tie.

Now, after Shillingstone, a little of the bile I had tasted in that draughty office resurfaced. Although driving to Richmond, negotiating the arcane traffic system and risking the chance of having to make conversation with Adrian was never really an option I had seriously considered, I did regret speaking to Erika on the telephone rather than confronting her face to face.

When I mentioned the plaque, the photograph, even the name of the railway station, I had been able only to imagine my mother's reaction. I wanted to see the light in her eyes dim or dazzle, to observe the curl of her lip and the flush in her cheeks, to judge the sincerity in her frown. Instead all I had was the tone of her voice and the insistence, genuine or otherwise, that no, *that* Edward could not have been my father and yes, *her* Edward, *our* Edward *did* die in East Germany.

Take it or leave it. I couldn't call my mother a liar to her face. The chances are she was telling the truth all along. And, anyway, as she had said, I had no choice. I had nowhere else to go. *Back up and drive away.* It made some sense. All I could do was leave it all behind and get on with my life: rudderless, guileless, fatherless.

PART THREE

THE AWAKENING OF ANDRIS FLEET CONTINUED

2015

1

Puttering up and down the wide expanse of grass on a brand new ride-on mower, with the sun on my back, sweet air in my lungs, and with a favourite shuffle turned up high on my iPod, I could not have been much happier. I had been so impatient to sit on it, rev it up, spin it over the lawns, but the rains had confined it to the old brick barn until this day: this bright, dry morning in June with the sundried grass ripe to be trimmed by the crisp, shiny blades rotating with intent between its thick rubber tyres.

"How's the new toy?" shouted Harvey from over the garden wall.

I heard not a word, but in the corner of my eye I noticed the old man waving at me. I finished the swoop I was on, piloting the machine with growing confidence, and brought it to a controlled stop a few yards from where he was standing. I switched off the engine, which quietened to a soft fading throb.

"What did you say?" I called.

I needed to reduce the volume on my music and settled on simply pulling the earphones out.

"I said, how's the new toy?"

"It's great. Like driving a Ferrari."

Toy, had he called it? It had cost well over three thousand pounds, more than I had paid for a few of the cars I had bought down the years.

"You fancyin' a cup of coffee after your next lap?" he asked with a grin.

"Tea would be great, thanks."

"I'll tell Lynne to put the kettle on. Happy mowin'!"

He turned away and wandered slowly towards the house, hands in his pockets, just as relaxed as you like. Never one in a rush was Harvey. He took his time; the job always got done in the end. *Time should give you a clear view*, he told me more than once, *not blurred vision*. I think he was quite proud of his little aphorism, so he would give it a regular airing. I had come to love this man, this sixty-odd-year-old rascal (not very much older than me), in his baggy work-jacket and worn corduroys, this wise, grey-whiskered countryman whose farm I lived on, whose grass I was cutting, and whose daughter I adored.

A little later we were sitting at one of the picnic tables draining our mugs, picking cake crumbs from our plates, when Polly's filthy 4x4 pulled into the driveway and came to a gentle, crunching halt on the gravel outside the farmhouse. Lynne, unofficial mother-in-law, stood to collect the crockery and waved to her daughter, who stepped out of the vehicle with shopping bags and a package wrapped in brown paper. She slammed the car door with a kick of her right boot.

"Hi!" she called. "I'll just put this lot indoors and then I'll join you. Any tea left?"

"I'll make some fresh," said Lynne, following her in through the doorway.

Harvey watched as I stood and gave his daughter a little hug when she reappeared and took a seat with us.

"How was town?" I asked.

"Busy, as usual," she said, getting her breath back. "Typical Friday, frantic, you know what it's like. More people than

96

ever, the weekend. There were plenty of tourists in town already and it's not even the school holidays yet."

I thought she looked a little tired, frazzled from the supermarket.

"You okay, Poll?"

"Yeah, I'm fine. I'll be fine after a cup of tea."

I had been living here with Polly and her parents for the best part of ten years but never grew tired of looking at her, at her bright-eyed, sun-kissed round face framed by her wild, wavy dark-brown hair, at her slight yet powerful body, sloppy tee-shirt and jeans, always jeans.

Harvey turned back to his newspaper. He had lit a cigarette and took a deep, satisfying drag; I knew he was trying to give up smoking but he was finding it impossible.

"What was in the parcel?" I asked.

"Just some new leaflets from the tourist office. I called in on the off chance. Most of the ones we have are out of date, I think. You know, last year's prices and stuff."

"I'll sort them out later."

"If you like."

"When I've done the lawns."

"Oh, so you got the mower working, did you?"

"Damn right. Started up first time."

"It's just like drivin' a Ferrari," said Harvey without looking up from his paper.

"She drives like a dream," I insisted. "Really she does. Better than your crappy old car!"

"Hey, lay off, I love my beast!"

Polly had been driving her battered tank for as long as I had known her. I hated it with more than mock derision; it was uncomfortable, unresponsive to drive and cumbersome to park. In retaliation she scoffed at my fondness for dinky two-seater sports cars, a type I seemed to have settled on and refreshed every few years ever since I found myself living alone. She mocked the inadequacy of the boot-space (*how are you going to fit a hay-bale in there?*) and always believed she had scored a point by relentlessly referring to the design as *feminine.*

At that moment a grey saloon swept past the house with a toot of the horn and headed out down the drive to join the road: one of the two families currently occupying the holiday lets.

Lynne re-emerged with a mug of tea and a chocolate biscuit. She had been digging up a batch of early potatoes and her fingernails were still rimmed with earth.

"There you go, dear," she said, placing the refreshments in front of her daughter. She shuffled up on the bench next to her husband just as the dog, who had dozily followed her out of the house, came over to sniff at Polly and then decided to lie down on the warm concrete by Harvey's feet.

"What's in the news, lover? Anythin' interestin'?"

Harvey grunted. I watched Polly bite into the biscuit, spilling crumbs, giggling, wiping away a stray lock of hair out of her face.

"Not really." Harvey had decided to answer his wife after all. "Stuff I've read about before. Same old. Here, take it if you want a read. I'll have another five minutes then I think I might split some logs before lunch."

This was my life now.

A happy life. It had taken a lifetime to get here but it had been worth the effort. It felt like I had finally built one of those towers made of wooden Jenga bricks. I had found the perfect partner, companion, lover and best friend, and with her had come the loveliest of families: her salt-of-the-earth parents and their dog Nancy, an old border collie who spent most of the day sleeping, and Sean, the gentle giant, her seventeen-year-old son, as handy and willing a lad as you could ever imagine.

Sean was born prematurely, his mother had quite casually told me over our very first drink *à deux*, and a lack of oxygen at birth had caused mild brain damage. He attends a special school but has no need to board. An outsider watching him interact with his family would never guess; he is a healthy, happy, sweet-natured young man with a sense of fun and a heart-warming innocence about him. And although his reading, like his speech, is slow and halting, he tunes an engine like a mechanic in a Formula One team and he can shear a sheep almost as fast as his grandfather. His passion is his model railway, a complex structure involving tunnels and functioning level crossings on which he will spend hours as the make-believe world unlocks his imagination. Set up by Harvey for him when he was about ten as a simple oval track, it now covers much of the floor-space of great-grandfather Stanley's old master bedroom.

Polly met the boy's father when she was going through what she admitted was her rebellious phase. She had been studying mathematics for two years when she decided to drop out of university, leave home and take up instead with a group of travellers she had met during the long summer months. She spent the best part of a year living from hand to mouth in a converted bus, hopping from one unofficial site to another across the south west. Lynne was beside herself, according to Harvey, but I can't imagine him losing too much sleep over what he would be confident was his daughter's very temporary detour. She'll be back, I can hear him saying to console his wife. Poll likes her home comforts too much to end up livin' in a leaky old caravan for more than ten minutes. Her eventual return to the farm was no surprise to him but, as he confessed to me once, the sight of her swollen belly was. Neither parent ever met Sean's father, a young charismatic Irishman who disappeared three months before the child was born. Over the sea back to County Cork, was the educated guess.

There were twenty years between us, Polly and me, but neither of us gave it much thought. Jibes about cradle-snatching or collecting pensions and free bus passes were rare. If she ever felt the need to have a little ageist dig, I would say how sorry I felt for her growing up in the dreary, regressive eighties, missing out on the previous two decades which had indisputably been a golden age of contemporary music, a flowering of creativity and invention unlikely ever to be repeated; and really, Poll, you had to have been there. At sixty years old I was still quite presentable, as Mrs Hussey might have said, more or less fighting fit: clean-shaven these days but thinner on top and with too many wrinkles, and the knee was no worse in spite of years and years of wear and tear. Some while ago, not long after I met Polly, in fact, I had an operation to rebuild a part of the joint; it was a limited success which meant that although I still couldn't walk without a limp, I was able to hop along at a decent lick, mercifully without the need of a stick.

*

We celebrated my sixtieth birthday in fairly low-key fashion. I was never one for extravagant parties, and frankly I would have struggled thinking of whom to invite to fill a decent-sized room. The family took me out for a meal in the poshest restaurant in Dorchester. Next April would be Polly's fortieth; she had already dropped heavy hints at a week in the Seychelles.

One of many small farms tucked among the soft green folds of West Dorset, the fortunes of Pattercombe, indeed much like my own life, had been dramatically transformed since the start of the new millennium. Polly had told me that on the night her grandfather died, New Year's Eve 1999, the rest of the family breathed a collective sigh of relief, and a new age of modernity could at last begin. Old Stanley was a twentieth-century man, born during the Great War, born to be a farmer, a man of the land, a man attached to *his* land, a man of very fixed ideas. To be stricter with the truth, he was a man whose guiding principles were those of *the first half* of the twentieth century. He eschewed everything that came along with the age of rock and roll, and then pretty much everything else that followed it.

He wouldn't see beyond the end of his nose, Polly had said. Not he couldn't, *he wouldn't. His mind was so narrow that no new thought could squeeze in nor out.* When his black and white television set finally expired, he allowed himself the rarest of indulgences and his wife was permitted to go out and choose a colour one. *You can get yourself a blue one or a green one*, he had said. So, he did have a sense of humour, at least, if that story isn't just another episode of family legend. His wife, the put-upon Ida, was a little different, apparently; she bought celebrity magazines and read them in secret, storing them behind the sheets and pillowcases in the airing cupboard where Stan would never dream of going. But she was too weak to stand up to him in the long run, and Ida lost her battle, dying many years before he did, a victim of serial wounds caused by decades of stabbing frustration. Meanwhile, and despite his son Harvey's attempts to modernise the farm, Stanley let the fortunes of the business decline, everything from the size and health of his dairy herd to the condition of the buildings and the machinery housed within them.

When Harvey eventually inherited, he had the freedom to rationalise the business just in time. He'd had years to formulate a plan of action, and wasted not a moment in selling the cattle and a large portion of the land they grazed on, and with Lynne and especially Polly at his side (practical, educated, highly numerate Polly riding shotgun), he cautiously turned his hand to the tourism industry.

"It's called agritourism," she explained to me the first time I met her.

"Tourists get a proper sense of country living, of life on a farm. They live amongst the sights and sounds and smells of the animals on a working farm, they can roll their sleeves up and muck in if they want to or just watch from the sidelines. Pattercombe's a great site, we've got fruit trees, a kitchen garden, a pond, a wood, sheep, chickens, tractors. Plus, the sea's not too far away if people want a change of scene."

I remember coming across Polly at a tourism fair in Bournemouth. I think *Hospitality Industry Conference* was the proper title in those days. It was an annual event but I had not seen her there before. She had an armful of brochures and an effortless, innocent charm. Pattercombe Farm had had its first summer of visitors: just a thin stream of single families in the only refit that was up and running at the time. I was still working for Cassis and was more than a little jaded; I'd had my fill of blackcurrants. Polly has always maintained that she headhunted me.

Over the years leaky outbuildings were demolished, with the best of the stone barns renovated and converted into a holiday home. A further pair of new cottages was built on the site of the old milking shed. The apple orchard was extended to cover two acres and I oversaw the construction of a cider press last spring. We had the grounds landscaped with new planting and the pond was drained, cleaned, refilled and bordered by young willows. The huge garage, a pair of smaller storage barns and the old family house remained, along with the sheep, Harvey's pride and joy, his small flock of around sixty Dorset Down which grazed contentedly in the top field.

Polly and her mother look after the holiday lets, Sean helps his grandfather at weekends and I just muck in whenever and wherever I am needed. I have marketing and hospitality expertise, of course, but these days I am just as likely to be found clearing out the chicken coop or driving a tractor down our lane, the blades of its clunky hedge-trimmer rolling and splicing, ripping and spitting out twigs and overgrown shoots in all directions. I even have my own pair of scruffy green overalls. City boy no more, it would appear.

Back at the beginning, as both Polly and I were in the hospitality industry, we decided we needed to meet each other in hotels for what we called research purposes. Bournemouth and its surrounding area suited us as it was more or less equidistant. In fact Cassis owned a splendid place near the town but out of discretion I avoided it, even though I was entitled to a fairly generous cut-price rate. We tried self-catering rental cottages, country house hotels, B & Bs with sea views and many more in between. I wasn't discerning in the slightest: every one was memorable, perfect, the ideal choice, as long as Polly was there to share it. On one of our weekends together, in Bournemouth itself as I recall, she invited me to give Pattercombe a try, both in the business and, more significantly, as part of a new home life with her. I was typically cautious; I had never lived in any place where the nearest shop wasn't two minutes away in a well-lit street with cars and people and noise. I asked myself if I really was an animal-person. The only cow I had ever had any proper interest in was the brown and white one on the cover of Floyd's challenging fifth album, *Atom Heart Mother*.

As a driver for whom time often meant money, I had always regarded tractors as the enemy. And I knew there was a family involved, including a teenage son who would resent me. I had met all them just the once before. But of course it was the best thing I ever did. It was a perfect time for me to change direction and the top and bottom of it was that I was in love with her and would have followed her to the moon, never mind to the far side of Dorset.

And so I left Southampton in 2005. I was fifty years old, irritable, restless, had been more than a little lonely if truth be told, and I desperately needed a fresh start. The Cassis Group was in new hands by then and was expanding, and moreover the management structure had been reorganised: *rationalisation* was the word. The result for me was a series of sideways moves into marketing, then website design. I was obliged to move into a new office in Winchester, where I was surrounded by a garrulous, sarcastic group of under-thirties. Meanwhile Upper Shirley had been transformed into a residential sprawl of new avenues of apartments and starter homes, and had taken on a suburban anonymity which I found depressing. The sports stadia had long gone: first the old Hampshire cricket ground was demolished, and not long afterwards followed the disappearance of the Dell. Weekends, without the noise and the colour and the energy they once bought to the area, were never the same again.

I took to Harvey straight away. Even though I was far older than the man he had imagined would one day make his daughter happy, I think he saw in me something of the son he never had. He delighted in teaching me the ways of the countryside, never missing a chance to tease me for my metropolitan manner and my innate suspicion of mud. It was a teasing I could trust because I knew that at its heart was a fondness, a respect, a kind of manly affection that I had never known before but which I recognised instantly.

He taught me how to split logs with a long-handled axe, how to put up fence posts and barbed wire, how and when to prune apple trees, how to fix a trailer on to a tractor and how to use a chainsaw without losing a limb. I remember we were in the bottom field removing a fallen tree and Harvey had hauled down the machine to slice the timber into manageable chunks.

"You ever used one of these bad boys?" he asked, flicking away a cigarette end before picking it up with one hand.

I shook my head in awe.

"Mind of its own, this one. You have to tame him, see. Show him who's boss."

He slipped on a pair of goggles, tugged at the starter cord and set about sawing a branch off the main trunk. He made it look as effortless as snipping a paper ribbon with a pair of scissors. After a minute or two he stopped the engine and beckoned me over.

"Here," he said, lifting the chainsaw towards me. "Your turn, city boy!"

I remember the time it took to get the heavy beast to feel comfortable in my hands. With the sweaty goggles over my eyes I felt slightly android.

"Don't forget, hold him away from you. Point him ahead of you."

I pulled the cord sharply and the saw immediately jerked into life, roaring like a wild animal suddenly unleashed. Knocked backwards as if by the recoil of a rifle, I gripped the handle but panicked that the thing would rear up and its spinning chain of chattering teeth would fall towards me. Harvey's strong leathery hands appeared in the blink of an eye, grabbing the saw over mine, his muscular arms around my body, holding both me and the machine firmly until the moment I could resume my own grip, when he calmly depressed the stop button.

He let go of me and laughed.

"Don't worry, Andris, lad, you'll get used to it."

"Thanks," I said, pulling off the goggles in relief.

"And by the way," he added with his tongue hard inside his cheek, "I expect all of this ash to be cut up into nine-inch logs before sunset!"

Another, less dangerous skill he tried to teach me, and this time more successfully, was how to play the game of indoor skittles. The pair of us went off to the village pub from time to time to play on the alley, and in fact we still do. Once we'd teamed up and beaten some of the locals, we were asked to join the pub team and play for them in a local winter league. It was an enjoyable way of meeting people and getting to know the area, and without wishing to blow my own trumpet, indoor skittles is a game in which I excelled. Like darts, billiards and sex, I found it to be an activity where a pronounced limp is not so much of a handicap.

*

With the inevitability of a homing pigeon's final flight, my mother left England for Latvia. It was a case of the stars aligning for her, I suppose: the political clouds clearing to reveal a new, independent country, eager to stand on its own feet, and an uncontested divorce from Adrian Plummer. It was not so much the man's obsession with materialism that wore her down (whatever the problem, large or small, public or private, his answer was always to throw money at it); rather the end came when he admitted a long-standing affair with the wife of the British ambassador to one of the islands in the Caribbean whose name I have forgotten. Smelling a rat, Erika had actually hired a private detective to follow him during a week in the West Indies. It was quite a mini-scandal, finding its way into the pages of a few of the daily newspapers. And not only had he split up the marriage, Adrian had also caused a rift between his two daughters.

Patricia took her father's side, considering that her mother's fixation with Soviet politics had driven him to a woman who would tell him more readily that she loved him. Tiffany had more sympathy for Erika, and, when the story broke, I believe my mother spent a week or two up with her and Rhys, hiding away in Hereford where they owned and ran a farm-shop. Neither daughter has produced a grandchild for Erika, a fact which she is prone to advertise abroad if she of a mind to score a cheap point. Tiffany is more interested in making a profit than making a baby, it seems, although I have no idea how Rhys fits into the equation. Not that it is too late to make both, I suppose. In spite of a diet of fresh country air and organic vegetables Tiffy has not aged well and she actually looks older than I do. As for Patricia, she has kept a very trim figure but she discovered in her late twenties that she preferred female company and she has lived with a woman I have never met, a veterinary nurse called Marlene, since the decision they took together while raising a toast to the new millennium. Perhaps it was at the exact moment that Polly's grandpa Stanley passed away.

I have seen very little of either sister in the past several years. And I have seen nothing at all of my stepfather, who, I was told by someone who thought I might actually care, now lives in the Cotswolds.

As for my own divorce, that never happened. Jacqueline and I simply never got round to it. There's no bitterness between us, just an empty space. At the time neither of us wanted to have lawyers thrashing around in our lives for weeks and months and then presenting us with bills for legal fees before they washed their hands of us and moved on to the next shipwreck. Actually our marriage was never a shipwreck, more a slow drift into separate oceans. I haven't seen Jackie for years. I still have an old address in Putney but I very much doubt if she is still living there. I have no e-mail address, no telephone number. But she is still my wife, strictly speaking, and I'm still her husband. Polly says she is fine about it, it's not an issue, and I do believe her. She says she's more interested in who people are on the inside.

*

Erika established herself in Riga as if she had been away for forty days rather than the forty-odd years which had passed since she had been smuggled out of the port in a fishing boat bound for Helsingfors. Many of her childhood friends were no longer in the capital, but other exiles she had been in contact with down the years were returning, and some old allies who had stuck it out with the Russians were delighted to welcome her back home after so long. Notably Leons Lapsa, widower, snowy-haired poet and professor of Comparative Literature approaching retirement: a flickering student romance, stifled in the very middle of the last century, was rekindled two lifetimes later.

In 1995 they married in a short civil ceremony at the city hall in Riga. Like a pair of teenage lovebirds they couldn't take their eyes off each other. As they repeated their vows I watched as he held her tenderly in his arms, pulling her close to his heart lest she were plucked away from him a second time. And when Erika said that, both being in their sixties, theirs was more like a love between sister and brother, a long-delayed meeting of minds, nobody really believed her, least of all me. Yes, I was there, toasting the happy couple in fizzy Russian *shampanskaya*. And I was genuinely happy for her, to see her relaxed in her homeland, surrounded by friends and what remained of her family. The gold in her hair was mostly artificial by now, touched to keep the white at bay, and her blue eyes, for so long dimmed, had their twinkle back. She was wearing more make-up than I had ever seen her with before; perhaps Leons encouraged it, perhaps she was disguising her lines for the wedding close-ups.

My half-sisters were there too, of course (Trixie rather reluctantly, I felt), and we found ourselves in a small pocket of well-wishers who spoke virtually no Latvian. I hadn't seen our Aunt Katarina for years. Resplendent in an outfit of shocking pink, purchased, she said loudly, on Fifth Avenue, she outshone the bride, whether deliberately or not. Erika was catty about her sister's lapsed Latvian, and she whispered to me that the facelift she'd had in Miami, apparently, would come back to haunt her. Kat was accompanied by her husband Robin, a pompous man with a dangerous superiority complex. He reminded everyone who was obliged to listen that he had been a *very* senior civil servant at the British Home Office. They had no children, which allowed them the cleanest of breaks upon his retirement to settle in coastal Florida. I have seen neither of them since.

For the three of us siblings it was our first visit to the home of our mother. It was February and I can recall the deep chill and the blanket of snow that covered everything. The trees were bare, the parks frigid, the people were in a hurry to stay warm, their faces masked in scarves and hoods. There were parts of the city that seemed to be in hibernation. I remember using the toilet in the cafe where a party was held after the wedding ceremony: there was neither a flushing loo nor water in the taps. Either the system was frozen up or the plumbing upstairs was too decrepit. The couple were sharing Leons' flat near the university at the time, housed in a drab complex of buildings in the neutral architectural style beloved of communist dictatorships. The Rigans had their freedom, they had discovered their voice, but their city remained at that time a plain image of constraint and mediocrity. There were fewer cars on the streets than I had imagined, and even fewer new ones: other than the rare sight of an expensive German limousine passing by, splashing wet snow on to the pavements, there was not even an illusion of prosperity. Seeing a car less than ten years old was like coming across a silver coin in a basketful of buttons.

Leons told me that unemployment was so high because of the Russian withdrawal: the communist economy had provided plenty of jobs and the change to capitalism and democracy would be painful. The Latvians had grown used to state intervention, he said, and now a free-for-all had filled the vacuum and there were so far more losers than winners. In a memorable turn of phrase he said that if Latvia was a phoenix, it was one whose wings were still covered in a layer of ash and whose eyes were still closed. He told me to come back in the summertime: *I am always more optimist in the summer*, he said. *I take you in canoe on the lake or maybe the river. We drink cold beer and catch fish maybe.* Leons was a decent man. I could see that he was making an effort.

I had no worries about my mother's welfare. She had squeezed a very tidy settlement out of Adrian, she confided to me. She'd screwed his nuts to the floor, I think was the phrase she used. I told her I genuinely hoped she wasn't joking.

We had a little time with Erika, the three of us, her children. She told me that she was glad that I had got rid of my moustache, which made me smile.

"It never suited you, Andris."

"But you once said it was a particularly fine moustache."

110

"Well, it was," she agreed. "It just didn't look particularly fine on you."

The women shared a conspiratorial hug and my sisters laughed together for the first time in ages.

One morning she took me to one side and touched my hand.

"I've kept your father's name, Andris," she said quietly, looking for a reaction. "If you were wondering. You know, at the wedding."

"I hadn't thought anything about it."

"I never took Adrian's. I was never Mrs Plummer, as you know. The girls have always been okay with that."

"Right."

"Leons is lovely. I can see you like him too."

I smiled and vaguely nodded.

"But your father was the one, Andris. Of them all, he was the one."

I was unsure if she was looking for gratitude or pity, and so, pulling away from her loose grip, I gave her neither.

On our last morning in Riga, Erika took the three of us to a favourite restaurant in Vecriga, the old city, where we had a kind of farewell lunch. There was a faded charm about the architecture there, in the narrow streets and alleyways that had been at the heart of the place for centuries of frozen winters like that one. Afterwards she led us down to the docks; it's only a short walk, she said, and she wanted to show us the building from where her father had once directed his business of processing and packing fish. In the distance a Swedish container ship dominated the port but the cranes were idle and there was little activity. Ripples of sleet blown in off the Baltic were turning to snow as the temperature dropped. We arrived at her destination across an empty, icy yard, passing groups of men smoking, huddled together for warmth, a few loading scuffed wooden crates into the back of a truck.

"You see what became of it, my Daddy's place," Erika said, pointing at a flaking sign above the chained gates, its words spelt out in Russian Cyrillic which she translated for us: Refrigeration Services of Latvian Socialist Republic.

"It's a tragedy," I heard her say under her breath, then more loudly, stamping her feet on the ground and rubbing her hands together, "Come on, it's too cold to hang around here."

The place was deserted, locked up, and, under a frigid grey sky, utterly depressing. I had the impression that our mother regretted bringing us there after all.

My sisters and I flew back to London later that afternoon. For many reasons I was glad to set foot back on English soil.

*

"Did you notice this one when you were putting out the tourist leaflets yesterday?"

Polly was standing in the doorway to the lounge where I was watching a DVD. She was holding a slim, shiny fold of paper advertising a local attraction.

"What's that?" I asked distractedly.

"It's one I haven't seen before. Shillingstone Station. It's a renovated station: trains, a museum, a platform made to look like it did in the 1960s. Sean spotted it."

Of course I had noticed them. Whether consciously or not, I had mentally blocked it out, filing them in the display frame with the castles and caves and gardens and amusement parks in a vacant, mechanical way. Since the Cassis group had declined to negotiate a second contract with Abbott's years and years ago, I had tried, successfully for the most part, to give no further thought to the station and specifically its small garden plot.

"Anyway, it's got him really excited." Polly was still talking. "I think I'll ask Dad to take him over one day. It's open three days a week, but weekends will be difficult. Shillingstone, that's over North Dorset, isn't it?"

"I think so."

"Near Blandford?"

"I think so."

"Under an hour's drive."

"Easily, I'd say. Well, maybe more if *you're* driving."

Polly had turned and gone, not even acknowledging my remark with a response.

The excursion was discussed over dinner. Sean was vocal, it was half-term, Grandad was free on Wednesday, I stayed in the shadows, everybody was happy. For a little while at least.

The same evening at around eight o'clock the telephone rang. It was a call for Harvey from his slaughterman. Polly's father had already selected about a dozen of the perkiest spring lambs to have killed as soon as the trailer was available to ferry them to the abattoir. The slaughterman was ringing to offer Wednesday as the only slot he had until much later in the month.

"I'm goin' to have to deal with the lambs on Wednesday," said Harvey, putting the phone down. "Sorry, Polly, you're goin' to have to tell Sean."

"That's annoying," she said. "He'll be really disappointed. What about Saturday instead?"

"You know what the weekends are like, Poll. Can't you take him?"

"I'm not around on Wednesday, Dad. There's that food fair on in Bridport. I've got people I said I'd meet there, suppliers I might use."

"What's Andris doin'?"

I looked up from the cup of coffee I was holding. I had

been listening, of course, and could see the inevitable proposition looming into view. And with it the inevitable pressurised reply.

"Yeah, I can take him, I suppose," I said, saving them the trouble of even asking the question. "What, this Wednesday? Morning or afternoon?"

"Morning, I'd say," said Polly.

"You can make a day of it," suggested Lynne helpfully. "Have some lunch. Is there a café? Or take him for a pub lunch somewhere out that way."

"Yeah, fine, whatever."

I had very few secrets from Polly, but she knew nothing about the memorial at Shillingstone Station and the wasps' nest it had disturbed in my mind, long since quelled. When we were together in bed that night, restless under a too-thick duvet in the warm air, I thought I might tell her but I hesitated: there was no need at all for her to know, really, no point concerning her with something I myself had all but forgotten after so long.

I rose early on Wednesday morning to give Harvey a hand with the young lambs. We had moved his pick of fourteen away from the rest of the flock and shooed them into a temporary pen he had fenced off at the near end of the orchard, where the slaughterman's truck could access them more easily. The little creatures were frisky, bleating and querulous. I was sent to the house to fetch out old Nancy to restore some order.

I had planned to leave at ten o'clock. Sean was not an early riser unless his grandfather was cracking the whip and I was in no hurry to drive over to the other end of the county. Stiff breezes were sending fluffy clouds scurrying across the sky; it was a dry day, which would make Harvey's job easier.

At the same time that the slaughterman's truck and trailer

eventually appeared at the top of the driveway, Polly poked her head out of the back door and shouted to me that Sean was nearly ready. I watched the visitor turn and reverse so that the tail-gate would drop back and provide a ramp for the lambs to run up and into the metal box from which they would get their last sight of the farm. I knew the man, of course; we had been through this sorry rigmarole many times. I nodded as he approached. He always wore a dirty pair of overalls, wellingtons and a baseball cap over his thick, wild hair. I could never remember his name.

"Mornin', Harvey," he called out, as if I were invisible.

Harvey was at the back of the pack, patting woolly back-sides, whistling, cajoling, pushing the animals towards the jaws of the dusty trailer. I was standing in the way, I knew, and felt slightly awkward: the return of metropolitan gaucheness in the face of rural ritual. One of the lambs danced up to me quite randomly and stopped to rub its neck against my knee, my weaker knee. I looked down, gave it a pat and ruffled its lovely, warm creamy head: a sturdy little chap, four months of life on this earth. It was looking back at me innocently, this trusting animal, fixing me with humble, questioning eyes. Did it know its time was nearly up? Had it some instinct, some premonition that this trailer signalled danger? Did I see a flicker of fear in those dark eyes, did I imagine a silent plea? I pushed the lamb away with a lump in my throat which I was ashamed of, for I am not a sentimental man. The animal bleated, jumped away and faced back to the rest of the herd who were colliding in confusion, one against another like woolly-sided bumper cars.

"Come on, you beauties, let's be havin' you!" sang the slaughterman.

Harvey had found a stick and was pushing the first one inside the echoey cell of the trailer with it. Some of the others, with a bit of a prod, would instinctively follow. Nancy was hanging back, panting, looking bored.

"I think I'm in the way here," I said, avoiding a small reverse stampede. "It's time I went anyway. Good luck with them."

Sean was standing by the cars, dwarfing his mother who had opened the passenger door of the 4x4.

"He's making a fuss, Andris," she said with a frown. "I'm sorry, he wants to go in my car."

This surprised me as Sean loved the two-seater and regularly helped me wash and valet it.

"Really?"

"He insists."

"I'm not taking that wreck."

"You'll have to."

"Not all the way over to Shillingstone."

"Sean is adamant. He's in one of his moods."

The boy had turned away from me, facing the road. We could all hear the commotion with lambs going on in the field behind the house.

"Hey, Sean!" I shouted over. "What's wrong with my car today?"

There was no answer and my heart began to sink. Was I to spend hours with a sulky seventeen-year-old, driving a nightmare of a car whose seats rattled and whose stereo system wasn't even compatible with my iPod?

"Here are the keys," said Polly, waving them in the air. "I'll take yours to Bridport later."

I was slouching across the gravel to join her as Sean began to shake. I thought he was having some kind of fit, but in fact he was trying to contain laughter.

"Sorry, Mum," he said suddenly, turning to face us. "I can't keep it up any longer."

"No, neither can I," she admitted, and grinned at me.

"These are *your* keys, lover. I was only kidding. I'm a rubbish liar, I'm surprised you fell for it. You know Sean can't stand being seen in my car!"

I was forced to smile along with them.

"Well, you kind of had me. But you're both rubbish liars, really."

Sean had come over, giggling like a six-year-old, and I watched as he gave his mother a companionable squeeze.

"And that's why," I said, "at least I think that's why I love you both so much."

2

I had read every word in the leaflet, had studied every detail in the photographs, had even spent ten minutes on the website, but I was still surprised to see for real the transformation that had taken place at Shillingstone Station. Many years of work borne out of love and dedication had gone into the renovation project, it was clear, and the main buildings looked as well-maintained as I imagine they ever were in the 1950s. The wooden canopy over part of the northbound platform, constructed for the visit of King Edward VII (*to protect the royal guest from inclement weather*, according to the website) had a fresh coat of cream-coloured paint, as had the doors and window-frames, shining in a rich mid-green. An old railway carriage sat moored at the platform edge, transformed into a buffet car with seats and little tables. The café itself, decorated with posters and photographs from the heyday of the Somerset & Dorset line, had taken the comfortable space where, twenty-five years earlier, I remember sitting with Mary White discussing the largest order of furniture she had ever had at the time. I noticed the little fireplace, the hearth polished, and, strangely for June, neatly made up with kindling and coals but unlit, just as it had been on that much earlier spring afternoon. Where the reception had been, what I fancied had once been a waiting room, there was now a jumble of a shop selling railway books

and souvenirs and other assorted bric-a-brac. A model railway, manned by a whiskered enthusiast, was displayed in
what had been the draughtsman›s office. Vernon, that was
his name, was suddenly sitting there in my memory, still
engrossed in front of his great clunking 1990 computer in
its white plastic casing the size of a microwave oven. Outside
there was a small museum in an outbuilding of timber and
glass which housed a collection of artefacts and photographs,
and beyond the station house, in the other direction, in as
healthy a state as ever, was the garden. It was a picture: picnic
tables stood before it, and the space was filled with herba-
ceous perennials of yellow and purple, lavender, marigolds,
ornamental grasses, and towards the back, tall orange lilies,
clumps of daisies, roses of white and pink and peach, and
leafy bushes whose names I didn't know.

The project was still a work in progress, as evidenced by
a small band of volunteers in overalls who were wandering
around with toolboxes and grubby gloves among the pockets of visitors, but of the furniture makers I had visited there
was not a trace; that was a part of the station's history that
had been long since swept away. The industrial park by the
station yard remained, but the buildings had all been replaced
in the meantime as had the names displayed outside them,
now identifying engineers, boat builders, a marquee hire
company. I remembered that Abbott's had moved to Poole
as the carpentry business expanded: I had dealt with them as
a buyer for Cassis for a couple of years in the early nineties
but had never been back to Shillingstone until today. I took
it almost as a personal affront when relations were broken,
when their next generation of furniture was deemed by my
bosses to be too expensive for us. Or did they say too extravagant? I thought again of Mary White, the sexy older woman,
and smiled. *If I were twenty years younger,* she had said to me

once with a wicked grin, *I'd be offerin' you bed and breakfast. And anythin' else you fancied in between.*

"Andris? Andris, can we have a drink, please?"

Sean was staring at me, a plea in his big grey eyes, his deep voice waking me from my thoughts. We were standing in the shop, browsing the books and memorabilia. I think he was getting fed up although he was too polite to say so. The model railway display in the next room was quite tiny and we both knew he had a much better one at home.

"Are you ready to go?" I said.

"No. I'm just thirsty."

I gave him some money and told him to join the queue for refreshments.

"I'll wait outside in the sun. On one of the tables, if there's one free. Get me a coffee, please. White."

"And a cake?"

"Why not. Get whatever you fancy. You should have enough money there."

I made my way awkwardly between couples, pensioners revisiting a bygone age, a family, parents talking to young children about steam power and tank engines and, *maybe if you're good boys*, a slice of chocolate sponge-cake. Out on the platform was an old-fashioned porter's luggage-cart laden with an array of boxes and old suitcases. Beyond the railings to the east the wide green valley was bathed in sunshine, soft and rich. My eyes were drawn instinctively towards the skyline and the distant arching silhouette of the rippled hill I had walked over on the day I met Mary White, the day I had discovered Edward Fleet's memorial.

I noticed there was an empty table at the far end of the platform, close to the garden where an elderly woman with white hair and an apron was weeding one of the beds, down on her hands and knees, loosening the tiny roots with a trowel before lifting them with gloved fingers into a black plastic bucket. Beyond her, almost completely hidden by tall, spiky grasses and rosebushes, was the familiar block of Purbeck stone.

I placed my jacket on the table as if to claim it and wandered on to the sloping patch of lawn to get a clearer view of the tablet. Nothing had changed; of course, why, indeed how could it have? The inscription was just as it had been on the day it was first engraved, and here today still highly polished and gleaming in the sunlight. This time the words held no surprise for me, and I reacted with a certain nonchalance as if the detail itself was of no great significance. Which, in truth, it wasn't. Granted, I could not stop myself from revisiting it out of blank curiosity, but I was no longer affected by such a freak of synchronicity. In twenty-five years I had grown quite a shell. Or was I deluding myself? The faint scent of roses hung in the warm, still air, and the only the lazy drone of bees fractured what seemed a moment of pure serenity.

I stepped back gingerly and attracted the attention of the lady gardener who looked concerned that I might tread on her bedding plants.

"Hello," I called across to her, "Sorry to interrupt you. Do you know a chap called Andrew White, by any chance? Or Andy, perhaps?"

"Sorry," she answered. "I was miles away. I was watching you, looking where you were putting your feet."

"It's okay. I haven't trodden on anything except the grass."

"What did you say?"

"Do you happen to know Andy White? He used to work here, did a bit of gardening on this plot. Actually a lot of gardening, I think, back in the nineties. His mother had the furniture place."

"Yes, of course I do. Yes, I know Andy. Nice lad. Well, he's a man now, of course."

"Does he still live here, in the village? Does he help out, you know, with the renovation work?"

"Well, he did. He looked after the plot here until he left."

"He left? Left Shillingstone?"

"As far as I know he went to join his mother when she retired."

"Where was that? It's alright, I'm not snooping. I did know the family back then. I did some business with Mrs White. With Abbott's, as it was called. The furniture place."

"Oh. Well, that's what it was called, alright."

The woman stood up, ostensibly to stretch her legs but perhaps to have a closer look at her inquisitor.

"She left Shill about, what, ten years ago," she went on. "Mary, we called her the Queen of Sheba. A wealthy woman, so they say. I suppose she must be, running a business like she did."

"So, you say she no longer lives in the village?"

"No. Not even local. She bought a big place somewhere in Cornwall, I think. At least that's where Andy said he was going once she got herself sorted. He never had a family of his own, Andy didn't. He was going to set up a garden centre on his mother's property."

"Andris! Here's your coffee!"

Sean arrived with a tray and placed it on the table by my jacket.

"Well, thanks for your time," I said to the woman. "I was just curious, you know. It's going back a fair few years."

"You're welcome," she said, getting back down on her hands and knees and moving the bucket a foot or two along the verge.

"She had a daughter too, didn't she?" I suddenly remembered.

"Mary?"

"Yes, a daughter who worked in the offices here. I don't know quite how long for."

"Anne?"

"That's right, Anne. Annie."

"She moved away years and years ago, she did. She went away to college, I think. Met someone, got married, you know how it goes. Anne lives, oh, I don't remember where. Not in these parts. Somewhere up country."

"Never mind. I'll let you carry on. It's a lovely garden, by the way. You're doing a great job on it."

"Thank you, but it's not just me. We're a team."

"Your drink's getting cold," shouted Sean, before emptying a can of cola in a couple of long gulps. "And I bought you some fruit cake."

"Thanks, Sean," I said, joining him on the bench with the slightest of backward glances towards the rosebushes. "That sounds perfect."

*

When we got back to Pattercombe I spent a little while researching Mary White on the internet. The gardener was correct in that she now lived in Cornwall, having sold the Abbott's furniture and furnishing business for what seemed to me like an enormous sum to a German company. She had earned several awards for industry and design over the years, both local and national, and in a photograph of her receiving a silver dish from a minor royal I could see that the vitality in her body and the sense of fun in her smile were still very much part of her. What I hadn't expected to read was that in recent years she had set up a foundation to promote environmental sustainability.

Sean and I did not leave the station immediately after our refreshment stop. He spotted an outdoor miniature railway on a raised square of land above the garden and so wandered up there alone while I drank my coffee and gazed out over the fields towards the flanks of Hambledon. After five minutes he came back down, greeted me with a non-committal shrug, and as we strolled along the platform in the sun, he reminded me that he had his eye on a selection of model railway accessories in the gift shop; meanwhile I was vaguely curious to visit the little museum. It was there that the station revealed its second secret to me, and just like the first a generation earlier, this one set my heart racing while at the same time it felt like a kick in the stomach.

I should have gone back into the shop with Sean. I should have gone and waited for him in the car. I could have set up a new playlist on my iPod while he was queuing to pay. Should have, could have, but didn't. What I did do was drift into the wooden outbuilding to examine the artefacts and photos of the station when it was in its pomp, if that is the right word for such a modest dot on the line, where many of the Bath to Bournemouth trains didn't even have a scheduled stop. Nevertheless, I have to admit that the place had captured my imagination, especially as the whole renovation gave a real impression of what it must have been like to be a traveller in the 1950s, say, steaming through the countryside, stopping at little halts like this one where a uniformed porter might meet you as you alighted with a polite doff of the cap and a welcoming smile. There was a certain romance about the place, what it had been in an age when the motorcar was still a luxury, when the slow pace of life gave you time and space to savour it, I suppose. *Time should give you a clear view, not blurred vision.* Thanks, Harvey.

Apart from framed images of the station staff from the post-war years, all smiles and puffed-out chests, what interested me especially was an album of seemingly random archive photographs of special trains I had barely heard of, visits of dignitaries I recognised even less, and other notable incidents from the station's past. There were other people jostling around in the small room and being conscious of hogging the album, I was flicking through the later pages quite quickly when my eyes rested on a scene that looked familiar. I found myself staring at a good quality print taken from the north platform, probably from beneath the canopy, looking out across the tracks to groups of men in sober flannel suits and trilby hats standing in twos and threes, some with notepads, one man kneeling as if to pick up a dropped coin. There was a clumsily typed caption: *Police and railway employees discuss the events surrounding the mysterious death of naval officer E.L.Fleet in October 1960.* It was a rather dull photo and even the more prominent characters were unnamed, but behind one of the detective inspectors I caught a face I did recognise: a young face, hatless, with wavy hair and intelligent, concerned eyes. I was sure it was Cooper. I struggled to recall the man's surname. He'd been invited to my wedding, not by me but by my mother, in fact: a great friend of my father's, she had said, he would be touched to be invited. Mr Arundel. Cooper Arundel. I remember having a short conversation with him: he had tutored my father at Cambridge in the fifties, took a shine to him, they became great pals, that was the tale, I think. A decent enough chap, quite intense. That would have been 1985. The bystander with the worried expression here in a black and white photo taken in 1960 didn't look very different from the man I had met on my wedding day. He had one of those ageless faces, I suppose.

Once again a wave of confusion broke over me and, as I closed the album and passed it on to a woman with bad breath and sunglasses standing irritatingly close to my shoulder, I almost dropped it. I was sweating. I forced my way out into the fresh air and tried to compose myself, gazing out blankly, vaguely towards the spot across the railway lines where the men in the photograph had been standing, *discussing the events*. I realised that although the sun was shining directly on my face, my chest, my arms, I had in fact begun to shiver.

If it were Cooper standing among a huddle of policemen, then what on earth was he doing there? As far as I knew, he was never a journalist, he didn't work for the railway company. I took a very deep breath and leaned against one of the canopy pillars for support. What was his reason for being there? What interest could he have had in the murder of the other Edward Fleet? There was, after all, only one plausible explanation: whatever my mother had told me, whatever she had insisted was the truth, the memorial in the station garden *was* dedicated to my father. There was nobody else who happened to share his exact middle initial. It was my own father, and nobody else's, who had been travelling south on that night, who had been killed on that train, who had been found dead in a Dorset ditch, back by the open track, several hundred miles across a sea and half a continent from Berlin.

3

"I knew you weren't keen on taking Sean to Shillingstone. That's why, isn't it? That seeing the memorial would upset you again? After all those years?"

"Well, I honestly thought I had got over all that. All the anxiety, the doubts. The plaque, the name, I thought I had pretty much forgotten all about it. I suppose there was still something right at the back of my mind. Something I hadn't quite managed to bury."

"I'm sorry I had to ask."

We were lying in bed, side by side, eyes wide open, staring at the ceiling through the darkness. We had gone up earlier than usual. Polly had said that she felt exhausted. I had found it impossible to concentrate on anything on the television.

"There's no need to be sorry. I dealt with it. I even deliberately went and had another look at the stone. I felt just, I don't know, just neutral. No, Poll, it's the photo of Cooper Arundel at the station that has really unnerved me this time. If it *is* him."

"You said you were certain."

"Yeah. I am. I'm sure it's him."

"There'll be a perfectly reasonable explanation, Andris. If, as you say, he seemed like a decent man, a friend of your father's, then he'll be able to explain everything."

"Maybe he will. If he can. If he even wants to. I don't know.

But the whole idea that my father's death even needs explaining to me after fifty-five years is what bloody upsets me. And why Erika has been spinning me a line about Berlin for so long."

"You don't know for certain if that's the case. Give her the benefit of the doubt."

"I think I've been doing that for far too long."

There was no reason to keep Polly in the dark any longer. When Sean and I returned to the farm, I took her out into the orchard, away from her parents, and quietly told her that our visit to Shillingstone Station had not been my first. I laid out to her the whole story, not that there was very much of it that I was sure about: Abbott's, Mary White, the memorial, Erika's insistence that my father did die in Germany, and now the photograph of Cooper Arundel on the platform.

Polly shuffled closer to me and, leaning on an elbow, looked into my face, trying to discern my expression, finding the reflection in my eyes of the faint glimmer of moonlight seeping through the curtains.

"There was a time," she said in a near whisper, "when I was around twenty, that I hated my dad. I despised him for what I saw as his close-minded, smug country ways."

"I remember you telling me this before," I said softly, turning to face her.

"I was very mixed up. I was away from home, in Bristol. What seemed to me to be the big, edgy, sophisticated city. Living with a very different crowd. I wanted to be something, somebody that I was not. That I *am* not. You know what happened. Having a child made me grow up fast. Made me appreciate what I was lucky enough to have here."

I raised an elbow, inviting her to snuggle up to me. She threw an arm lazily across my chest and, as our heads touched, strands of her hair settled over my neck. For a moment or two we lay in near silence, the only sound in the room the light fluttering of young leaves on the branches outside our window, rocked by a delicate evening breeze.

"And Sean," she said quite suddenly, "he will never know his dad."

"You can't say never, Poll."

"I haven't had a word in seventeen years. He isn't going to appear out of the blue now, is he? And in any case I wouldn't want to see him again. Honestly, I wouldn't. I could never forgive him. Like you, he's a part of my life I have tried to bury. If he came back tomorrow I would show him the door."

"What about Sean?"

"Sean never talks about it. Never mentions him. He hasn't since he was a little boy. I told him the truth. Which, I think, I know, brought us closer together."

She reached over and brushed my lips with the tips of her fingers.

"And, anyway, he's got you now."

"Well, I'm not his father, am I?"

"As good as."

"It's not the same though, is it?"

"Andris, Sean loves you. He might never tell you, but I know. He loves you like a father."

"Yes. Yes, I think he does, doesn't he?"

She stretched her neck and kissed me, finding my lips intuitively in the gloom. I lifted my free hand and laid it gently on her shoulder, stroking it dreamily.

"So, you'll confront this man Arundel?" she asked.

"If I can find him I will. If he's still alive even. He must be close to ninety by now. Mind you, confront him? Confrontation isn't really me, is it?"

"You have every right to push him."

"The guy was a university lecturer in philosophy. Even

at ninety he could probably tie me up in knots, run rings around me."

"Andris, *ninety*? Come on, I think *you'll* have the upper hand."

"I don't know. I guess I'm just a bit nervous about the whole thing."

"Don't be. You've no reason to be."

"It's just the way I am."

"You just go and ask him the questions you want answers to. If he's such a decent man, then he'll help you."

"I hope so."

There was a muffled sound of tyres on gravel as a car crawled past the side of the house, its lights casting a milky glow which ghosted for a second or two into our room: one of the families renting a cottage back from an evening out.

"Do you want *me* to do anything to help?"

"No. No, this is my business. It's nothing to do with any of you. You, your parents, Sean; you must stay out of it. No, I have to deal with it myself. But thank you, love. I mean it. Thanks. It's great to have you in my corner."

"Of course I am."

"You don't know how much that means to me."

"Yes, I do. You've told me before."

We both laughed quietly. It was true, of course it was.

"The whole thing has knocked me back," I said presently. "I admit it has. And years ago I would have just felt sorry for myself. Since I met you, I have a resilience I never had before."

"I know."

"And that's down to you, that is."

"It's us. It's both of us. Together."

"Well, whatever it is, I love you for it."

I squeezed her gently. The curtains caught a breath of wind and danced.

"You'll be careful, won't you, Andris? You don't know what you're getting yourself into, really. Spying, a murder. You don't really know where it'll end up."

"I'll be careful. It's my nature to be careful. Don't worry."

"I'll try not to. But I do need you. So much. *We* need you."

We kissed again, my hand drifting over her breasts, down beneath the bedclothes, resting lightly on her soft, warm belly.

*

I arrived in Clifton in the middle of a thunderstorm. It had not been especially difficult to trace my father's mentor at Cambridge. I had a clear memory that when I had met him at my wedding thirty years ago he had given me his calling card printed with his position at the University of Bristol and a telephone number within the department. He told me that if I were ever in a jam I should call him. I wondered at the time why he made such an offer, as I didn't really know him at all, and was puzzled by what he could mean by being *in a jam*. He wouldn't have been at the wedding at all had it not been for my mother's insistence. I assumed, and still do, that there was an element of guilt in his voice. On the back of the card he wrote his home number for good measure. I never got in touch, of course, but I did keep the card and within hours of seeing his face in the Shillingstone photograph I located it fairly easily in a box of keepsakes.

When I rang the number I spoke to the current owner of what I assumed was a residential property somewhere in the city. I found myself in conversation with Arundel's nephew, a man with an easy-going manner and a slight lisp who called himself Nick. He seemed to trust my voice and explained that he and his wife had bought the house when Uncle Coop could no longer manage it. He accepted that my father had known his uncle once upon a time, and passed on without question details of the old man's current whereabouts.

I drove slowly through the puddles which were forming over the uneven paving stones leading to the ornate entrance of the Avon Acres Residential Care Home. The rain was battering off the fabric roof of my car, testing it beyond its limits. At one of the seams there was a small leak and, under such pressure, droplets of rainwater had already dampened a patch of my trousers above my right knee. I parked, got out, slammed the door and ran across to shelter as quickly as I could. Once inside the building, batting myself down, kicking rain off my shoes, I was ignored for a good thirty seconds by a receptionist who was too entranced by something on her computer screen to acknowledge me.

I was standing in a wood-panelled hallway with reinforced glass doors leading off in three directions, and a wide, carpeted staircase took the eye up to a landing with what looked like watercolour landscapes on the walls. There was a faint smell of disinfectant. I guessed that the house had at one time been the private home of a wealthy family, maybe traders down the years in wine or fabrics or slaves. Or all three. I was daydreaming, imagining things wildly, waiting for the woman to pull her gaze away from the monitor. Eventually she did.

"No, Mr Arundel is not expecting me."

"A relative, you say?"

"No, I said the son of a very close friend. Mr Arundel will recognise my name. Unless he's beyond that..."

"No, Cooper is not one of our dementia residents. At least not yet. He's all clued up, and no mistake. Just rather frail in his movement."

"I see. Well, that's to be expected at his age."

"Indeed."

"So, may I...?"

"I'll give his team leader a call."

"Fine. Thanks."

"Excuse me, while I..., " she said, picking up a phone. "Take a seat, if you like."

Presently a big-boned woman of about forty in matching pale blue tunic and trousers appeared through one of the glass doors and introduced herself with a firm handshake as Christine, Duty Manager.

"Hello, nice to meet you. I'm Andris Fleet."

"I've told Cooper that you are here, Mr Fleet."

"He must have been taken by surprise," I said.

"Actually, not really. Perhaps he was expecting you."

"Unlikely."

"Well, whatever, I've moved him back into his own room. You can chat there. He was in the conservatory, but what with this rain you can't really hear yourself think in there with the battering on the roof."

"Yes, it's a horrible morning."

"You'll need to sign in," said the receptionist who had been listening to our conversation and was now standing behind her counter offering me a visitors' book and a ballpoint pen.

"And wear one of these badges," she added.

"Then, if you follow me," said the Duty Manager, "He's on the ground floor. He's got a nice view out over the gardens."

The badge was no more than a sticky circle of yellow paper printed with the black letters AA arranged one above the other. I attached it to my jacket lapel and followed her along a corridor, feeling like a mechanic who had been called up to repair a broken down hatchback: a silly thought I put down to being a little nervous.

"This is it," said the woman, tapping on a door already ajar, with the laminated name *Cooper* stuck on it at eye level.

"Cooper, here's your visitor," she said, raising her voice. "Come in, Mr Fleet."

The room was spacious, nicely furnished with good quality pieces including a neatly made bed and a pair of heavy upholstered armchairs, sitting in one of which, facing into the room, was Cooper Arundel. He heard me come in and looked up in my direction.

"Hello, Mr Arundel," I heard myself say.

"You'll have to get a bit closer," said the woman, who was pulling the curtains open wider.

The rain was easing up, but on the vast lawn, sloping down to a line of trees, large puddles had already formed.

"He's a bit deaf," she went on, "and as his eyesight's fading he can probably only see your outline. Why don't you take the other seat? Move it a bit nearer to his, that's better."

"Hello, Mr Arundel," I repeated, limping towards him. "How are you today?"

"Is that you, Andris Fleet? They said you'd come to pay me a social. Is that really you, young man?"

"Yes. Yes, it is."

"Then sit down there where I can see you. Foul day for gadding about."

"Yes. Very true."

I offered him a hand which he saw, took hold of and shook with more strength than I had anticipated. I pulled a small bottle of vodka out from a pocket and placed it on the table by his chair.

"For you. I thought you might appreciate this."

I wondered if he could see exactly what it was.

"It's vodka. I thought you might still like a drink occasionally."

"That's very kind. Very kind indeed. Only in medicinal doses these days, Andris. You can leave it there. The staff won't mind. They trust me. Can't think why."

He winked in my direction.

"Yes, sit down. That's better, I can see you there."

In spite of the handshake and an energy in his voice, the man was reduced, understandably. His hair, still thick and wavy, had turned white, and the skin on his face and neck was loose and flaccid. He was dressed in a shirt and tie and a thick grey cardigan even though it was a warm day, corduroy slacks which covered what I could tell were bony legs, and a pair of claret-coloured carpet slippers.

"It's been a very long time since I saw you, Mr Arundel."

"Call me Cooper, please, for heaven's sake. I've known you since you were born. I don't think we need to start right at the beginning again."

His voice, although thin, was brisk and lively.

"You're looking well, " I restarted.

"Not so bad for a geriatric, I suppose. Eyes are letting me down but I manage. You did well to find me. I'm a recluse these days here at this prison camp."

"I managed to trace you through Nick, your nephew."

"Yes. Yes, you would. Not a difficult trail. How's your mother?"

"She's well. I don't see her much, to be honest. She lives in Latvia now, with a new husband. I say new, they've been married for twenty years."

"Yes, I did know that. And how time flies."

I realised that Christine was still in the room, needlessly patting down the old man's bedclothes. I looked across to her.

"Are you alright, Cooper?" she said. "Can I leave you two?"

"What's that? Oh yes, leave us. This fellow won't bother me. He's practically family."

"Shall I bring some tea?"

"Not for me."

"Mr... Fleet, wasn't it?"

"Yes. Well, a coffee would be great, thanks. White, please."

She turned and left the room, placing a rubber stopper at the foot of the door to keep it ajar.

"It was very good of her to invite me to *your* wedding, you remember," Arundel picked up.

"Yes. Now that *was* a long time ago. You know we split up..."

"Oh, yes. I was told that you live apart now."

"Have been for years. It's a lifetime ago."

"Yes," he said, almost to himself, "most things seem to have happened in a different age."

Unwilling to agree, I left his observation to hang.

"She said I was all that was left of your father, Erika did."

"Really?"

"She wanted me to be there, at the wedding, to, I don't know, to represent him in some way."

Whether or not he had any idea what was on my mind, he had given me an opening.

"I have a few questions about my father, Cooper," I said. "Actually, that's the reason I have come to see you. I was hoping you might be able to shed some light."

"Can't your mother help?" he interrupted.

"She seems to have a pat answer to anything I ask."

"Which is?"

"That he died in Berlin."

"You're asking about Eddie's death?"

"Yes. Yes, I am."

"Well," he said, casting his eyes over the frames of his glasses to read the label on the vodka bottle, "Of course your mother is quite right about that."

This was the last thing I wanted to hear but the first thing I had expected.

"Cooper," I pressed, as firmly as I felt I could. "Look at me, Cooper. Please don't treat me like a child. We're past all that, aren't we? I've been lied to most of my life. At least it feels like I have."

The old man struggled to find a comfortable position in the armchair. He was wheezing under the effort.

"Be a good soldier and fix my cushion, would you?"

I stood and rearranged a pillow that had slipped down behind his shoulders, so that it supported his head.

"I assume you have a good reason for coming here, Andris. Something that gives you cause to query your mother's account?"

His gaze was now firmly back on me, his fading eyes straining to hold mine in their grip.

"Am I right?"

I cleared my throat before setting him a question of my own:

"Are you familiar with a railway station in Dorset, in the village of Shillingstone?"

"Shillingstone? Well, I've heard of it."

"There's a museum there now, with some very interesting archive photographs."

I waited for a reaction, but none came.

"In one of them, in one of the photos, I saw you, Cooper. You were standing in a crowd of policemen on the southbound platform in October 1960."

"Really?" he said, looking puzzled. "I'm quite sure it wasn't me in the photo. October 1960? It couldn't have been."

"There's a memorial at the station to a man killed in a railway accident, also in October 1960. My father's name is engraved on the plaque."

"Is it? That's very odd."

"Odd? Well, I suppose that's a word you could use for it."

I had already taken the photograph of P from my inside pocket. I raised it and leant towards him.

"Do you recognise this woman?" I said, and sensed immediately that his focusing and refocusing was a charade. There was an instant in his sham confusion when I saw a flicker of recognition.

"I can't really see her properly, Andris," he insisted. "Should I? Who is she?"

"I imagine you know a lot more than I do about her, Cooper. All I know is that signed herself with the initial P."

He took a long breath and slumped once again deep into his chair. I rested the portrait of the actress on the plump arm of my seat.

"Listen," I said, "I'm not asking for state secrets. It was over fifty years ago. I just want to know how my father died. And perhaps even why. Is that too much to ask?"

Arundel was staring at the bottle again. I regretted having brought it.

"My dad was in the navy. I know that. So was the man in the memorial. I also know that the memorial was controversial at the time. There were rumours he was a Russian spy, a traitor. I'm right, aren't I? Aren't I?"

The man refused to answer. I wondered if he were even still listening.

"I was tormented as a child over that. Bullied for being the son of a traitor. I never understood why. Can you imagine that, how that felt? Can you? Whatever he did, whatever treachery, whatever crime, that made my life hell. Are you listening to me? Cooper, can you hear what I'm saying?"

There was a sharp knock on the door and, without waiting for a reply, the Duty Manager reappeared in the room with a tray. She must have heard me raise my voice but made no comment.

"I brought your coffee," she announced. "There's sugar if you need it. And a biscuit. You alright there, Cooper?"

The man had turned his head awkwardly to look out into the garden.

"That rain has finally stopped," she said.

I hadn't noticed, but she was right. For several seconds we all watched the dripping leaves of the potted plants out on the patio.

"Thank you," I said. "For the coffee."

"You're welcome. We might be able to take you out for a bit of fresh air later, after all, Cooper."

He ignored her; he seemed lost in his own thoughts.

"Are you sure you don't want a drink, Cooper?"

He shook his head, almost imperceptibly.

"Not even a glass of water or something?"

"Leave us!" Arundel suddenly shouted.

"I beg your pardon?"

"I said leave us, woman! This is a private conversation, for fuck's sake!"

I was taken aback but to a lesser extent than the woman who retreated, muttering something under her breath.

"And shut the door behind you! Shut it properly, damn you!"

A moment or two after she had disappeared, Arundel faced me once more and offered the hint of a resigned smile.

"She's a nosey bitch, that one," he said.

"Did you hear what I said, what I was saying before?" I picked up, desperate to regain momentum.

"I heard every word, Andris," he said quietly with a sigh. "I'm sorry about the bullying, I really am. Listen to me. Listen to me carefully. Be sure that your father was not, I repeat, not a traitor. That's the truth, I guarantee."

I searched his wrinkled old face for sincerity.

139

"I'm not going to be around for much longer, Andris. And you deserve to know. Telling the truth won't hurt anybody now. It's all too long ago, you're right."

I waited in silence for him to gather his thoughts. Eventually he spoke again:

"You must make peace with your mother."

"My mother?"

"Erika was involved, Andris. She was involved in what she believed would be Eddie's arrest. That was all. Not his murder. Not the slander, not the smears."

"Why would she expect him to be arrested if you're telling me he wasn't a traitor? What had he done? What had he done wrong?"

"It was all a terrible misunderstanding, Andris. Miscommunication. Human error. An avoidable tragedy."

"You're not making any sense, Cooper. I don't believe you. You must tell me the truth. Tell me everything. Everything there is, there was. Who is this woman? Who is P? You knew her, I know you did."

He looked across again to the little bottle.

"I think I'll have a shot of this vodka," he decided. "Can you reach me a glass?"

There was a glass by his bed. It looked clean. I quickly fetched it, twisted open the bottle and poured him an inch.

"More," he ordered. "Give me a proper drink. I know it's not even midday, but, hell. You'll join me?"

"No. No, thanks," I said, nodding at my coffee cup. "Cooper, please. Who was this woman?"

He took a stiff draught of the alcohol, swallowed and let its warmth slowly invade his bloodstream.

"Andris," he said after a moment, a sadness in his raspy voice, "Your father, dear man, had a weakness for women. The prettier they were, the weaker he was. It was an Achilles heel, I suppose. It's not a crime."

I said nothing, leaving space for him to fill.

"There was a girl in Copenhagen, for a start. I've forgotten her name. He told me it was the real deal, he couldn't live without her, all that hearts and flowers stuff. I told him to drop her, to keep his eye on the ball. He said it was too late. She was expecting a child. We had to be brutal. It was a horrible time for Eddie, of course. We paid for the Danes to abort the baby, relocate her, somewhere he'd never find her. Terminate the whole thing, the whole sorry episode. Eddie never really forgave us."

"You were more than his friend by then," I suggested. "You were his mentor, his controller, is that the right word?"

He nodded slowly, before going on:

"Eddie was working for the Secret Intelligence Service, MI6, if you prefer. We both were. You knew that, I think."

He paused for another drink, then pushed the glass away so that it was almost out of reach.

"I recruited your father. At Cambridge, of course. He was a brilliant young man. Had all the charm in the world. Made people want to love him. I encouraged him to join officer training for the Navy. Then he worked for me at Six very soon after passing out."

"You can't have been much older than him."

"Six years, I think. But six years is a significant gap, Andris. And they were important years for me. I interrupted my own studies in '42 to become a cadet. Then I trained as a paratrooper. Just in time for Normandy. The first wave. Soften up the Germans, blow up a few bridges, make contact with the Resistance. Sabotage. It's a lovely word, don't you think, *sabotage*? Our language has been blessed with so many wonderful imports from French."

I noticed that behind his glasses his eyes had misted over. Arundel wasn't seeing me any more, he had eyes only for the target, he was part of a team of *saboteurs* crawling in the dark through the muddy shallows of the Orne. I let him drift a while. I was of the opinion that pressure on a very old man would be self-defeating.

"And Russian, too," he said presently, rubbing his eyes behind the lenses. "*Babushka. Babushka.* Is there a more delightful word to roll around your mouth?"

I nodded impatiently.

"It sounds like a glorious war," he went on eventually, "But it really wasn't. I returned to Cambridge in '45. They offered me a post. So, there I was, tutoring, lecturing, and, quite out of sight, taking the shilling dangled by the Secret Services too. Still had two masters when I transferred to the university here. Meanwhile, as recruits go, Eddie was one of my best. And that's the truth too."

"And this woman?" I said, picking up the photo again. "Tell me about this woman."

"It's Primrose Smith. She was a long-time girlfriend. Eddie met her at Cambridge. She became an actress, quite famous in her day. I think she ended up in the US. I had no idea your father was on that train, Andris, and that is God's truth. She was in some revue in Bournemouth and he had taken a detour to visit her. He was supposed to be going directly to Portsmouth, to the naval base."

"I was five years old in 1960, Cooper. And so, you're saying, he was having an affair, you're saying he was sleeping with this actress at the time. And what about the Danish girl? Was that sick episode before or after my birth? Was he cheating on my mother with her too?"

"Yes. Yes, he was. I'm sorry, Andris. That's what he was like. A slave to his dick."

I felt a nausea rise in my hollowed-out stomach. My father was no less a cheat than Adrian Plummer, whom I despised to this day. A brick had been ripped out of my wobbling Jenga tower. Arundel hadn't noticed my expression. Nor the blood rising to my cheeks. He was picking up speed.

"I spoke to him that day. That morning, in Bristol. He was due to meet a man in Portsmouth the next day. A man working for the Soviets. A man called Gints Bendiks."

"Why?"

"Listen, Andris. Listen to me carefully. Your father was a very brave man. It is important that you don't forget that. We had set him up as a triple agent. A *triple* agent. Do you understand what that means?"

"I think so."

"He was behaving as a double agent, spying for the enemy against his own country, but this was a deceit. He was onside all the time, playing the Russians. It was the late fifties. We knew who most of the spies were at the Soviet embassy. Eddie arranged to meet one of those we guessed would take the bait. Your father was brilliantly convincing."

Arundel paused to watch me take a sip of coffee. It had already gone cold and I placed the cup and saucer on the floor.

"We were giving them scraps," he went on. "Authentic stuff but scraps all the same. Nothing to undermine our own security. Who's who in NATO, pure fluff, names of discredited agents. There was a cell of ex-Nazis, for example, still working for Six in Graz with links to members of the Hungarian resistance. Yes, I know, don't look so shocked. When Stalin was putting the shutters down we found ourselves smooching with some rather unsavoury characters. Expediency is the word you are looking for. Opportunism is another."

He shot me a glance over his glasses. I felt he was looking for acceptance rather than approval. I held my expression of neutrality long enough to oblige him to continue:

"Well, this lot were taking the piss. They were washed up, we knew that, they were getting money for nothing. They were disposable. So Eddie wound them up with Russian help. On top of that he was feeding misinformation. You'd call them lies: details with explainable errors on troop deployment, British naval strength, NATO exercises, to confuse the Russians, to slow the buggers down.

"This went on for a couple of years, at least, Andris. The Russians loved him, couldn't get enough. They knew the game, of course. They were under the illusion that he needed cover for his bosses at Six and so in turn we got their scraps too: Soviet agents in Britain and western Germany, mostly obsolete, but not all. Plus details of their infiltration of the Baltic resistance groups. That's how he met Bendiks."

"You have a very good memory."

"It's like it happened yesterday. It was a moment in my life, and in Eddie's too, when we were totally alive: every sense heightened, every sight the most vivid, every word the most significant we'd ever heard."

Arundel had left me again; he had returned to the reassuring warmth of the Cold War. In the corner of the room by the door I saw a walking frame and wondered why I hadn't noticed it before.

"So why was Bendiks important?" I said eventually, resolving to pull him back.

"Bendiks? Bendiks was a sleeper. He was a Latvian, a Russian agent allowed to leave for Britain with a group of exiles from Riga in 1950, ostensibly to escape the Soviet grip on his country. He embraced England. He knew your mother and her sister, your aunt. He was a year or two older than them, an educated man, spoke four or five languages. He ended up working as a freelance journalist and of course he was close to the Free Baltic movement that had been established in London. Your father met him several times, and was already using him as a conduit, had been doing for months when Erasmus was murdered."

"Erasmus?"

"Erasmus was the unofficial leader of the Free Baltic cell. Larger than life, that sort. A charismatic man, by most accounts. A fearsome bully according to a few. I never met him. He was energetic, a successful fundraiser for money and materiel which found its way to the so-called Forest Brothers, the underground army back in Latvia."

"He sounds like somebody MI6 could have done business with."

"Very perceptive, Andris. As I said, I never met him, but I believe he did have some admirers on the third floor."

"He was murdered? In London?"

"Yes. Yes, he was. According to Eddie, everything pointed to Bendiks. It was a bomb, and he'd had the training. We knew that. But we didn't bring him in. We wanted to play a longer game. Erasmus was collateral damage, I'm afraid."

Arundel looked at me again for a reaction, an expression of distaste for state-sponsored cynicism. Again I tried to remain impassive.

"Your mother was disgusted too. She knew Erasmus well. In fact..."

He paused discreetly to let me guess the rest.

"But he was no great loss to mankind, Andris, believe me. We suspected that he had collaborated with the German SD during the occupation. There were stories that he was responsible for the imprisonment of scores of Jews and Communists who were later transported out of Latvia. After his death, several credible witnesses came forward to verify the rumours."

"And, as you say, he'd been on our payroll."

"Just for titbits, as far as I know. And moral support, yes."

"Expediency."

"You're getting the picture, Andris. And MI5 had been watching him. They also had Bendiks in their sights. As I said earlier, your mother was a party to what happened next. Somehow she had been made to believe that Eddie was a traitor. I suppose it wasn't so surprising as that was the impression he had given, but only to the Russians, absolutely, strictly to nobody else. Erika had been shown a photo of your father with Bendiks. They undermined him. I honestly don't know the full story; you'll have to ask her yourself. She denied any involvement to me at the time. Understandably. The crux of the matter is that MI5 had your father killed."

The tale was unravelling so quickly I had no time for emotions.

"Wasn't there any attempt to clarify things with you, with MI6?"

"Your father's role as a triple was extremely secret, Andris. As I said, miscommunication. Or no communication. Partly our fault, probably, but Five needed no excuses. They were not slow in jumping to conclusions. It was like that in those days: competitive, unhealthily so. Anything to get one over on Six, and ask questions later."

Arundel stopped talking. I watched him heaving for breath, lifting his glasses, glancing out of the window, tailing a young gardener who was pushing a wheelbarrow of bricks. The old man's vitality, not to mention his power of recall, belied his age. The gardener disappeared from view. While Arundel stared blankly at the space he had vacated, I spent some time idly studying the rather ugly geometric pattern in the pale blue curtains; I was trying to put all the information he had fed me into a kind of order. He turned back to me presently.

"The man who killed your father," he said quietly, "his name was Macduff, by the way. Like in Shakespeare. He used a cyanide compound."

"Sorry?"

"Sodium cyanide, if I recall. Astonishingly rapid. That did for Eddie. Sorry, Andris, you didn't need to know that, I wasn't thinking."

I accepted his apology with a curt nod.

"Macduff, he was a specialist. I have to tell you that he did some work for us too. I didn't know it was him at the time. I saw records after his death."

"Macduff's death?"

"Yes. Not long after killing Eddie. He died in Berlin: shot at the Wall helping two Easties trying to cross."

He saw my look of disbelief.

"It's the truth, Andris. That's where Macduff fell. He was working for us on that mission. They said that he led a charmed life, but Berlin was where his luck finally ran out. Eichendorffstrasse. I saw the report; and the East German one, bizarrely. Much later, of course; we're all friends now, aren't we?"

He paused to smile at the irony: ancient spies free to read each others' old mail these days.

"He was Castille's man, really, though," he said. "Macduff did a lot of work for Castille at MI5. I don't think it's a coincidence that Castille had a country house less than three miles from Shillingstone. A place called Sturcote House. A family estate for a family man, and *Sir Mark* these days. And *Lady* Castille, of course, the fragrant Angela. That's where Macduff was spirited away from on the night of Eddie's murder. At least that's *my* theory."

Arundel was trying to get comfortable. The pillow had slipped again and he had started to droop to one side. For a second time I helped to rearrange his support. He thanked me brusquely and then set off again:

"Castille and I go back a very long way. All the way back to Cambridge in the early 1940s, in fact. He was a couple of years older than me, a St John's man, a great sportsman, a great rower. As was I in those days. I turned up at Trinity and was ambushed by the intense rivalry between the colleges. NATO and Warsaw Pact, MI5 and MI6, Cambridge and Oxford, these pale into insignificance compared with Trinity and St John's. And Castille and I seemed to embody it every time we rowed the bumps or ran cross country. I don't mean friendly rivalry, Andris. I mean bitter and nasty and personal. As bitter as you can get."

There was another pause. I began to worry about how much all this was taking out of him. He took off his glasses and then put them back on.

"He was called up in '43 into military intelligence," he said, scratching his forehead with a bony finger. "He was part of the second wave invasion post D-Day. Spent a few years in Germany after the surrender. Later on he was given a nice job at the Home Office, thence a hop into bed with the Security Service."

He hesitated once again and coughed weakly.

"Are you alright, Cooper?" I said.

"I'm fine. Pass me that drink again," he ordered. "This is doing me no harm, getting all this off my chest."

I put the glass into his outstretched hands. He took a sip and swallowed.

"The girl was the key," he resumed eventually, indicating with a vague forward gesture of his hooked index finger the photograph still at my arm. "That girl, Primrose Smith. Eddie was being tracked by Five, we now know. They had photos of him with Bendiks. Your mother had seen them. So now somebody must have shown them to Primrose Smith. They knew more about your father than we did, which is embarrassing for me to admit. At least they knew about the girl's relationship with him. They did their homework, so hats off. Her father served in the Great War. She was a patriot just like him, as English as rhubarb and custard; she wasn't part of Eddie's Soviet game. They tried to persuade her that she was sleeping with a traitor. She wasn't convinced. As I said, she'd loved him since she was a teenager, but she wanted to confront him. She was in a play in Bournemouth, I think I told you. The plan was hatched around that. She invited him down to see her there. I do not believe for one moment that she knew that he would be attacked on the train, but she was the reason he was on it, that's clear. If I'd known, if I'd had an inkling about her, I'd have told him to stay away, of course I would. But Eddie kept her hidden from me, just as he kept her hidden from Erika."

"There was a theatre programme in the attaché case the police found."

"Indeed."

"And a novel."

"You are well informed, Andris. Yes, it was *Mother*: a book I had recommended to your father."

"Really?"

"Gorky. A sentimental view of the Revolution. But a valid one."

Gorky. My thoughts hurtled back to boarding school, to kind Mr Hussey's study, to the quotation on his desk about truth being the god of the free man.

"And there was money, actually. A good deal of cash that was never discovered. It was Six money: over nine hundred pounds. That's close to, I don't know, probably around twenty thousand today. Macduff must have helped himself."

Now I had a brief vision in my mind of Mary White, née Abbott, paying for supper at the Old Fox Inn. The embers in the fireplace were glowing orange. Somebody in the bar exploded with laughter. Good luck to you, Mary, you crafty old girl.

"You look uncertain, Andris, unconvinced."

"No. I was just thinking of something else."

"If you think I'm still telling fibs, then you're wrong. I no longer have a professional default option of deceit. And I can back all this up. Belt and braces. If you really want me to."

"What do you mean?"

"I can probably get access, for a short time at least, to Macduff's archive report on the operation. I'm owed a favour or two. It might be abridged or edited but you'll see a flavour of what I saw back then. His escape route had to be through Sturcote House. Give me your address. There's a pad on the side table."

He was pointing to the wide pinewood desk on the far side of his duvet whose top was designed to swing over his lap when he was sitting up in bed. By the notepad I noticed a large half-completed jigsaw and a box upon which lay a magnifying glass. It looked like a cheap reproduction of one of Van Gogh's sunflower paintings. He saw me studying it.

"Oh that. One of the few pleasures I can still have fun with. But a bugger with my eyes the way they are. And that one, well, too many shades of yellow."

He was laughing to himself quietly. I wrote down the address of Pattercombe Farm.

"Will you be there for the next forty-eight hours? I'll have something sent over. It'll be on tablet, I imagine. You're comfortable with that? You'll need a password. I'll set it up with your father's middle name, the name he hated! Alright? Capital L, the rest lower case."

"Alright."

"And you'll need a question for your ID. Mention to the courier something about his shoes."

"Shoes?"

"Just a throwaway remark. So he knows he's dealing with the right chap. And don't worry, you'll recognise him as bona fide."

I realised that I was still standing. It seemed inappropriate to sit down again.

"I think it's time I left. I have probably exhausted you, Cooper."

"No, you did right to come, Andris. You deserve to know the truth, of course you do. I'm sorry it's taken you so long to find it. I thought, we thought, your mother and I, that you would be better off living your life without it. That was hubristic of us, presumptuous, and I regret it. And yes, you were quite right, it was me in the photo. You'd have made a good spy," he said with a short laugh. "I had no idea there was a copy on public display. And the memorial. It's funny you saw the memorial. What were the chances of you even being there? I imagine nine in ten visitors to the station will miss it."

"I saw it first in 1990 when the station was closed. I did some business with a furniture company who leased the premises back then."

"You must have been shocked."

"I put it out of my mind."

"I paid for that stone, Andris. I wanted it to exonerate Eddie somehow. There was a huge row, even though several years had passed since his death: was he a traitor or not? All the doubts resurfaced."

"Why wasn't he ever cleared?"

"That's something else I regret. His role as a triple never

151

saw the light of day. It was an operational decision, above my pay-grade, as the coward might say. We wanted to keep Bendiks dangling, *active* as it were, we didn't want to spook him. The thinking was he would lead us to richer pickings. You can imagine the job we had convincing Five to leave him be."

"And was it worth it?"

"Well, we did pick up a high-ranking officer in our own service whom he was running. A year or two later, that was, so patience was rewarded. Bendiks himself was never caught. He was talented, slippery. He escaped to Latvia some time in the mid-sixties: home free, out of reach."

Another question had been gnawing at me for several minutes:

"Does Castille still live at Sturcote House?" I said abruptly.

"I believe he does, but he is a very old man. I can find out. Be careful what you do next, Andris. If I were you I'd do nothing more. You've got the truth, so now let it lie. What I've told you was dynamite fifty years ago; even twenty years ago. Now it's the dormant past. You hear, dormant."

I shook his hand. His grip was a good deal weaker second time around.

"Don't get up, Cooper."

"As if I could. Not in any hurry, anyway. Do you mind if *I* ask *you* a question before you leave?"

"What's that?"

"How did you get hold of the photograph of Primrose Smith?"

I hadn't anticipated him turning the tables. Not wishing to bring Mary White into the frame, I bluffed:

"It came to me anonymously. Through the post."

Arundel's watery gaze froze to ice.

"I said you'd make a good spy," he said. "You've already

learned to lie a little to protect your source. Am I right?"

I felt faintly embarrassed, like a schoolboy caught cheating in a test.

"I'm glad you came," he smiled, releasing me. "I'm glad I've told you what I know. I'm ninety-two next month. I've lived most of my life in the world of secrets, and I don't want to take too many of them to my grave. It feels good to unburden."

"When did you stop?"

"Being a spook? Oh, I retired in the 1970s. Still quite a young man. I returned to academia full-time, here in Bristol. I still know people. I'm consulted even now, but less often, naturally. Things turned very sour in the seventies, Andris. We were doing good things in Ulster at the time, but, for reasons known only to the sainted few, Six were shunted out and Five took over. Politics. It was all a bit bruising but, you know, a long time ago."

"Any memoirs?"

"No, of course not. That's not really encouraged."

"So there's still plenty you will take to your grave after all?"

"Yes. Yes, I suppose there is. Most of it good. Most of it worthy. I've nothing to be ashamed of any more. You may not believe me, but honestly, I haven't."

4

The office computer at Pattercombe provided me with as much background information about my father's English lover as I could possibly ever want. Primrose Smith was the third and youngest daughter of Sir Francis Clarendon-Smith and his wife Lady Charlotte. Websites I visited confirmed that Sir Francis had served as a British Army captain in the trenches. They told me that Primrose, born in January 1930, the same month and the same year as my father, had followed the standard educational path trodden by thousands of upper middle-class girls before her, finishing at Newnham College, Cambridge, where she read English and threw herself into student drama. Following her graduation she was invited to train at the Royal Academy of Dramatic Art. Her earliest work was for the radio: plays, announcements and a little writing. She joined a variety of touring companies and made her television debut in 1962 as a presenter. A few minor acting roles followed and she rose to a degree of prominence as one of the female leads in a popular period drama of the mid-sixties. Sadly it appeared that this was not the stepping stone she had hoped it to be. I read that, as she approached forty, a series of parts in plays staged mainly in provincial theatres followed, and with them, irregular spots in pantomime. In 1970 she moved to the USA, adopted the professional name Rosa Smith and secured small roles in a string of

154

long-forgotten comedy series. The woman who should have been playing Lady Macbeth in Stratford was being cast as a caricature of a ditzy Midwest housewife. In 1972 she met and married Chet Montana, singer and bass-player with the San Francisco soft-rock band Instinct, and settled in California. The couple rapidly produced four children and then divorced, the break-up predominantly caused by Chet's cocaine addiction. Primrose never worked again and suffered from severe bouts of depression. I was genuinely upset to read that she spent the final two years of her life in an institution, and died aged 54, penniless and a desperate alcoholic. If it hadn't been so touching, her life would have seemed such a sad cliché.

Before I even started reading a word of her potted biography, my eyes were drawn to the photographs in the margin. There were two images to illustrate the article, and the first one, flanking the paragraphs on her early years, was exactly the same studio portrait as the one I had been given by Mary White, the one still tucked away in my jacket pocket. Looking at it again, this time on a computer screen, I saw an underlying fragility behind the beauty, her perfect skin so easy to blemish, the lace at her throat so delicate it might melt like snowflakes. A second picture, lower down in the text and this time in colour, showed her as Rosa in an American TV role, still striking but fatter and cheaply dressed. Perhaps she was in character for the show, I would never know for sure. Later that evening when the house was quiet I found myself sitting in the dark wondering what had become of her children.

*

There was plenty to be done at home and I had no need to leave the farm for the next day or two. The school holidays were around the corner, and thankfully the cottages were fully booked for the season, give or take. With Harvey mostly occupied with the farming, I found that over the years I had become a glorified odd job man during the summer months, a willing factotum who was expected to repair breakages, leakages and seepages, and remove any other encumbrance that could make the paying guests' time under our roofs anything less than perfect. I didn't mind at all, to be honest. I had lost track of the new practical skills I had learned. Well, partly learned. On one occasion I had even mended a satellite dish with nothing more than a screwdriver, a pair of nail scissors and nine inches of gaffer tape. That was a fluke, I admit. I usually steered well clear of electronics, preferring low-tech jobs like paintwork or grouting or clearing blocked drains.

I was in the process of replacing a bulb on an outside light on one of the rentals when I heard the sweet throb of a motorcycle engine in the lane. Harvey was down in the orchard with his pesticide sprayer. Polly had taken Sean into town for something. Lynne was inside, probably in the kitchen, probably baking. The cottages were all empty; it was a sunny day, the middle of the morning, everyone had gone off with their plans for a few hours under clear blue skies. I looked up to watch a helmeted rider steer a beast of a machine into the driveway and carefully decelerate to stop out of sight around by the front door of the farmhouse.

I stepped down from my ladder, placed the light attachment on the grass and hobbled back up to the house as quickly as I could. I heard the engine fade to a low growl.

"Hey!" I called out before I could even see him. It didn't really matter if he met Lynne before me but I was certain this would be the courier sent on cue by Cooper Arundel. I turned the corner to see a tall, slim figure dressed in black leathers from throat to ankles effortlessly pulling a shiny white BMW on to its stand.

"Hey! Hello!" I shouted again, and arrived to greet him just as he was removing his helmet. I need not have rushed, for there was no sign of Lynne.

"Good morning, sir," he said, slipping off his gloves.

He was a young man in his twenties with coffee-coloured skin, short black hair and shiny eyes the hue of burnt caramel. People of Afro-Caribbean descent are still a rarity in Dorset, even in 2015. In spite of myself I was staring a little too hard. On the front of his jacket, somewhere over his heart, was crafted a small gold emblem with the words *Trinity Couriers*. There was little doubt that here before me stood Arundel's winged Mercury. He looked back at me with an open, engaging countenance.

"I'm here from Trinity," he said redundantly, waiting for a sign.

"If you'd like to come into the house," I said, remembering my instructions, "I think you could leave your boots on, they look perfectly clean."

"I would prefer to wait outside as a matter of fact, sir," he replied. "If you don't mind."

His voice was steady, mellifluous, accentless. He could have read the news on the BBC radio in the 1950s.

"But I do have this for you. One moment, please."

He opened a side compartment on the motorcycle and produced a slim cardboard box, also labelled *Trinity*, about the size of a hardback novel.

"Here you are, sir. Special delivery, as I think they used to say."

"Thank you. I'll ..."

"Take it inside, if you wish, sir. And please, take your time. I'm happy to wait here in the sunshine. Stretch my legs a bit."

"Right. Fine. Thanks again."

I felt him watching me as I limped into the house, clumsily

removing my working shoes, and disappeared into the shadows of the hallway.

The room we used as an office looked out on to the kitchen garden. There was nobody in view, I checked: no-one weeding the onion bed or lifting early potatoes. I closed the door quietly behind me, found a pair of reading glasses, and sat at the desk to open the parcel. Inside was an iPad, its shiny plastic shell marked on the reverse in tiny capital letters: PROPERTY OF H.M. GOVERNMENT. I pressed the tablet on, a pale blue screen was illuminated and, above a keyboard, a box demanding a password appeared.

I composed myself before typing, very deliberately, my father's middle name: L a n c e l o t, and then touching Enter. I was almost instantly looking at a page of old-fashioned typewriter print, presumably a photograph of an original operational report produced in the 1960s. A narrow pink band at the foot of the page told me that this was the first of four. I imagined a title page had been skipped, for page 1 began partway through a sentence. I read avidly, hopping from line to line, leaping over blacked out words or phrases; as Arundel had warned, the text was somewhat redacted, which I found frustrating.

It amounted to a third-person narrative in which the protagonist, M, boards a train and, *at a professional distance*, follows a Target. Some names were hidden, presumably those of passengers that were either irrelevant or sensitive. Surprisingly, the departure point, Bristol TM, was there to be seen. My father, and I think I knew now that it *was* my father, was simply referred to as Target. I read on, pages 2 and 3, pages lightly edited in which M confronts Target, administers a syringe of ███████████, and at a precise moment which he has calculated, tosses Target's body out of the moving carriage, followed by his belongings.

Reading this section affected me less than I thought it

might. I rationalised that I was not after all discovering the truth about my father's murder, merely having a known truth confirmed.

Suddenly the name Shillingstone also appears without disguise. The report mentions M jettisoning a ███████████, which I guessed to be the attaché case. He then describes his escape from the platform and his disappearance into what is described as *the shadowy undergrowth.*

Harvey kept a collection of OS maps of Dorset some-where in this room, and I spent a minute or two checking the shelves. The only small scale Explorer maps he seemed to own were of the south and west of the county. Number 117 came maddening close but Shillingstone was missing, just beyond the edge. I opened up a larger scale Landranger, Number 194, and found the spot straight away, but in much less detail than I had hoped to see. It was a battered old map, a 1989 imprint, but the older the better, I was thinking: little would have changed since Macduff was here, and the fields around this stretch of the Stour certainly would not have altered.

Returning to the tablet screen, and with a finger on the paper map, I gained a decent insight into the route the killer had taken. He mentions the weather conditions, the inter-mittent moon, the strength of the current of the river, the composition of a copse. He ignores a road bridge, preferring the seclusion of a footbridge. I checked the map once more: he is heading almost due north, confirmed by the mention of the lights of a village at his right, name ██████████. Page 4 is more heavily redacted: a destination is arrived at, shielded by a black oblong large enough to hide the words Sturcote House perfectly in this typeface. And now other characters appear, detailed only by further black boxes. The protocol of a rendezvous, entry through the rear of ████████, the transfer of a case, the offer of a meal. Here not only are names redacted but also pronouns, even the *he* and the *him* and the *his*. The text must run on to a further page or more: page 4 ends in mid-sentence, blacked out in its entirety.

I stood up from the desk to stretch. I peered out of the window for signs of life: it was going to be an excellent year for the onions. I took a deep breath and sat down at the iPad again. I read the whole account again, slowly. It struck me how much less functional a report it was than I had expected. Macduff, or whoever else had written it, had displayed to my mind quite a poetic flourish: he mentioned the vagaries of the moonlight, for example, the fleeting sight of a fox, the shapes and names and even the texture of the trees.

Turning my attention to the map again, I traced what I imagined had been his winding path in the dark. I regretted not having a magnifying glass like the one the old man had to help him see the shades of yellow in his sunflowers jigsaw. Distances in the account were vague, but even the loosest of directions lead my finger indisputably to Sturcote, a building shown sitting by a narrow country road, about a quarter of a mile from an oxbow in the Stour. Arundel must be right: Macduff headed here and was spirited away with the collusion of the landowner.

A programmed timer must have activated a pulse in the pink band. It had started flashing, and a line of text ran across it indicating that by pressing its strip on the touch-screen a message would appear. A little pressure produced a new page on which was a short warning from Arundel himself, I assumed. I read it twice:

Dear A,
You have what you wanted. Please make sure device
closed down before return.
MC still owns SH. However advise avoid. Sleeping dogs
and so on.
Much love, C.

I switched the machine off and absent-mindedly refolded the maps that were scattered across the desk. The house still felt empty, deathly quiet. I needed a moment to gather my thoughts. I carefully placed the tablet back in its cardboard folder and tucked in the stiff ends to seal it.

*

After a few minutes I shuffled back into the hallway, and even before I stepped outside into the fresh air I could hear voices and laughter. One of the picnic tables had been carried on to the front lawn and at it, sharing some kind of joke beyond guessing, were sitting the motorcyclist and my unofficial mother-in-law Lynne. It appeared that she had offered him refreshments and he had just finished what looked like a cream tea, dabbing crumbs of scone off a jam-stained plate with his fingertips and licking them lovingly. No doubt sweating in the heat of the late morning, the young man had removed the top half of his leathers, and a tight white cotton tee-shirt barely concealed the contours of a lean, muscular torso. At his boots lay Nancy, eyes open for a titbit he might drop but otherwise content simply to be close to him.

"Andris!" called Lynne as I emerged into the sunlight. "There you are. You've been keeping poor Lyle waiting."

Lyle? She knew the man's name? Wasn't everything supposed to be hush-hush?

The courier looked up from his tea cup and shook his head.

"Don't worry, sir. The lady is exaggerating."

Lynne let out a high-pitched girly laugh.

"There is no hurry," he went on, smiling at her indulgently. "Have you had enough time with the delivery, sir?"

"Well, yes. Yes, I have," I said, offering him the box, "Thank you. Yes, I have finished with it."

"The lady..."

"Lynne," said Lynne.

"I'm sorry, yes, Lynne saw me outside and offered me a scone."

"I'd just baked a fresh batch."

"Delicious."

"Andris," she said, "can you believe that Lyle here had never tasted clotted cream before?"

"Really?" I said looking at him.

"Never," he said, raising an eyebrow in mock apology.

"I offered him a sandwich," Lynne continued enthusiastically, "but he said no, didn't you, Lyle? Mind you, you don't look like you need much feeding up from where I'm sitting."

Christ, Polly's mother was flirting with him, and probably had been for the past quarter of an hour. Lyle stood up and carried the parcel back to the BMW. I watched Lynne's eyes follow the sleek movement of his backside as he went. Lynne, get a grip, woman!

Suddenly from the other side of the motorbike Harvey appeared. How long had he been there, crouching behind it, examining the wheels, admiring the engine, stroking the bodywork?

"What a lovely machine, eh, Andris?" he said. "K series. 1600. Gran Turismo."

"Yes," I agreed, still wondering why he wasn't up a ladder in the orchard. "It's a superb bike."

"Virtually brand new, eh, Lyle? Just a couple of thousand on the clock?"

"But, sadly, not mine," said the young man with a stage frown.

"Well, at least you get to ride it," said Harvey, running his hand lovingly over the seat.

"Yes, there is that. And I'm afraid I must ride it straight back to London imminently."

"Do you need the loo before you leave us?" called Lynne.

"I'm fine, thanks," he answered, zipping up the jacket and adjusting the straps of his helmet.

"It's a damn shame Sean wasn't here to see it," said Harvey. "Gran Turismo, like this."

I thought he must like hearing himself say those words. *Gran Turismo. Babushka. Sabotage.*

"He would have loved to sit up there. A pity they're both out."

Actually no, it's not, I thought. Polly would have gone weak at the knees had she been around to watch the courier in his tight leathers and even tighter tee-shirt, the golden image of a certain type of male perfection, smiling his winning smile and licking clotted cream off his thumb.

"You must come again, Lyle," Lynne was saying, mouthing the words deliberately. "Can he hear me with that big helmet on?"

The rider, now fully dressed and ready for his return journey, nodded.

"Come and stay! We've got plenty of beds! Bring a friend!"

Come and stay? Bring a friend? I looked at Lynne, perplexed.

"He's not married, Andris."

"Oh, really?"

"No. I did ask."

"I'm sure you did, Lynne."

Harvey was shaking the man's hand as if he were the son he never had setting out on a long, meaningful adventure.

"Take care, young man," he actually said. "And enjoy the ride!"

I made to approach the bike but the rider was already revving the engine, kicking away the stand, and preparing to move off.

"Thank you," I said, but I don't think he actually heard me over the low tiger purr of the bike. Well, thanks for coming, anyway.

With one hand in the air, a theatrical wave, he steered the machine up the drive, turned smoothly into the lane, and with a sweet burst of acceleration, he was gone. Lynne and Harvey, still under the spell, carried on waving. I had to smile. Meanwhile Nancy had sauntered over to the exact spot in the sun where the motorbike had been standing and was making herself comfortable in its aura.

Later that day, when I had a little time to myself, I pulled out the Landranger map again and studied the significant right-hand corner. Could I be mistaken? Was my finger sitting over the wrong destination after all? And yet, if I were in some way vindicated, did I actually feel complete?

You have what you wanted.

Well, yes and no.

Advise avoid.

Why did you write that, Cooper, having confirmed that MC still owns SH? You could have said he'd sold up years ago and gone to spend a happy retirement in the Bahamas. You could have told me he'd died and gone straight to Heaven. Then I would have avoided without need of advice, wouldn't I? And I'd have believed you, Cooper, in this new era of openness between us, this time of *glasnost*, of finally telling the truth.

Sleeping dogs and so on.

How dangerous can a sleeping dog be if he's in his nineties? Dogs don't live that long, not even clever ones.

I had to give myself more time to reach a decision. In the meanwhile I came to the conclusion that I needed another angle. I needed to square the circle. Firing up the computer, I logged on to an airline ticket site, dredged up my credit card, and booked a seat on the earliest flight I could manage from Gatwick to Riga.

5

It was strange to see Leons Lapsa wearing summer clothes. In addition to his snowy white hair he had cultivated a matching little beard which I thought suited him perfectly. He was wearing a loose tee-shirt with the Dynamo hockey team crest, baggy shorts, scuffed trainers and a wide smile. He looked genuinely pleased to see me. For a man in his early eighties, the outfit suited him less well than the facial hair, but I had to admire him for his spirit.

"Andris!" he called excitedly as I emerged into the arrivals lounge. "Andris, over here! Welcome back!"

The airport was busy with tourist arrivals, and our way to the car park was encumbered by hotel reps, tour operators, taxi-drivers and even gaggles of children selling fizzy drinks: people loitering, dawdling, scurrying, voices raised in a language I could not understand. Leons seemed to know where he was going and the best way to get there, so I followed him, my bag slung over my shoulder, trying to catch the flow of his running commentary. We weaved in and out of human traffic, and into the sunlight flooding the concrete of the terminal concourse.

"The heat is not normal," he said, pointing in the direction of the car park. "This way. Attention of the cars. We have heat, sun, for one week and is not normal, even for summer in Riga. Thirty degrees, I think so. But do not be worried, Andris. In the car I have climatisation."

"Air conditioning?"

"Yes, I have it. Follow me, please."

I could tell Leons was very proud of his new car, a silver VW Golf GTI. It must have been brand new: he was still deriving a sensual pleasure from unlocking the boot, placing my bag in the spotless compartment, opening the passenger door for me (after reminding me it was the one on the right-hand side), then settling into the comfort of his pristine driver's seat, and turning over the engine, responsive and thrillingly obedient.

"You've got rid of the old Saab, Leons?"

"Pardon me?"

"You have sold your Saab, the blue car you had before?"

"Oh, yes, Andris. It was good car for me, but it was very old. Lot of problems in the winter. This will be my last car, I think so."

"Really? That's a sad thought," I said, acknowledging privately, however, that if he kept it as long as he had driven the Saab he was probably right.

"I buy German car, Andris. And I pay it with euros. What have we become? It seems we are all Europeans now."

"In England we are not so sure, Leons."

He laughed and braked suddenly to avoid hitting a delivery van.

"You live on island. It is different mentality, yes?"

"Yes, you are probably right."

He turned up the air-con to somewhere close to maximum.

"This is very smart," I said, looking around at the interior.

"I am lucky, Andris. Here in Latvia we have weak economy in spite of euro. Maybe because of euro, you understand? You know how it was in the crisis. In England also. The crisis of the banks, yes? Our good times in the years after 2005 end like that," he said, clicking his thumb and middle finger. "Have you heard of the Baltic Tiger? He was shot by the bankers. You live by capitalism, Andris, you can die by capitalism also."

He was laughing but we both knew it was hollow laughter.

We were already beyond the airport complex and had joined the traffic heading north-east towards the city.

"But I am lucky, Andris," he said, cutting in sharply as a motorbike overtook us, ignoring the speed restrictions. "Your mother has money. I have money. I have small pension. And selling my poetry. Yes, Andris, I am selling my poetry! Now more than when I write it!"

Leons was enjoying practising his English. As he steered his VW along the main artery through dreary suburbs and high-rises, he told me, with the excitement of a teenager who has just kissed a new girlfriend, about the unexpected wave of fame that had engulfed him in the past twelve months. A sample of one of his very earliest love poems had been set to a rap theme which had been a surprise hit in not only Latvia but, once translated, in Estonia too, downloaded by the tens of thousands, and had become a staple in the night-clubs of Riga and Tallinn throughout the winter. Since then a lawyer he knew had drawn up a contract whereby Leons was being paid handsome royalties for further adaptations of his lyrics. And there had been plenty already: the rapper, whom he described as a lovely boy from the resort town of Jurmala, had recorded six more tracks based on Lapsa's juvenile collection, and the old poet had suddenly become a cult figure among the younger generation.

Faster cars were recklessly overtaking buses and trucks, Leons too was not averse to moments of brutal acceleration, and I wondered if this is what he meant when he had said that the Golf would be his last car.

I remember Erika once telling me that Leons' poetry was

unfathomable, even for her, one part political, one part philosophical, a third part metaphysical, and that it translated very badly into English. Perhaps she had been talking about his later compositions. I have to admit I had never read a line of it, in either language. I wondered if the goatee had anything to do with new photo opportunities in the pipeline for the old boy.

"I spend afternoon in studio," he enthused, "Recording studio, one month ago or so, I have invitation to watch musicians."

"It sounds like great fun," I said, genuinely envious.

We crossed a river bridge and merged with the slow, honking traffic burrowing its way into the chaos of the narrow streets of Vecriga. I had been here before with my mother and half-sisters, but I recognised very little. The slate-grey spire of the Dome cathedral we had visited loomed up to our left. For all Leons' pessimism, I thought that the city looked more alive, with its fluttering maroon and white flags, a more prosperous, confident place than when I had seen it twenty years ago. It was as if it had discovered a richer, more colourful palette. Mind you, twenty years ago the grey days of the Soviet occupation were still fresh in the memory, and, of course, I had been here in the middle of winter. The last time I had seen these streets, now dotted with outdoor cafés and bistros, with paved stages for street theatre, now teeming with tourists in sun-caps and pink skin, then the gutters were clogged with brown snow and the sky was a constant, frigid dusk.

"And how is my mother, Leons?" I asked.

"Your mother? Your mother is of good health. You will see, Andris. And she looks forward to see you again, naturally. When you telephone, she was very happy, I think. Very happy to see her son again after so long time, I think so."

Erika was standing by the hob wearing a cotton headscarf and a long apron, a wooden spoon to her lips, tasting a casserole that was steaming in a cast-iron pot.

"Andris, darling!" she gushed. "Come and give your mother a kiss! Careful of the apron, you'll get grease on your clothes. That's it, a little peck will do. It's lovely to see you, my dear."

The kitchen was a bright, spacious area with wide windows and an open glass door that gave on to an undulating lawn. They had moved out of the city centre several years ago and had bought a modern chalet-style house in Mezaparks.

"You too, Mother," I said, and taking in the unfamiliar surroundings, "This is nice."

"Well, we thought, we'd like to retire somewhere a bit quieter, didn't we, Leons?"

"To end our years with better view than back of streets and car parks, you said," added her husband, who had followed me inside.

"Well, of course. And why not? This is a lovely area, really, the best suburb in Riga."

"Historically it was always the, you say, *posh*? The most posh part of city for residential."

"There are some fascinating examples of early twentieth-century architecture, Andris, you must see them. You'd love it. You studied architecture, didn't you, darling?"

"Design, actually."

"Design?"

"A foundation course."

"Well, it's the same area, isn't it? You appreciate the *design* of a fine building, I'm sure."

"Yes, Mother, I do."

"The only disadvantage is we are so close to Kisezers but we don't actually have a lake view. Not even from upstairs."

The last time I was in Riga we had gone for a short walk by the side of the lake, my mother, my sisters and I: less than half a mile, a quarter of an hour or so, it had been bitterly cold and the lake was frozen flat, motionless, covered in a white dusting of fresh snow, its grey ice six inches thick below the surface. I remembered the forlorn, frosted jetties, the hard, stony shores, deserted and drained of colour, patrolled only by grim ranks of stiff, dreary pine trees.

Leons picked up my bag from the floor where I had dropped it.

"I take your luggage upstairs, Andris. You have guest room, of course."

"Thanks."

"And put some different clothes on for dinner, Leons!" said Erika, and then, addressing me:

"He looks like a poor student, doesn't he? Or at least he thinks he does. He forgets he's nearly eighty-two. Has he told you about the rap music?"

"Yes, he did. In the car."

"Of course he did! It's all he talks about. That and his new car. He's behaving like an adolescent."

"I think it's great."

"Well, don't tell him that. He's becoming unbearable."

"Too late, I did tell him."

"Andris, I've got to live with him! He's actually quite famous! Here, taste this," she said, offering me the spoon. "Enough salt? Yes? It's a pork stew with mushrooms. We'll be eating in about half an hour, okay?"

*

171

As luck would have it, the home produced cider from Pattercombe I had brought as a gift complemented the meal perfectly. Erika served it with cold potatoes in sour cream and a green salad. Leons was effusive in his praise as if this were a meal of a higher standard than the norm. Once she had removed the headscarf I saw that my mother now favoured a crop cut to her pale grey hair; I thought it suited her well. She had put on rather too much make-up before dinner, which went only part way to disguise the lines of age. She looked, nevertheless, *quite presentable*. And what was undeniable was that she still moved well. I watched as she lifted the heavy pot off the hob, as she rearranged the chairs around the table: she was strong and agile for a woman of her age, with no obvious signs of arthritis or anything worse.

Leons took much pleasure talking about his grandsons, a pair of twin boys, now in their early thirties, both married, still living in Riga, just two streets apart. They were due to come over the next day and take him out on the lake. They would hire a rowing boat for the day, he said, take a picnic, maybe catch a fish, listen to the radio, find a little beach, read, play cards.

"It's the boys who take me out these days, you see. When they are little, it is me taking them out, teaching them to sail, to row boat. Now they are in charge. In charge of me, the old grandfather."

"It must be nice to be still close to them," I said.

"Ah, of course. It's normal. We are good friends. Then and now. But you must come also, Andris. You must come and see our beautiful Kisezers under the sun. The boys speak a little English. You must meet them."

"They get up very early," warned Erika, tidying up the plates.

"Sadly, not this time, Leons," I said. "I plan to stay only one night."

My mother had anticipated my response, I thought, and she carried the dishes over to the sink without another word.

"One night?" complained her husband. "This is no time. One night is too short stay, especially for your mother, I think so."

"I have things I need to get back for. I have a flight back to London tomorrow afternoon."

"But then I cannot drive you to the airport."

"Don't worry, Leons. I'll get a taxi. It's not a problem."

"If you are sure. But a taxi, a taxi is not Golf GT, Andris."

"No. No, it's not," I smiled. Not *Gran Turismo*.

He picked up some unused cutlery, the empty bottles and followed Erika to the far side of the kitchen.

"Leave all this to me," I heard him say, then a few words of Latvian. And then, perhaps for my benefit, "If Andris is here for one night only, then you must talk, you and your son together. I am sure he is here to speak with his mother, not to listen to me all the night."

"We'll go outside," Erika said. "It's still quite warm."

"Maybe I write a little," he said. "You speak with Andris. I bring you coffee on the terrace, okay?"

*

When I joined my mother on the wooden decking beyond the French windows, she was already sitting in a rattan rocking chair with her eyes closed, basking in the orange glow of a smudgy sunset. She was holding a miniature cigar and, hearing my footsteps, she opened her eyes and raised it to her lips.

"I didn't know you smoked those," I said, finding a matching chair across a small low table from hers.

"I've started again," she said, "Yes, I know, it's a very bad habit. They're not going to kill me, Andris, don't worry. Not now, at my age. Not one or two a day."

I scanned the shadowy garden: an expanse of lawn, flower borders, geraniums mainly, daisies, petunias, then a line of bushes and mature trees at the far edge. A faint smell of barbecued sausages drifted across from a neighbour's patio.

"I smoked them a lot more as a student. As a younger woman. An affectation, I suppose. Mind you, everyone smoked in those days."

"My father too?"

"Of course he did. Everybody did."

She inhaled slowly and the tip of the cigar glowed in the fading daylight, wisps of its aromatic smoke coiling into the air.

"This is more than a courtesy call, isn't it?" she asked. "You have a problem, Andris? I'm right, aren't I? You need money or something? Is it the woman? Pauline, is she called? I can always tell."

"Polly. Her name is Polly, and no, she is not the problem. Not at all."

"I'm sorry. So she is well, Polly, and her son? Isn't he always ill?"

"They're fine."

She was feigning concern. She had never met my not-so-new family; she had shown no interest in meeting them and I doubt she ever would.

"So, you have money worries?"

"You're offering me money? Well, Leons did say you were doing well these days."

"Everything is relative. Latvia is not a rich country. But, of course, I can help you if you are in trouble."

"Mother, it's nothing to do with money. I'm fine. I've come to talk to you about father. About Edward."

"Edward?"

"Yes, Edward. The man who you once told me was the one."

"There's no reason to be sarcastic, Andris."

"I was in Bristol last week. I spent an hour speaking to Cooper Arundel."

I thought this would knock her off balance but she took it in her stride.

"Arundel? Why?"

"I had to. I needed to know the truth."

"But you already do. Why now? Andris, it's all such a long time ago."

"It doesn't matter why now, but you're right. It was a long time ago. And yes, I do know. Now I do. At least most of it I know. Arundel told me everything. Well, everything he knows."

I studied Erika's expression: she remained impassive, took another short drag of the cigar, and looked beyond me, out towards the sky. There was a barely audible monotone hum of neighbours' voices in the background.

"It's a pretty sunset tonight," she said presently. "We're lucky to have a south-westerly aspect."

"Are you listening, Mother?" I broke in. "He told me most of it. Not all."

"For a spymaster he has developed a very loose tongue," she said. "So why bother me with it? Why now?"

"I want to know it all, the whole truth, can't you understand? I want you to tell me your part."

"My part?"

"And why you told me father died in Berlin."

She was reluctant to answer immediately. I could almost hear the mechanics in her brain formulating a convincing reply.

"It was Cooper's idea," she said eventually, with a half-

175

laugh. "A story he invented, one we agreed to stick to, to protect you."

"Protect me? Protect me from what? From the shame of believing my father was a Soviet spy, a traitor? Did you believe that? Did you? What did *you* think of your husband?"

"Darling, I didn't know what to believe. I was in the dark, just like we all were."

"You know he was a triple agent? Did you know that? He was playing the Russians. They thought he was a double but he was still working for Arundel."

For one so slow at recognising sincerity, even I saw in her eyes the impact of information she had never had before. She pressed her cigar stub into an ashtray, took a deep breath and faced me.

"I guessed as much, Andris."

She smiled to herself, irony upon irony echoing back from an age of youthful naivety.

"Deep down I never believed he could be a traitor. I didn't. But Cooper wouldn't say. He wouldn't tell me anything for definite. They wanted to maintain the fiction of treachery. *It's not how it seems*, is what he said to me. That's all I had to hold on to. But then later he pushed for the memorial at the station, Cooper did. He believed in Eddie, I know he did. So, I felt in some way that I could too."

She rocked back in her chair and only spoke again when the momentum had subsided.

"He paid for your education, Andris. I don't think you ever knew that, did you? Did he tell you that himself? I think he felt he owed it to your father, to give his son a step up. The service might have abandoned him, but to give him his due, Cooper never has. That's why I believed there was more to it. More to it than him being a rogue spy. *It's not how it seems*, he said, he told me at Eddie's funeral."

I listened in silence. I had never heard her speak in this way before.

"Where is Dad buried, if not in Berlin?" I said presently.

"Berlin, Berlin," she sighed. "Andris, I am sorry for the lie. You must understand my reason."

Before I could say anything, she went on:

"Your father was not buried. He was cremated. There must have been no more than six of us at the ceremony. There's a small plaque in his memory on his mother's gravestone in Highgate Cemetery."

Suddenly a pair of outdoor lights came on, spilling a yellow glow over the terrace, and Leons emerged from the lounge carrying a tray.

"I bring you coffee," he announced. "And sugar if you want it."

"Thank you," I said. My mother did not respond.

"And here is your cardigan, my love. If you plan to stay longer outside. I am in the study, if you want me," the old man said, retreating.

There was no sound from the neighbours now, I noticed; they must have taken their food indoors. The coffee smelt strong. I took a cup, a tiny fine china cup half full of a dark, thick brew. I stirred in a little sugar. Meanwhile Erika paid no more attention to the tray than she had to her husband.

"Do you want it? Are you drinking it?" I asked, moving forward as if to lift the cup into her reach.

"No," she said with a blank smile. "Not at the moment."

I drank the coffee in one mouthful, its bitterness reaching the back of my throat as I swallowed.

"I am going to visit Mark Castille," I said suddenly.

"Castille?" repeated my mother, alert once more. "Is that wise?"

"I'm not sure. What would you suggest? You knew him, didn't you?"

"Yes, I did. I did know him. He was a bully." She paused. "Is he still alive, still with Lady Angela?"

"Yes."

"Still living at Sturcote House?"

"So you knew that?"

"After the event, I did. Cooper told me that. Painted me a picture. You know, his house being so close to where Eddie was killed. Painted me a picture and then hung a big Do Not Disturb sign over it."

"He did something similar to me."

"Nobody wants a fuss. Especially now. What is it, fifty-five years later."

I hesitated a moment before putting a simple question to her, one I had framed days ago:

"Mother, why did you betray my father?"

She looked at me in surprise.

"Betray?"

"Yes. Tell me why you betrayed my father."

"That's a very long way from the truth, Andris!"

"You helped them ambush him, didn't you, Mother? Didn't you?"

"What on earth do you mean?"

"Tell me, for Christ's sake. Just tell me. Don't you want to get it off your chest once and for all? I'm his son, aren't I? Your son? Don't I deserve the truth from my own mother?"

I struck the table with my fist, setting the coffee cups dancing off their little saucers. I was shaking with frustration, my hands trembling from both anger and caffeine. I waited impatiently for a response which came at length:

"They said they would arrest him," she said softly. "Believe me, Andris. I understood that he would be *arrested*. Only arrested. Not murdered. Not left dead in a ditch like some common criminal."

I watched her, waited for more.

"Things weren't right between me and your father, you have to understand. You never really knew him, you were too young. Eddie could be a lovely man: charming, kind, but it never lasted with him. He was one for the next chance, the next pretty girl. I found it out too late: I was already married to him. I was the fool he could always come home to."

She looked away from me again, then continued, as if talking to the darkening sky.

"Katarina warned me about him. He'd had a thing with her even before we were together. I knew about that, of course, that was no secret. I remember the exact moment I knew it was over between them and that he would be mine. We were all in a pub somewhere near the colleges, a whole group of us undergraduates, drinking, celebrating a birthday, I think. All in a cosy little backroom with a narrow serving hatch into the main bar."

She paused to allow herself the hint of a shallow smile.

"I can see it now," she said, "a little coal fire burning, just enough room for about a dozen of us. Eddie called it a snug. Isn't that such a lovely word? He'd just made a gentle joke at Kat's expense, everyone was laughing, Kat was pouting, and he just looked up across at me, directly at me, on the other side of the room, and gave me a smile and a little wink. He was so beautiful, Andris, my heart literally fluttered."

She stopped again, this time to sigh and gather her thoughts.

"But much later," she went on, "after we were married, it was Kat who told me he was a philanderer, and that he'd been in trouble with the police in London more than once. You remember her husband, don't you? Robin? He worked in the Home Office in those days, quite junior, but very alert, on the up, finger in all the pies, eyes at every keyhole. He had doubts about your father, stories coming to him from police sources. Eddie had been picked up drunk again in the West End. He'd been seen with a woman, a translator with links to the Soviet embassy. There was evidence of hotel rooms booked. He was involved in a fight in Soho: the police arrested him but he was released the next morning. And so on, and so on. I knew nothing of this, Andris. Nothing until Katarina felt she had to tell me what she knew. Robin showed me photos: photos of Eddie with the woman, with men in shops, then in a park, one with a different woman outside a Tube station."

"How did you feel?"

"That's a bloody stupid question, isn't it? How do you think? I felt used, cheated. I felt worthless. And angry. The final straw was a photo they showed me of your father with Bendiks. MI5 had been on his tail. They caught them together on film."

"Cooper spoke to me about Bendiks. You knew him, didn't you?"

"Gints Bendiks was a creep. He was on the boat with us when we left Riga in 1950. I remember him flirting with my sister, in fact with all the girls on board. When we arrived in England he stayed in London and as far as I know he hung around with some of the volunteers at Free Baltic. After Cambridge I saw more of him. I got more involved in the movement and he was still around from time to time, drinking coffee, smoking cigarettes, snarling at Stalin and Malenkov. He regularly brought money so he was popular. Money for the cause."

Above us the blue was growing ever deeper, almost black to the east. The first stars to show sparkled in the early night sky. Erika had stopped talking. She pulled on the cardigan, picked up her cigars, changed her mind, reordered her thoughts.

"I saw them together," she went on after a moment, "Bendiks and Eddie. With my own eyes. One day your father told me he was going up to Trinity to see an old tutor. Coincidentally I had been in the same room as Bendiks the day before; he had said, quite casually to somebody else, that he was going to see a publisher the next day in Cambridge. I overheard him bragging about some pamphlets he had written. I decided to follow Eddie's car. The tutor couldn't have been Arundel; I'd heard that he'd already moved to Bristol by then. Whether I was going to see Eddie innocently chatting with some other old teacher, or meeting another woman or some shady Russian spy, whoever it was, I needed to know for myself. They met in a coffee shop on King Street. I watched them both go in, five minutes apart. First Eddie, then Bendiks. And leave five minutes apart. I saw them sitting together, deep in conversation. I felt sick. Three days later Erasmus was murdered."

"Erasmus?"

"Don't be so disingenuous, Andris. If Cooper didn't mention Erasmus to you then he must have Alzheimers. Erasmus was the leader of our movement in London, you must know that. He was a great man, our champion. Always an inspiration, always positive even when things back here in Latvia were at rock bottom. Did Cooper mention the Forest Brothers?"

"Yes. Yes, he did."

"The Brothers were what was left of the resistance to the Russian occupation. Many were betrayed by a British spy. A man called Philby. Maybe you have heard of him, Andris? Eddie wouldn't have been the first Englishman to whisper secrets to the KGB. It became a lost cause after '57, but in the early days, Ras would send money, clothes, weapons, even people over to help them, to support their efforts. By the time of his death, Free Baltic had virtually wound up. The Forest Brothers were finished and Ras himself was deflated. He was realistically of no great concern to the Russians any more, he was no threat to them unless they thought he could spark a revival at some point in the future. His death was the result of a personal vendetta, I am sure, a feud with Bendiks."

She was beginning to run out of breath, beginning to wheeze.

"How well did you know Erasmus?"

"I think you know the answer to that," she said after a moment.

"You were lovers, of course. Of course you were."

"Yes. For a short while. Yes, we were."

I had anticipated the reply and had been deliberate in asking, but now was powerless to prevent the pressurised little bubbles of air floating up across the grey veil that was covering my eyes, unable to halt the swell of sickness rising in my gut, the bile at the back of my throat.

"My father was a rat! *You* were a rat!" I screamed suddenly, blinking free of the veil, staring hard at my mother's anxious face. "And how old was I exactly? Five years old? Younger than that when you were both at it, both fucking strangers? Did I actually matter to you, for fuck's sake? Did it matter that you had a *child* at home? A little child who had no idea that not one but both his parents, the two people he trusted the most in his world, both of them were living lives of deceit? Cheating, lying, did that child matter to you? Did I matter to you at all? To you, to him, to either of you? Did I? Honestly?"

Spitting the words across the table at her, I could hardly breathe.

"I thought I was strong," whispered Erika. "You must understand, darling."

I could see that she had started to cry.

"I thought I was strong," she began again. "Strong enough to deal with your father's ways. I thought I could manage alone, but I was wrong, Andris. I was wrong. I was weak, I know I was weak. And Ras was..., he was so kind to me..."

If you had been stronger, Mother, just a little bit fucking stronger, then we might, you and I, we might have had a chance of a proper relationship all these years. I would have respected you, been able to trust you. And you could have found out who I was, and trusted me with the truth. Just a little bit stronger, Mother.

I didn't say any of this. Perhaps I should have done, part of me wanted to, but I could see her shaking, sniffling uncontrollably. She was already suffering enough.

"I am sorry. I am, truly I am," she said eventually, wiping her face with the back of her hand. "I admit I was weak. My marriage felt over no sooner than it had begun. I'm sorry you're hearing this, Andris. Erasmus was a rock, a support. And I couldn't forgive your father for his death."

"My father?"

Her make-up was smudged, she was trying to control another shudder of sobs. Presently she looked up pleadingly and said:

"The evidence pointed to Bendiks. According to Robin. I had seen him with Eddie three days earlier. It was a brutal, calculated murder. Ras was passionate about two things in his life: the freedom of our people from Soviet enslavement and his motorbikes. He fell in love with the British motorcycle. Silly, isn't it?"

She picked up her cigarette lighter and turned it over and over in her hand.

"By the time of his death he was riding a Triumph Tiger. He was so proud of it. He said it matched his nickname: he'd always been called Tiger because he was such a fighter, even as a small boy. To own this bike with its tiger emblem was everything."

I could hear the affection for him in her voice. It was genuine, I knew.

"One evening somebody booby-trapped his motorbike. That's how he died. It was parked outside a pub in Clapham. He turned on the ignition and the explosion sent shrapnel and body parts all across the street."

I gave her a moment. I needed a moment too. I stood up to stretch my legs and felt my weaker knee throbbing. I limped out into the darkness of the lawn and stared into the shadows. As I turned back to face the house I could see, in the thin yellow light of the twin lanterns, the rocking shape of my eighty-three-year-old mother staring into her lap: she was fiddling with the pockets on her cardigan. Framed by the canopy and the raised decking, she looked as if she were on a stage, an actor preparing for a pitiful soliloquy in the final act of a melodrama but having trouble remembering her lines. The closest things to her were a cup of cold coffee and a dirty ashtray. Upstairs there was a light on behind the closed curtains of a bedroom whose window was open. Briefly I wondered if Leons Lapsa, metaphysical poet and hero of Latvia's musical youth, had heard any of the conversation that had rumbled on below.

After some time I rejoined my mother on the terrace. With her head still bowed, she appeared not to notice me. I took my seat and cleared my throat to rouse her.

"Does Leons know anything about all of this?" I asked. "All of this ancient history?"

She had found a tissue and was wiping her nose.

"Leons? No, of course not."

"I just wondered."

"Katarina persuaded me to meet Castille," she went on, eager to finish her story. "By some Byzantine hierarchical arrangement he was indirectly Robin's boss. It also turned out that he was employed by MI5. They had been suspicious about Eddie for months, if not years. We looked at the photos again, I heard all the accounts over and over. He was desperate to convince me that he was a traitor. I couldn't make my mind up whether Eddie was betraying his country or just betraying me, his wife. Castille wanted me to sign up to an operation to nullify him. That was his word, Castille's. I would give my blessing, not run to the police or the newspapers or my MP the moment he was stopped. Nullified. By which I understood arrested. Andris, you must believe me. I had no idea that they would have him murdered. No idea."

I wanted to believe her, but that's normal. I've wanted to believe my mother's word all my life.

"Did Cooper ever speak to you about a man called Macduff?" I asked.

"Macduff? As in..."

"Yes, as in Macbeth. Did he mention his name?"

"No, never."

"Macduff was the man who killed my father. I've already seen an archive report of the operation, thanks to Cooper. It was a redacted version, but reading between the blanks it's clear that Macduff was working for Castille. His escape route, as you must have suspected, involved Sturcote House."

"What else did it say?"

"Father was identified simply as Target. Macduff details tracking him, the murder, then his escape. There are enough pointers to guide you northwards through open country, following the river. I only saw as far as his reception at the anonymous house, by which time names, key objects, even pronouns were blacked out. It was like a child's puzzle book. But, to my mind, conclusive."

For a moment Erika had nothing to say. Finally she asked:

"What became of Macduff?"

"He's dead," I said. "He died shortly afterwards. In Berlin, as a matter of fact."

Erika shrugged at the irony. She shivered. The heat of the day was dissipating quickly.

"What will you do, Andris?"

"Cooper told me to stay away. To let sleeping dogs lie. I don't think he meant it."

"What do you hope to achieve? Really? Raking it all up again?"

"I don't know. But this thing is driving *me* now. It's taken over. I'm just following an instinct. I have no choice, it seems to me. I want to hear Castille confess. I want to smell the guilt on his breath."

"He will deny everything, believe me. I think you are wasting your time. He will pull up the drawbridge. That's what happens. Silence in the name of national security. That's what they do, you know that."

"As I said, I have no choice, Mother. I can only try, can't I? I want to see his face, read his eyes. I want to hear the strain in his voice."

"Please be careful, Andris. These people are still powerful. If he lets you see him, please let me know what happens. Please promise me that. Above all I need to know you are safe."

"I promise."

She lifted her hands towards me, she wanted me to hold them, to show solidarity. She wanted me to forgive her.

"Come here, my son. In spite of everything I've done, and I know I could have been a better mother, you and I, we are both on the same side, believe me."

Believe her? Here on this chilly terrace, under these shining stars, with my hands in hers, with so much finally said, this time, for once, I did.

6

Steering my car slowly down the muck-splattered road with the village of Child Okeford a mile or so behind me, I was struck by the feeling that I had made a mistake. I was heading in the direction I was convinced was correct, but I was confused, at the point in the lane where I expected a driveway to Sturcote House, to find a neat, highly varnished sign at the turn-off advising arrival instead at the Sturcote Stables & Riding School. I pulled over, stopped and peered through the windscreen: the drive was partly hidden by high, dense hedges around the perimeter of a large acreage of land. From my position, sitting in the empty lane with my left-hand indicator clicking away fatuously, the buildings were hidden. But this had to be the place. Had the house been demolished, or transformed into a business premises just like a certain nearby railway station had once been the base of a furniture makers? I wondered if Arundel's information, for all his tablet technology, had been up to date. I needed to speak to someone from the twenty-first century, someone dynamic like Lyle. Alternatively I just needed to drive on a little further, take the turning on to the property and investigate for myself.

The driveway took me through an alley of trees for about twenty yards before it forked. The more substantial track to the right was marked by a second, smaller sign for the stables,

SS&RS Reception. To the left, barely visible within an abundant beech hedge, I spotted a flaking sign indicating the way to Sturcote House, *Private.* I crawled along the rough track, flanked by holly and rhododendron, for a further fifty yards until it opened beyond the bushes, turned to gravel and gave a first view of the house. I knew enough about English architecture to recognise a classic Georgian manor, this example built in blocks of pale grey stone, Portland at a guess. Two storeys tall, edged on both sides by proud chimneys, it was fronted by a wide, stepped portico, and was geometrically perfect with the thirteen tall, mullioned windows of its façade spaced evenly six and six and one above the double door, the whole rectangle topped with a beautifully proportioned roof of black tiles. The drive swept around a lawn and gave the option of parking at the side of the building or directly by the main entrance. There was already a car there, a small red Renault, so I decided to creep up to the side of it.

My heart was beating faster than was good for it. Once out of the car, I took a moment to survey the scene. As I looked back to the lane I had taken, I could hear only the low rumble of a tractor as the road was hidden by the line of bushes and trees. What sounded like a motorbike accelerating provoked a murder of crows to rise out of the distant branches into the milky sky, cawing fractiously. There was the faint whinny of a horse, maybe two, from the opposite direction, then silence. A light tang of manure and the scent of cut grass hung in the air. I turned to face the house once more: this was the moment I had been imagining ever since I flew out of Riga three days ago, my mind filled with the words I had been rehearsing to say and the ones I had anticipated hearing in response. As I limped towards the steps I realised my gait was that of a condemned man. Yet I had every right to be here. I searched my soul for a greater self-belief, and my rap on the heavy brass door-knocker was satisfyingly less of a polite tap than a frontal attack.

My first knock was answered, however, by only the rasping bark of a dog from within, then nothing. I waited, then rapped again, even more loudly, more insistently, and was rewarded after a moment by one half of the sturdy door opening a foot or so and the sight of a plump, middle-aged woman in a housecoat who wordlessly fixed me with a suspicious stare. I coughed to clear my throat.

"I believe this is the home of Sir Mark and Lady Castille, isn't it?" I said, more forcefully than I had intended.

"Yes, it is," she replied, without taking her eyes off me. "But Lady Castille is not at home at the moment."

"Oh," I said dully, not quite ready to respond to unnecessary detail.

"She has a hospital appointment this morning," the woman went on instead, giving me more.

"Is Sir Mark at home, perhaps?"

"Yes, he is. But he is resting, I believe."

"Do you think he would see me?"

"I don't rightly know. I imagine that would depend. Who shall I tell him is calling?"

"Please could you tell him my name is Fleet. Andris Fleet. Edward Fleet's son."

"Andrew Fleet," she muttered to herself, committing the name to memory before turning away.

"Andris," I insisted. "Andris, not Andrew."

She looked at me with what I sensed was not a little contempt.

"Just a moment," she said, withdrawing. "Wait here." Then she closed the door in my face.

It was a good three minutes later before the woman, who I assumed was a housekeeper and the driver of the Renault, reappeared and announced that no, Sir Mark would not see me.

"It's out of the question," she declared with an air of satisfaction.

"Tell him Arundel sent me," I improvised. "It's extremely important. Please, mention Cooper Arundel."

"He said no. I'm sorry. You must leave."

"Please!" I repeated. "Just tell him I've been sent by Cooper Arundel. It *is* urgent."

"Cooper what?" she said, sucking her teeth.

"Arundel. Like the town in Sussex."

"Arundel? Cooper Arundel?"

"Exactly. Please tell him. He'll understand, I guarantee."

*

The interior of the house had a faded grandeur that I had seen in properties protected by the National Trust or English Heritage, homes whose owners could not maintain them without allowing paid access to the hoi polloi. It seemed that Castille had not quite reached that point of discomfort yet. I had given the housekeeper my most gracious smile as she left me to wait in the spacious entrance hall for an audience with Sir Mark. Filled with the scent of beeswax, the hall had plain, cream-painted walls, a stone staircase with mahogany balustrades rising to a hidden landing, and in the exact centre of the shiny stone floor stood a large, round polished oak table supporting a huge glass vase filled with wild flowers. On two opposite walls were twin dark oak settles, on one of which I had been invited to sit.

A large black dog, a lurcher, I thought, suddenly appeared and wandered inquisitively towards me for a sniff at my shoes, my knees and, before I crossed my legs and pushed its pointed head away, my groin. I gave it a perfunctory pat on its rear end and it strolled off down a corridor unimpressed.

I uncrossed my legs and tried to relax. I felt like I had been summoned to see the headmaster and I was outside his study anxiously waiting for the green light above his door to come on. I reminded myself that it was me who had called this meeting, not him: come on, a little self-belief. However I was feeling, and I really couldn't make up my mind, when the woman suddenly appeared where the dog had been loitering, I was as startled as if I had seen a ghost.

"Right," she shouted at me. "He'll see you now."

I followed her obediently down a short passage where she knocked lightly at the first door she came to.

Mark Castille was in the library, a ground floor, wood-panelled room whose two large windows were partly shuttered to keep out the late morning sun. Though there was no reason why I should have been, given his age, I was actually surprised to find him sitting in a wheelchair, fully dressed down to polished loafers and paisley cravat. As the housekeeper pushed open the door, he turned the chair to face me and beckoned me into the centre of the room with the wave of a hand. The woman retreated and closed the door.

"Come in," he said in a weak voice. "Did you say your name was Fleet?"

If he had stood he would have been much taller than me, I was sure, even at his advanced age. I had found only scraps on the web to flesh out what I had been told about him, and only one photograph: a press picture taken outside the Palace on the occasion of his knighthood. He must have been about sixty at the time, a huge man in top hat and morning suit, smiling self-consciously, dwarfing his wife. Slightly slumped in his chair, he now appeared still heavy-set yet flaccid, wider around the neck, and the years had left his once smooth face as saggy as a deflated soufflé. His remaining hair, silvery and wispy, grew around his ears, and behind wire-rimmed glasses his eyes were reduced to dim flickers at the back of deep, dark caves.

"That's right, Sir Mark," I said. "I'm Andris Fleet. I believe you once knew my father, Edward."

"I believe I did," he muttered before slowly pivoting ninety degrees to face a table that was standing in the shadows. It was only then that I realised that there was a third person in the room. Sitting across the table was a much younger man who I guessed had been watching me in silence from the moment I entered the room. His blond hair was cut short, and he was wearing a polo shirt and shorts, both black, and white ankle socks and plimsolls. He looked like he was dressed for a table tennis match, but as I walked into the middle of the library I noticed that it was in fact Scrabble that he was playing. Castille hadn't actually been resting, not in the way I had imagined; he had in fact been contesting a board game with a man who might have been a personal trainer.

"You have met Peggy," the old man continued, eyes still on the pattern of words forming on the board. "And this is Roland."

The younger man remained seated but made eye contact with me in a distant, who-the-fuck-are-you kind of way.

"Roland is from the agency. As you can see, we are playing a game of intellect, something to keep my brain from turning to jelly." He laughed, wheezing slightly. "I still do the Telegraph crossword, you know. With a little help sometimes, eh, Roland?"

The table tennis player nodded and smiled back.

I coughed.

"I'm sorry to appear like this, out of the blue. And sorry to interrupt your game, but I was hoping I might speak with you for a few minutes."

"In what regard?"

"I have some questions relating to my father."

"You do?"

"I met Cooper Arundel a week ago, and..."

"Arundel?" he broke in. "Is that rascal still alive?"

"Yes. Yes, he is. And in good health. A mine of information."

"Information? Really? Misinformation, more like. Slippery as a bag of eels, Arundel. No lie black enough for that man."

Roland continued to consider the options his tray of lettered tiles afforded him, seeming to pay no attention at all to the conversation being conducted around him.

"So," I said. "Would that be possible?"

"Mm?"

"Please could you spare me a little of your time, perhaps?"

I looked towards Roland, then back to Castille.

"In private, ideally?"

Roland looked up inquisitively from his neat line of letters. For a moment the old man refused to answer. I wondered if he had heard my request. Was he in fact wearing a hearing aid? I was on the point of repeating it when he turned the wheelchair towards me and said:

"Yes. Very well. I *will* talk to you. Roland, could you leave us, please?"

"Sir Mark?" the young man said, betraying an Australian accent in just two monosyllables.

"It's alright, Roland. I'll be fine. Go and get some air. Take Hansel down to the meadow. Give him a run out. Dog needs a good run out."

Roland stood up. He was slim, athletic and, I noticed, had particularly hairy limbs.

"If you're absolutely sure, sir."

"Go. I'll be perfectly fine. I won't touch the game. I won't peek at your letters, if that's what's bothering you! Peggy is indoors. If I need you, I'll sound the alarm. Man overboard, eh?"

He made a display of touching a white plastic pendant the size of an Olympic medal hanging at his chest, which I hadn't noticed until then. The cord was lost somewhere between the folds of his neck and the loose silk of the cravat. Roland nodded and left the room through a shuttered door which I had believed to be a window; as he opened it to slip into the garden, the shaft of light widened to briefly fill half of the room with a pale, dusty glow.

"Sit down, Fleet." Castille gestured me towards a small sofa, suddenly illuminated. "Go on, man, sit."

We were alone at last. With hands on the wide wheels he slowly manoeuvred his chair squeakily over the parquet floor, so that we were barely a yard apart.

"You have five minutes, young man," he said quietly, firmly. "And I must warn you that at my age my memory is not what it once was."

I was amused that he had chosen to play the dementia card quite so early.

"Cooper Arundel and I had an interesting conversation about my father," I started. "About his death, in fact: his murder. It happened in 1960. Your memory does stretch back that far, doesn't it?"

"Good old Cooper," he said with a sarcastic smile. "Last of the great bastards. We go back a hell of a long way, Cooper and I."

He spoke slowly, allowing each phrase to resonate in his ears before picking out the next one. He was staring through his glasses into a space beyond me, as if searching for a book on the shelves at my back.

"A long way back. A lot further back than 1960. We served in the war, of course. On the same side for once."

He smiled to himself.

"We were great rivals, in many ways. At Cambridge. Did he tell you? The old St John's-Trinity warfare. The dirty tricks. Grease on the oar handles, that sort of thing."

I was in no hurry to hear all this again, but if he wanted to talk, then I would listen.

"Did he tell you about the time they paid a couple of rogues from town to kidnap our cricket captain the morning of a final? Brilliant player, a match-winner you would have called him. Forgotten the chap's name but his father had played for Surrey. They drove him twenty miles out of town, dumped him in a village that wasn't even on a bus route. By the time the poor chap turned up the match was already lost. Trinity denied any involvement but it sounded like Arundel. Wicked man. I have to admit he *was* a better rower than me. Just about. I'd give him that. But he'd have to agree that I had the edge as a runner. Cross country, and on the track. Legs not much good any more, though," he said, tapping his knees. "And cricket, too. Arundel was a big hitter alright, but he hadn't the finesse. Never could play a half-decent spinner."

I gave him a hollow smile, not sure how much longer to indulge him. He was already a little out of breath but seemed determined to carry on.

"After the war he came back to Cambridge, as you probably know. I stayed in military intel, which lead to MI5. Arundel, of course, inevitably joined SIS, the other lot. Two sides of the same coin, him and I. That's what they said about us. One always trying to get the upper hand over the other."

"And you had a mutual acquaintance?"

"We had many of those."

"I mean my father."

"Fleet? I hardly knew him. What was his name? Edwin?"

"Edward."

"Edward. Yes. I remember him. Not too draughty for you?" he suddenly asked, tilting his large head towards the outer door. "Roland hasn't closed it, has he? I don't think he trusts you with me, Mr Fleet."

"It's nice to have a little air," I said. "But we were talking about Edward."

"Fleet was Arundel's boy, wasn't he?" he picked up at half-pace. "Targeted, recruited, polished; all by Cooper, all his own work. Then sent out to spy for England, only for him to turn into a bloody KGB man. What a cock-up. Poor Cooper. Like having your prize lab piss all over the judges' carpet at Crufts."

"You seem to remember a version of the story very well, Sir Mark."

"Bits and pieces are coming back. 1960, you say? That is such a long time ago. I think we still had an empire then, didn't we?"

"MI5 were watching my father, weren't they?"

"Were they? I suppose they must have been. If they were doing their job properly."

"So why would they do that?"

The old man had stopped, lost in thought, already tiring, or at least appearing to.

"Why would they do that?" I said again, more loudly.

"What's that, Fleet?"

"Have my father watched, followed. Why?"

"I imagine they had their reasons. He'd been in a few scrapes, hadn't he? Been seen with the wrong people. Wasn't that the story?"

"You mean people like Gints Bendiks?"

"Who?"

"Bendiks, the Latvian."

"I can't remember that name, I'm sorry."

"He was embedded. He'd been in the country for ten years. Worked for Free Baltic but was passing information to Moscow."

"I wasn't managing your father's case. I don't remember all the details, all the names."

"You remember my mother, I expect, don't you?"

"Do I?"

"I think you do, Sir Mark. My mother's name is Erika. Erika Fleet."

"Erika?" he said, maintaining an expression of puzzlement.

"She supplied you with evidence. She testified that she had seen Bendiks and my father together in a café in Cambridge."

"Bendiks? That fellow's name is a mystery, I'm afraid. Perhaps I knew him under an alias. That's what happens: Six calls him Smith, Five might call him Jones, and to the Russians the very same chap is Ivan. "

"She talked to her brother-in-law," I cut in. "Robin, Robin..." Just at that moment I could not recall the name of Katarina's husband. I was annoyed with myself; I should have been better prepared. "I'm sorry, I have forgotten his name. A junior in the Home Office. Robin..."

"You must mean Robin Montgomery."

"Montgomery, yes."

"Unpleasant chap."

"He told her to speak to you."

Castille turned the wheelchair at an angle to me and gazed out at the slice of garden visible between the shutter and the open window.

"She met you," I insisted. "She told me she did."

He seemed to have stopped listening. Where had his mind wandered?

"Pretty woman," he said unexpectedly. "Striking, in fact. Golden hair."

"You *do* remember her?"

"Yes. Yes, I do. I do remember her, Fleet," he sighed. "She seemed more convinced than anybody that her husband was a traitor."

"And you came to an arrangement with her?"

"Yes. Yes, I think you've got that bit right."

"And what was the arrangement, Sir Mark?"

"The arrangement? Well, I suppose it was a matter of national security. We'd have to have him arrested. Your mother would have to keep quiet. No histrionics, no weak-mindedness after the event."

"Arrested? You were going to have him arrested?"

"I imagine so. I can't remember exactly but that would have been protocol. Absolutely. The fellow was a double agent after all. We had to take the keys to the sweet shop off him, didn't we?"

"What about having him nullified?"

"Nullified? That's a fine word. That sounds like a word I might have used."

"Meaning to arrest him?"

"Of course."

"Nullify could mean eliminate him, eradicate him."

"I think you are letting your imagination run away with you, Mr Fleet."

"The truth of the matter is he *was* nullified, wasn't he, Sir Mark? Nullified in the sense of murdered."

"Yes, I do remember the case now," he said, unperturbed. "The killing, that was regrettable."

"An MI5-authorised killing?"

"Is that what Arundel told you?"

"Isn't it the truth? Did you give the order, Castille?"

"Don't be preposterous. There was a murder, I grant you, but no killer was ever caught. Accusations like that are beneath you. I think you should leave now, Mr Fleet. I feel rather tired. I think your time is up."

"I haven't finished yet."

Instead of an indignant reply he simply hardened his stare. I pressed on regardless:

"What do you think my father was doing on a train to Bournemouth?"

He looked away. I was tempted to shake his chair to regain his attention. Eventually he coughed, wiped flecks of spittle off his chin with a handkerchief, and spoke again.

"That is a question I asked myself," he replied, indulging me.

"What do you mean?"

"As far as I was concerned we were going to pick him up in Portsmouth. *Arrest* him. We suspected he had a meeting there with a Moscow agent: a woman, I think."

"Primrose Smith?"

"Who?"

"Primrose Smith. An actress. She was having an affair with my father."

"Oh, yes. Yes, she was. I had forgotten about her. No, it wasn't her. It was a different woman, an older woman. Or was it a man? I really don't remember."

"Didn't you meet her? Primrose Smith? Didn't you try to convince her that my father was a traitor?"

"You must be thinking of someone else. Old Cooper's confused you."

I held him with a look whose intensity demanded more.

"Listen," he went on slowly, sighing again. "I wasn't running that operation personally. You need to understand that. I did talk to your mother, but not in private. There were others present, including, I think it was Kingfisher who was managing things."

"Kingfisher?"

"Yes. He was a lovely chap. He worked with me for several years. He was a deputy of mine at the time. 1960? Yes, he must have been.

"Mr Fleet," he said quietly, raising himself in his seat, "let me tell you something you really should know before you make your accusations. I wasn't in the country when your father was killed. That may surprise you, but it really shouldn't. The Cold War wasn't the only thing on the agenda at that time, you know. I had South Africa on my plate, I do remember. There had been a referendum, it was clear that that country would become a republic very soon, independent of Britain. I was down there in talks on the repatriation of British subjects. It was a glorious spring in Cape Town. Such a delightful climate down there by the ocean."

He was looking past me again.

"I'm not interested in the weather in Cape Town. Are you passing the buck here? Saying it was all down to Kingfisher?"

"What? Absolutely not. No, no, I don't actually know *how* he played it. He was an honourable chap, I do know that much. Six wanted his head on a platter, I remember, for your father. Mine too. But I wasn't having any of it. If they couldn't keep a closer eye on their own spook then they had no-one but themselves to blame. And before you ask, he died years ago. Kingfisher died of Aids, poor sod. I remember speaking at his funeral. St Albans."

Unruffled, controlling the tempo all the while, Castille had succeeded in tangling me up in knots. Denials, memory loss, an alibi, a dead suspect thrown in out of nowhere to muddy the waters, I didn't know where to go next. This is what he's done all his career, I thought: with a silver tongue and a sabre- sharp mind he's been keeping smarter opponents than me at arm's length for years. Then I remembered Macduff.

"Isn't it strange that the murder occurred just a couple of miles from here? And that the killer headed for this house after the event?"

"Did he?"

"I think you know he did."

"There was a very tiresome theory along those lines."

"You know damn well he did!"

"Mr Fleet, keep calm. The police investigated it all thoroughly. They visited here several times. Spoke to me when I returned from Africa."

"This has got nothing to do with Africa!"

Without realising it, I had sprung off the sofa and was standing over him. He made as if to reverse the wheelchair.

"Stop the lies, for Christ's sake, Castille!" I shouted. "Admit the truth!"

Sensing danger, his next move was an instinct to find the pendant alarm and press it. Before he had chance to adjust his glasses and pat his chest for the device, I was already closing in on him like a wild animal.

"Tell me the truth, you bastard!"

I reached the alarm before he did and tugged at it so violently that it was ripped away from his body with a sharp crack. His head jerked forward and his glasses flew to the floor. I thought I had broken a bone in his neck but the brittle noise was that of the clasp breaking apart. In spite of the pain, Castille was trying to reach one of the wheels to direct his chair away from me, but he was slow, off balance, and my momentum threw me into his chest at such an angle as to tip the seat over, sending both of us sprawling to the ground. The upturned wheelchair caught the legs of the table and I heard the patter of Scrabble tiles landing on the wooden floor. I easily gained the upper hand and found myself kneeling over his large, flabby body with my hands free and threatening, my burning face looming over the old man who, coughing and wheezing, looked up at me in pure dread. His breath smelled of stale coffee.

"Tell me the truth, for fuck's sake!"

I had seen that look once before: it was the same look of trepidation I had caught in the eyes of the desperate young lamb in sniffing distance of the slaughterman.

I could hear the fizzing of the tiny bubbles in my head. And my hands were already at the man's throat. Frantically he squirmed beneath me but was helpless to resist, and any words he tried to say were lost in a feeble gasping and cackling from his limp mouth. I pressed harder, my thumbs inching into his gullet through the flimsy material of his wayward cravat. I squeezed deeper, I felt the tendons in his neck yielding, then his windpipe collapsing. Roland hadn't come to his rescue. Peggy hadn't burst in to see what all the racket was about. The lurcher hadn't bounded into the library to help his stricken master. Lady Angela's taxi was still on its long way back from the hospital.

And then there was no resistance at all. Castille's eyelids were flickering like tiny candle flames in the thrall of a sudden draught. And I stopped squeezing. I let go of the man's throat, fell away from his body, and lay on my back, panting, staring at the ceiling. My limbs were twitching, my eyes were blinking furiously, I felt light-headed and desperately thirsty. What the fuck was I doing? I had physically attacked a helpless invalid in his nineties. I was seconds, inches from killing the poor bastard. What had I become?

I picked myself up off the floor and checked to see if Castille was still alive. His breathing was as shallow as it could be, he was moaning almost inaudibly, his swollen head was moving sluggishly from side to side. I hadn't killed him. Thank God for that.

One of the wheels of his chair was still spinning lazily in mid-air, dozens of the tiny lettered tiles were scattered under and around the table, and not far away lay the pendant with its broken cord. I didn't want to stay in that room one moment longer. My heart was thumping. I felt nauseous. I limped across to the French window and peered out to see if there was any sign of Roland in the garden. Fortunately the lawns at the rear of the house appeared empty, and I made my way as quickly as I could over the gravel path that skirted the building: deep breaths, two right-hand corners, a length of flower beds with roses in full bloom, and I was back at the front of the house. I fell into my car, fumbled ineptly with the key as my sweaty, strangler's hands were still trembling so much. I took a gulp from a bottle of water but I had no time to recover myself: I had to make a hurried escape, to abandon the scene, to become invisible, and to leave Sturcote House as far behind me as I possibly could.

7

I have tried to rationalise the events of that sad morning many times since. Mark Castille remains for me an enigma, a man whose life's work had infused deceit into his blood, a man for whom lying was second nature, yet a man whose denial, no matter how many times I tried to unpick it, was not altogether unconvincing.

I thought about attempting to verify his alibi, his timely involvement in South Africa, but everything had fossilised years ago, I had no tools to retrieve something buried so deeply under protected strata, and to be frank, I hadn't the energy either. I briefly considered investigating the life and death of a man called Kingfisher, whose first name I didn't even know, whose very existence I didn't fully believe in. Cooper Arundel's first response to me had been that the whole sorry episode was the result of human error, misunderstanding, it had all been an avoidable tragedy. I hadn't believed him. It seemed preposterous that the operation hadn't been planned, and I had come close to discovering the architects, but a definitive answer remained beyond me. Suspicions and conspiracy theories were all I had. No proof, no irrefutable evidence. Nevertheless, I felt I had done all I could, I'd exhausted every avenue with the means at my disposal and, in the end, I could not be accused of letting my father down. There are still times when I wonder if he even deserved my efforts. He had already been exonerated, after a fashion, but to a large extent his life and his death had been forgotten. I realised it was for me, not for him, for my own peace of mind that I had felt obliged to pursue the truth. And in the end it proved to be a vain pursuit. In the first moment of calm after the final, brutal act, I sent a blunt text to my mother: I told her Castille had denied giving the order to have Edward killed, I told her I had reached a dead end, I told her the case was closed.

As for my own behaviour at Sturcote House, I felt both shocked and humiliated. That I had come so close to committing a murder of my own in retribution for an unsolved crime was truly alarming: the very opposite of peace of mind. The old man would probably die in the next twelve months anyway. I lived on edge for the next few days. I couldn't get my mind to settle on anything for long. I was half-expecting a visit from the police: I could have been charged with assault at the very least, but I was not unduly worried. I judged that Castille was happier with the events of ancient times tucked away and out of sight, and although I had been as real and as present a threat to him as he could ever have imagined, I was still, in effect, just a visiting phantom from his past.

I wondered what it was that had held me back from administering the fatal blow. Proof of sorts that even in a moment of extreme frustration my anger was somehow controlled, it brought an awareness that limits of decency were etched into my nature. It was a confirmation that brought me relief and joy. I had almost killed a man but I had failed, and that failure made me proud of who I was.

And if there was a voice somewhere in my soul that had whispered *Stop! You bloody fool!*, then I was grateful for it. Grateful too that on that day my heart was not so full of vitriol that my rage and my obsession could ever run out of control. For on that day there was a part of me that was already softening, mellowing, warming; a part of me that has since grown to a stage where I now feel that looking back has no further role in my life. The chapter is closed. The train has left the station for the last time. I don't want its rattling wheels disturbing the foundations of my tower of wooden bricks. For me the future has already opened up with a bright new face.

The previous evening, the very night before I was to face Castille, Polly had told me, warm tears falling from her eyes, that, after seventeen years, she was pregnant once again. After my fruitless first marriage, this shock was news I had scarcely dared even to dream about. To watch a child of my own growing up at Pattercombe, to see that happy path stretching out before us, I melted at the very thought. And at sixty, well, I was clearly functioning pretty well in most respects. I wouldn't care if all the other parents at the school gates thought that I was the kiddy's grandfather doing mum and dad a favour: I'd had a lifetime to anticipate this joy, my pride would be all the more intense. We laughed that we'd have to put the Seychelles project on hold after all, decided that neither of our cars was really suitable for travel *en famille*, and realised that before too long I'd be collecting child benefit and an old age pension at the same time.

As we sat outside the farmhouse, Polly lying on the bench with her head resting in my lap, looking up at the starry night sky, making plans with a smile fixed on her lovely face, I could feel the beat of my heart quicken as though it were fighting to break clean out of my chest and fly free.

PART FOUR

THE RESOLUTION OF
ERIKA FLEET

2015

1

Polly had a scan today. All looks to be fine. Baby's heart pumping like an athlete's. So excited! Love, A x

Erika Fleet read the text for a third time and smiled. Her son was so blissfully happy and she could feel nothing but happiness for him. She would have her first grandchild at last, all being well. Why the caveat? She had never met his wife, or partner to be accurate, but she knew she was closing in on forty, well into the grey zone where nothing can be taken for granted with regard to the health and development of an unborn. Didn't she already have a teenage son with special needs? Andris would be a wreck if anything unpleasant happened. Erika had shunned superstition but she had taken to offering a prayer each night to the bedroom ceiling for the safe delivery of a healthy babe. Her son deserved it, it was time he had some good fortune; he'd always been a fine man, she knew that, a better son than she deserved. She felt more than a little unworthy of him, and the prospect of becoming his child's grandmother gave her a strange sense of diluted, unmerited pride.

She realised that she was starting to cry again.

She closed down the phone and wiped her eyes with a tissue from a box on the kitchen table. This was the second text she had received from Andris in as many weeks. And in between there had been a ten-minute telephone conversation in which he had announced, with an audible lump in his throat, that Polly was expecting.

*

Erika Fleet had stains on her soul that were troubling her now more than ever. The older she got the more pronounced they appeared. She wondered if Andris had truly forgiven her for the years of neglect, the excuses, the lies she had spun him. Once, for pity's sake, she had been skiing in the Alps when she should have been at home in London to welcome back the little boy for a holiday from his prep school. From those days to this he had been a constant in her life; undeniably, she should have shown him more respect. He had ended the second text with *Love* and a single *x* : something trivial, lower case, a throwaway, yet a straw that she wanted desperately to cling to.

Of course she knew where the lying had started, and she should have been ready for it. Her parents had always told her to trust no-one, but that was Riga, under the Russians, under the Germans, under the Russians again, with spies and spivs, tricksters and traitors around every corner. She was taught of the danger of sailing too close to the wind; you could never tell when its direction might change. Her father told her cautionary tales including the story about the lobsters, but she believed he kept so much more from her. Some time around 1942 a supervisor by the name of Sofija Kozlovskis was caught stealing a crate of frozen lobsters from her father's depot. It transpired that this was not the first theft she had committed, and all as a series of gifts to a *Kriminalkommissar* of the Gestapo in an attempt to persuade him to stop short of investigating her husband, who was a suspected communist agitator. She was betrayed by a colleague called Podnieks who had in fact been an accessory to the theft. Erika's father was obliged to dismiss Sofija, and her husband was arrested the following winter and sent to the detention camp at Salaspils to the south of the city, where he later died of malnutrition. At the end of the war Podnieks himself was exposed to the Russians as a Nazi collaborator, which was itself a lie, and he was arrested and shot by a firing squad.

When they were children, Erika and her sister Katarina had always allied themselves each to one of their parents. For the elder it was the mother: the pair would bake, embroider, play the piano together. Both girls learned to play but Katarina was the more gifted and it seemed natural that the mother gave here more attention. There was no envy from the younger sister; instead Erika would gravitate to her lovable old father, listen to his stories, go sailing with him, go swimming, chat about this and that, let him indulge her with little gifts that Katarina knew nothing about. (The girls went to school, to the shops, to the parks, even to the cinema: they could do all those things during the war, during the German occupation. People could do what they liked so long as they obeyed the rules, kept out of politics and were polite to the soldiers; unless they happened to be Jewish, of course.) Much of this happened across the city, not so far from where she was now, but it was all such a long, long time ago. Quickly, instinctively, Erika learned how to play her father, to flatter him, to exploit him. From childish origins she became wily, feisty, seductive, an expert in manipulating men.

Exile, a temporary exile as she hoped it to be, gave her a fresh beginning, a taste of freedom after the constraints of life in Riga. Cambridge was different, the air seemed purer, people spoke to you without fear, and, of course, an Englishman's word was his bond. The Latvian girl learned how to lie in English from Edward Fleet, a professional, and when she was sure he was lying to her, she invented lies of her own for him to swallow. Little Andris, poor lamb, he was born into a cesspool of deceit.

She'd had three good years with Edward, three years of what she thought was pure love: a charmed romance, a brief engagement and the early bloom of marriage in spite of straitened times in Harrow with the father-in-law forever trying to be helpful. Her writing for the group of exiles brought her into contact with Erasmus, a man she had briefly met before, a man so brilliant that she thought his dazzle made him unattainable. She had flings with others in that odd, fretful community: Gustav, for example, the dishy professor and his younger brother Mattias, who ended up working as a postman and who had the most gorgeous pair of thighs. The women in the group, small in number, had become wary of her. She remembered upsetting a cheerless woman from Tallinn called Ester, like her own mother a school teacher, whose teenage son she had seduced at a party. They were both drunk on too much of Ester's cheap Beaujolais wine, but even at the time she did feel a little ashamed of herself. It was a New Year's Eve party and the following day she resolved to be more sensible, more responsible, less selfish. Yet when a former tutor from Cambridge turned up at the house in north London one afternoon, quite unexpectedly, she had invited him into her bedroom before he had time to take off his jacket. He was a tutor who had offered to give her extra English lessons in her early days at Newnham. She wanted to pay him but he adamantly refused at first, only to agree to payment in kind when a month or two had passed. No, it wasn't Mr Arundel; Cooper's love was reserved only for Edward. Before they climbed the stairs together she had gently pushed the sleeping baby in his pram out into the back garden where he could slumber to the songs of the birds. By the time they were sated and finally resurfaced, the sun had gone in and it had started to drizzle. To her shame she found Andris awake and shivering under a sodden blanket.

*

The noise of the lawnmower outside the kitchen window had stopped. Curious and yes, just a little concerned, for Leons was not as strong as he once was (neither of them were), she walked over to the French windows. There he was, the dear man, sitting on the edge of the porch, sweating through his shirt, lighting up a cigarette.

"You alright?" she shouted through the glass.

"Oh, I'm alright," he called back. "Of course I am. Just having a little pause."

"I'll make us some coffee."

Erika had justified her behaviour, her excesses as a young woman, by telling herself at the time that she was snatching what she could, living for the moment, because you never knew when the good times might end. She'd said as much aloud to Edward. Even though she was rapidly become English, she still felt like a stranger in her new country, a tourist, a girl from Riga just passing through. Sometimes in the middle of the night she would be roused from her sleep by two huge men in dark coats who had come to take her to Moscow. *Your parents can wait for you no longer*, they always said to her in an odd, discordant unison. For a while her futile struggle against their strong arms was a recurring nightmare. She would wake up panting, sweating, clinging to Edward for safety and only much later would she fully recover. Nevertheless she retained the uneasy feeling that her good fortune would soon evaporate and that her life in England was itself nothing more than a dream.

Just as her marriage was becoming a drudge, just as her suspicions about Edward were hardening, Erasmus began to show a real interest in her. She was flattered, of course, and in spite of what some people said about him, to her he was never less than a gentleman. He was affectionate, bought her gifts but put her under no pressure; they slept together only when she was ready. They had only a tantalising taste of happiness thanks to the bomb planted by Bendiks. And to find out that the snake was a conspirator with her own husband was the last straw. She willingly spoke to Katarina and to Robin, listened to their concerns, and then less willingly with Mark Castille and the obsequious John Kingfisher. Arundel, to give him his due, was a rock of support in the dreadful aftermath and she was relieved to follow his advice, agree to all his arrangements, and even to embrace the myth of Berlin.

Suddenly sexual gratification had become less important to her than financial security. She met Adrian, had a second family and her life was quite perfect until they began to loathe each other. They had shared two beautiful daughters who wanted for nothing; neither paid her much attention these days. Tiffany and her miserable husband Rhys had sold up their ailing health-food business and had bought a caravan park on Anglesey; even in the winter it seemed to take up all of their time, allowing for a superficial phone call to Riga once every blue moon. She heard even less from Patricia who had always favoured her daddy and just like him had drifted from one woman to the next in search of happiness. She was a barrister too, and the last word was that she and Marlene were looking to buy a house close to Adrian's, in the same desirable village in deepest Gloucestershire. The pair were such fun as girls: Trixie and Tiffy, both bubbly, mischievous, highly intelligent. And in the meantime poor Andris, the little boy lost, pushed around, the tormented teenager cast aside, skulked in the many shadows of her luxury home; how abject she suddenly felt again!

Erika ambled over to the sink and filled a kettle and, having switched it on, waited for the water to boil.

Moments of reflection like this always seemed to make her feel not only sad but also very old. She had arthritic joints, high blood pressure and each morning took a palette of pills to keep her bouncing along. She would have only a few years to make a better impression on a grandchild. At least that was her hope: she longed to be allowed back into her son's life but she knew that she had not yet done enough to earn that right.

The earlier of the texts had come through on the day of his confrontation at Sturcote House. She didn't need to switch her phone back on to remember every word of the curt, definitive message:

Castille denies giving the order. It looks like I have reached a dead end. The case is closed.

Resourceful as ever, Andris had already moved on with his life, and with every good reason.

She reached for a pair of matching mugs and pulled from the back of the counter the coffee jar and a stainless steel cafetière. She ran the fingers of one hand through the soft tufts of her short white hair. Outside Leons was gingerly getting back to his feet.

Her thoughts were returning to Andris' visit to this house less than three weeks ago, when it was Leons who had made him coffee, after supper, and the two of them had sat outside in the rocking chairs on the terrace as the sun set. In her mind she had replayed her son's words to her several times over in the interim: the conversation he had described with Arundel, his anger, his question to her about Castille, and in particular the details of Macduff's redacted report that had somehow come into his line of vision. She had never seen such energy in him before. He had been galvanised that evening, his heart full of ambition, decisively set on finding the truth.

2

A return air ticket to London (expensive at short notice in July), two nights in an unassuming hotel in Earls Court, a round-trip rail ticket to Bournemouth and a twenty-four hour car hire (*economy, VW Polo or similar*), all booked and paid for. All in less than an hour. All from the comfort of a cushioned rocking chair, using a smartphone with a touchscreen the size of a playing card. And then a potted background of the owners of Sturcote House digested, even a detailed aerial survey of the said property viewed and memorised. What a strange and wonderful tool was the worldwide web.

*

It was the hour after lunch, the time of day on a sultry summer afternoon when people of a certain age might want a moment or two off duty, time to take the chance for a short nap, for a light stroll around the gardens to aid digestion, for a spot of mindless daytime television. Morning tasks completed, visitors been and long gone, Thursday's newspaper part-read and folded up for later, it was now the empty hour, dead time, the point when a chap's defences might be down.

The sight of a dusty red Renault heading in the opposite direction, with a round-faced, grey-haired woman gripping the steering wheel, would not have registered to Erika Fleet as being of any significance, but had she recognised the driver as Peggy Lynch, housekeeper and sometime nurse to the subject of her mission, then she might have silently congratulated herself on the timing of her approach.

The turn on to the Sturcote property was exactly as she had visualised it from the bird's-eye photograph: the fork in the lane, left to the house itself, right to the business that had been set up, twelve years ago, she had read, when the stables and adjoining land had been sold off by the Castille family to cover debts. She turned the wheel to pilot the little car to the right, down a short stony road which lead to a wide car park already occupied by half a dozen vehicles. A little further away there were several people about: groups of twos and threes, parents in conversation, impatient daughters holding saddles, stable girls leading ponies into a paddock. Between a pick-up truck and a bulky 4x4 Erika found a space to leave her car, turned off the engine, and pushed open the door with her elbow. The sun, held behind a film of unthreatening cloud, had been turned into a hazy white glow, while its heat, stored up for days, was trapped in the humid air. She picked up a thin pale yellow cardigan, changed her mind and threw it back on to the passenger seat. She locked the car, covered her white hair with a silk headscarf the colour of straw, and with her small leather bag slung over her shoulder she walked back to where a thicket of young trees hid her from view.

It took less than a minute to pick her way through the copse and she soon emerged into the fringes of a short avenue of holly and rhododendron. Peeping through the thick green leaves, she saw for the first time, just as she had imagined it, the exquisitely realised, perfectly proportioned, grey stone manor house.

Some moments before the large door was slowly opened to her, Erika could hear the high-pitched Germanic shouts from behind it:

"Hansel! Hansel! Where has that dog disappeared to?"

Erika rapped again on the knocker and Lady Angela Castille was suddenly standing directly in front of her.

"Yes?" she said dismissively.

"Good afternoon, Lady Angela. My name is Erika Fleet."

The woman looked at her blankly. She was tall in spite of a slight stoop, her grey hair was scraped back into a tight chignon and her complexion, if lined, was rudely healthy. She wore a loose blouse and a grey cotton skirt and carried a round-handled walking stick.

"I'm sorry. I have no idea who you are. What do you want? This is private property, you know."

"I'm surprised the name Fleet rings no bells in this household."

"Fleet? Fleet. Oh, my God, that horrible man who was here, the beast who attacked my husband."

"My son."

"Your son? You should be ashamed of him. Have you come to apologise? My husband has barely recovered. He is a sick man, Mrs Fleet, a man of ninety-three. It was an outrage."

Lady Angela was a deal younger than her husband. She looked to be in her early eighties, around the same age in fact as Erika herself.

"Did you involve the police, Lady Angela?"

"I really don't think that is any of your business. No apology? No? Not a word? Then please leave. If you've come here for no other reason than to gloat, then I might very well phone the police right now."

"That wouldn't be wise," said Erika, and before Lady Angela could interrupt, she went on, "I want to come in. Let me in. I want to talk."

"I'm afraid that really is out of the question," the other woman declared, tapping her stick against the door jamb. "Sir Mark is taking a nap. I will certainly not disturb him on the whim of his assailant's mother."

"No matter," said Erika. "It isn't him I have come to see. It's you."

"Me?"

"Yes. We need to talk."

"No, I'm afraid not, Mrs Fleet. I have no wish to continue this conversation. Good day to you, madam, and do not think to come back and disturb us again."

And at this point she retreated a pace and began to close the door, but Erika was already advancing and she pushed out a steady hand to stop it.

"What are you doing?" Lady Angela barked. "Get your hand off the door, damn you!"

"I'm afraid I cannot."

"Hansel!" she shouted again, "Hansel!", and to Erika:

"Get away from the door, I said! For God's sake, you're not welcome here. Go away!"

"We need to talk about Macduff."

"I beg your pardon?"

"I think you heard me. Macduff. We need to talk about a man called Macduff. A man you knew, Lady Angela. Before you were Lady Angela, when you were..." and here she hardened the g, "just *Angela*, the German girl rescued from the ruins of the eastern zone."

The woman had released her hold on the door and stared at Erika as though she had seen an apparition. On closer inspection it was clear that the glow in her face was the result of many applications of expensive moisturiser. For a moment neither woman spoke.

"You *do* remember Macduff, don't you?" said Erika at last.

"You had better come in," said the other.

They crossed an airy hallway, passing a polished circular table on which stood a large glass vase filled with assorted roses. Apart from the two women, the ground floor of the house seemed empty. Castille was upstairs, she guessed, sleeping. Andris had mentioned another man, a younger factotum, plus a housekeeper, yet Angela had not called out to them when she needed help at the door; for whatever reasons, neither was in evidence this afternoon. All was well.

Without ceremony Lady Angela led her into a drawing room, sparse with decorative furniture yet tastefully appointed. Both large windows were closed and a stuffy scent of pot pourri lingered in the sultry air. Over the marble fireplace hung a large black and white photograph in an ebony frame, a family portrait showing Castille, his wife and presumably his son several years ago in more relaxed times. Although close to an armchair, the woman remained standing, leaning on her stick, and Erika received from her no invitation to sit.

"Say whatever it is you have to say," she commanded, "then leave. I do not wish that my husband sees you."

"As I said," Erika began, "I have no issue with your husband. I want to know what *you* knew about my husband's death."

"I really don't know what you are talking about," she answered with an innocent yet mocking smile.

"October 1960. I'm sure you remember. An agent called Macduff killed Eddie on board a train near Shillingstone and turned up at this house later that night. By the back door, I believe."

The smile melted away but the woman remained aloof, impassive.

"Mark Castille was abroad at the time, wasn't he?"

Still no reaction other than a twisting of the wrist, which made the tip of the walking stick ruffle the tight pile of the carpet.

"Which would make it difficult for Macduff to be answerable to him, wouldn't it?"

Lady Angela's neck stiffened. She drew back her shoulders, and swallowed, wondering if she hadn't perhaps left a glass of water somewhere in this room.

"Macduff was working for you, wasn't he, Angela? Or should that be *Angela*," she asked, hardening the g again. "Which pronunciation do you prefer?"

"It's no secret that I am German by birth, Mrs Fleet. As far as I know, that is not a crime. I have lived in England for over sixty years and nobody has arrested me for that."

Now that she was speaking, Erika let her ramble.

"You still hear the slight trace of an accent, do you? A hint of the old Prussia? Our son now lives in Frankfurt," she said, glancing at the portrait. "He is a banker. Yes, he is wealthy. When I met his father I had nothing. You know what it is to have nothing, Mrs Fleet?"

"I too was an immigrant," said Erika, "I escaped from Latvia as the Russians bedded in. I knew difficult times."

"Then we have something in common, you and I," she said, lifting her stick a few inches off the carpet in the direction of the visitor. Erika allowed the silence that fell between them to encourage the woman to reminisce.

"After the war we Germans in the east also found the Russians on our doorstep, taking revenge on our men, destroying our cities. The lucky ones like me escaped. Like you, I imagine. In my case from Magdeburg. I was lucky because our city was close to the British zone. There was a good road to Hanover, at least in the days before the Russians locked everything down. My mother sent me along that road, just like yours did, yes? That road to freedom. She wanted to wait for my father, we hadn't seen him since '42, the winter when his division was sent to fight on the eastern front. She waited for him in vain, of course: he never came back. On my first day in Hanover I met Mark. He was working for the army, intelligence, administration. He took me under his wing, we fell in love..."

The woman's voice tailed off. Erika needed to pick up the pace.

"You knew that MI5 recruited your husband, didn't you?" she asked. "Didn't you, Angela?"

"Yes. Yes, I did. That was much later."

"And when would that be exactly?"

"I don't remember dates, Mrs Fleet."

"But you were aware he had become a spy-catcher?"

"There was no reason not to tell me. We were married by then, I think. We were very close, Mark and I. Always have been. He could trust me, for Heaven's sake."

"But you spied on him, didn't you?"

The woman looked shocked.

"You have a vivid imagination, Mrs Fleet."

But it was not Erika Fleet's imagination at work here, rather her powers of deduction.

Two days ago Katarina was surprised that her sister had made a transatlantic phone call to Florida specifically to speak to her husband, a man she had always shown little time for and even less warmth. Robin, meanwhile, albeit distracted from a barbecue, was happy to chat a little, indeed gratified to be in demand, more than willing to give a brief insight into the marriage of his former boss at the Home Office:

Whenever I met him, socially you understand, Lady Angela was always at his side. And I mean always.

Yes, I would say she was well informed.

Yes, she had proper, intelligent opinions on the issues of the day. She was rather more than a plus one, if you know what I mean, Erika.

His equal? Intellectually? Yes, I would say that she probably was. At least that was my impression.

Thank you, Robin. Most helpful.

The trace of smugness on Lady Angela's face vanishes as Erika suddenly produces from her handbag a heavy-looking, old-fashioned revolver and points it directly at her face.

"What on earth?"

"Sit down!" orders Erika, advancing on the other woman, who, although taller and more robust, topples into the armchair behind her when her stick is kicked away and she is pushed violently in the chest. She clutches her ribs and, now breathing arduously, stares up at her attacker in disbelief.

"Hansel! Hansel!"

"I don't think the dog can hear you."

Erika's own face is flushed, her hands trembling, still aiming the gun at the German.

"I want to hear what you know about Eddie. All of it. Start talking."

"You are a fool," she splutters. "There are cameras all over this house. You cannot get away with this. Put that thing down, I am begging you."

She is bluffing, Erika thinks. She noticed none on the façade of the building, no little black spy boxes, nothing allowed to detract from the architect's original vision.

"Sit down," Angela goes on, catching her breath, regaining a little composure. "Put the gun down, please. I will tell you what I know."

"I prefer to stand," insists Erika. "So, let me first tell you what I know. I have seen a report. An operational report filed by Macduff."

"I don't believe you."

"Sturcote House is mentioned by name."

"I don't believe you."

"And so are you, Lady Angela. So are you. By name."

Two can bluff, Erika Fleet is thinking, unevenly. She feels she may be on firm ground but she cannot be sure. Andris had told her the report in the form he had seen was redacted. Of course it would be. Arundel may still have a little influence in his dotage but he was no longer a magician. But the redactions themselves were interesting: *names, key objects, even pronouns were blacked out.* Pronouns? Why hide a *his* or a *him* if it wasn't to disguise a *her*? What could be concealed in place of a *he* if it wasn't a *she*?

"So, tell me. Tell me the truth."

The woman, suddenly looking her age, appears cornered like a scared rat, helpless in her own comfortable home.

"I was valuable to MI6 in the 1960s," she suddenly says, wistfully.

"MI6?"

"Yes. Six. They recruited me here. After we were married. They knew I'd escaped from the east, the Russian zone. They trained me in secret, when Mark was away, when Toby was in prep school."

She has paused. Erika gestures for more with the gun, for it has already become, in spite of its weight, an extension of her right hand.

"Mark never knew. I answered only to one man. It was as if I were a secret among secrets. Even Arundel had no idea."

Tell me more, Erika said with her eyes.

"I worked extremely seldom."

She stops, eyes moving shiftily across the room, calculating the odds.

"Don't stop," says Erika; she wants this to be over quickly.

"I ran a small team of agents in East Germany for Six for about four or five years. It was the least I could do, for what England had done for me."

"So why did you have Eddie murdered?"

"Fleet was a Russian spy, for God's sake," she sighs.

Erika has been determined to stay strong today, not to melt in the heat, but Fleet is her husband, her lover, her greatest friend and he is gone; Fleet won't ever be coming back. She sees him at twenty with a pint of beer in his hand, smiling, winking at her across the snug. In spite of herself, she can feel the heavy tears ready to fall from her eyes. She takes a deep, shuddery breath and claws at the woman again:

"That's not a reason to have him executed, not in this country."

"It was reason enough, as far as I was concerned. He was betraying the west to those evil bastards in Moscow. Mark would have played it by the book, I know. He never had the balls to make a positive statement."

"So you knew about the case."

"Only superficially, at first."

"You knew there was a doubt about whether or not he was a double agent?"

"Most were convinced."

Erika is crying now, almost invisibly; her cheeks are wet, but her eyes have hardened.

"You were working for the same fucking agency!"

"As I said, in many ways I was an independent, a loner."

"So you spied on your husband."

"And on Kingfisher, his deputy, who assumed operational control."

226

"And you employed Macduff?"

"Yes. He was a man I had met before. I offered him a generous reward."

"How did you know Primrose Smith?"

"Mark's records."

"Of course. And so you went to speak to her?"

"I went to meet her in Bournemouth, yes. To tell her her boyfriend was a KGB agent and to persuade her to play our game."

"You mean *your* game."

"She was a sweet girl."

"You told her about Macduff?"

"Of course not. She was still at the station in Bournemouth that night when the train arrived, several hours late, I remember, especially to meet him. I thought that was very touching."

"So you used her?"

"Of course. Don't be so naive, Mrs Fleet. You knew what kind of world your husband lived in."

The revolver is heavy and her wrist has drooped under its weight. She wipes her nose and cheeks roughly with her free arm.

"Now leave," says Lady Angela, reasserting herself and shuffling to the edge of her seat.

"Don't move!" says Erika, lifting up the gun to point it once again at the other woman's head. This time she doesn't flinch, but calmly raises both open palms to show cooperation.

"I won't. But *you* must. You must go, Mrs Fleet. You have your information but will tell no-one. No-one will believe you in any case, I think."

"Tell no-one?"

"It would be pointless. I would deny everything, of course. This will remain between us, you understand? I will say you

227

never came here. I will say I was threatened at gunpoint, that I made up a story to placate you."

"Then what am I to do with this?" Erika asks, pulling out her smartphone from her left-hand trouser pocket and holding it up in the space between them: "My voice recorder?"

Lady Angela, eyes burning towards the device, then back at Erika, finds the strength in her ageing limbs to spring forwards off the chair in a vain attempt to grab at the phone. In the same instant Erika steps back, drops the phone, picks up a small cushion resting on the corner of the sofa and covers the end of the gun barrel with it before pulling the trigger and sending a scattering of tiny feathers into the air. She knows the whip of the recoil will feel like she has broken her wrist, she knows the Webley has a loud, cracking retort (she has already fired a practice shot), and as the bang echoes through the shell of the house, she watches as the other woman grabs at a fat red stain filling the centre of her blouse. She is falling back into the armchair, a look of horror on her face, a shriek of pain forced from her throat.

"*Was haben Sie getan?*" she exhales in no more than a raw, breathy croak.

Quickly Erika moves closer to the woman, covers her face with the remains of the cushion as if to smother her, and fires a second shot through it in an area she guesses is somewhere between her eyes.

"Bitch!"

A fistful of blood and down and hair splatters hard against the back of the chair and Lady Angela's body falls limp. Erika steps back. She is shaking, sweating, the warm gun is hanging in her fingers, there are flecks of blood on her forearms and a faint smoky sourness in the air.

Gunshots in the countryside are not uncommon, especially in the summer months. She has to hope that anyone who has heard the double crack will not imagine anything more sinister than a stricken brace of pheasants. Upstairs Castille will be awoken but in his state is unlikely to be capable of finding his wife for at least five minutes. She places the weapon back in her bag, her phone back in her pocket, and without a second glance at the gory mess she has left behind, turns to leave the room.

As she walks briskly through the hallway she stops for a moment to examine the roses. The best two specimens are a delicate pink and a deep, rich red, both heavy buds on the cusp of bursting open. Edward was never what you might call a delicate man. She chooses the crimson one, plucks it roughly from the display and continues to the door with it dangling in her hand, dripping its water on to the stone floor.

The front lawn and driveway are deserted. She ties her scarf over her head with a loose knot under the chin, looks under the portico, then up to the corners of the building for evidence of security cameras, decides there are none and, breathing heavily, bursts into a trot to quickly rediscover the rhododendron bushes. Just as she is about to disappear into the copse she notices that the dead dog's hind legs are still partly protruding from underneath the leafy hedge. She stoops to move the animal further out of sight. She hadn't planned to shoot the creature but in a way it had been a fortuitous meeting: for her at least, not for the trusting, inquisitive, shiny black lurcher patrolling his mistress' grounds. The bullet in the dog's skull had shocked her: not so much the impact as the sound that the old gun made when discharging its fateful load, masking the yowl of the beast and provoking the instant flapping, squawking flight of dozens of blackbirds from the nearby trees.

The trick is now to rejoin her car and make as if she has been a visitor to the riding school. She is a grandmother booking in her granddaughter for a course of lessons in the autumn term. She has paid a huge deposit on her credit card. She has been shown around the yard and met Pippa, one of the full-time trainers. She has even patted the nose of a lovely grey pony called Prince who is often frisky first thing in the morning. In her head she has done all these things and now she is on her way home. In the middle of the car park a young woman in dungarees is chatting to a man wearing jodhpurs who is holding a greyhound on a short lead. Erika has to pass them to reach her car and they both look up to smile at her as she approaches, but she chooses to avoid eye contact, and, mumbling to herself, plays the part of the dappy old duck with her mind elsewhere. Which, truth to tell, it very much is.

She flings her bag heavily on the passenger seat, then the rose, tries to get comfortable, takes a deep breath and turns on the ignition. She can feel her tee-shirt sticking coldly to her damp back. Her wrist is aching and there are pains in her neck and shoulders from the tension. At her temples too. The car is stuffy; she lowers the window for some air. She steers the vehicle over the gravel and as she is driving slowly along the short, twisty lane taking her back to the road, she is forced to stop to avoid a cyclist swinging recklessly around the corner, breathing frantically, pedalling hard up the narrow drive towards the house. She does not know the man, of course, a young athletic man in black lycra, his blond hair visible in short tufts beneath a ribbed helmet. By his hairy arms alone, however, her son Andris would certainly recognise him, returning to base after a thirty-minute spin around the lanes: the table tennis player, the Scrabble partner, the agency man from New South Wales, the moodily laconic Roland.

3

Leons Lapsa had a formal, tortuous way of responding to a telephone call. He had heard it before, but in spite of a familiarity with the texture and tones of the Latvian language, very few of the words were actually understood by the monolingual Andris Fleet.

"Leons, it's me, Andris."

"Andris! Hello, Andris. How are you?"

"Fine, thanks. And you?"

"Oh, you know. I am surprise to hear you, Andris. I am watching the sports on the television. We have new TV with very large screen. Your mother has told you this? It is fantastic picture. Fantastic for sports."

"What's on? Hockey, I suppose."

"Andris! We are still summer! It is athletics meeting. Athletics from Stockholm, Sweden."

"Well, I'm sorry to disturb you. As you might guess, it is my mother I really want to speak to. I called her mobile but it must be switched off."

"Your mother is not here, Andris. She does not tell you?"

"What do you mean, Leons?"

"Erika is in England. Just a little visit, I think so."

"A little visit? For how long? Where is she? London?"

"Yes, London. London, I think so. She is in England for the burial, yes? Is that the word? Or the funeral?"

"Funeral, yes. Whose funeral?"

"She says it is friend she knows at Cambridge. Old friend, you see, from university days, I expect. Judith? Is that her name?

"Judith?"

Andris imagined the old man fingering his little white beard, an expression of confusion on his face.

"Maybe. Judith? I have forgotten. I am sorry. It is a woman she knows, friend from long time ago."

"So, she is going back to Riga, when? Tomorrow?"

"Yes. Yes, tomorrow. Tomorrow morning. I am to meet her at the airport, of course. I have written the time somewhere."

"So she isn't planning on coming to Dorset?"

"Dorset?"

"You remember, Leons; where I live."

"No, no. She has no time to go there. She is in London for two days: funeral, maybe shopping, then fly home. Back to Riga. Tomorrow morning. Are you alright, Andris? You sound anxious, yes?"

"No, it's fine. I'll call again, maybe at the weekend. It's not so important."

"And by the way, Andris, congratulations on the news."

"The news?"

"Of course, the news! You will be father! It is wonderful news. Erika is delighted, you can imagine. Her first grand-child! Finally! She has waited very long time, Andris. Good for you!"

"Thanks, Leons. Yes, of course. We are both very happy, Polly and I."

"Polly. Of course. I am forgetting her name. Give her our love, yes?"

"I will. And thank you. Please tell my mother I rang."

"Of course."

232

"And get back to your television."

"Yes. Yes, I get back. Goodbye, Andris."

"Goodbye, Leons. Take care."

*

Andris Fleet switched off his phone and breathed a sigh of relief. The moment he had seen the story on the regional news he had panicked. A gunman had shot and killed Lady Angela Castille, the reporter had announced in sombre tones, the wife of retired civil servant Sir Mark Castille who was also in the family home, asleep at the time of the attack. The body was discovered by an employee so far unnamed but described as Sir Mark's personal assistant, who had been detained for questioning. It was understood that the family's pet lurcher was also shot dead. The grounds of the manor house, Sturcote in North Dorset, had been secured, as had been the premises of a neighbouring equestrian business. Dorset police were appealing for witnesses and at this early stage detectives were keeping all their options open.

So they have no idea where to start, thought Andris. They are kicking around in the dark.

Even though it looked like rain, he had left Polly and the others after dinner for a walk through the paddock and up beyond the top field. He needed to stretch his legs, to clear his head from a fog of thoughts. Would the police call *him* in? Would Sir Mark suspect a second attack from the madman of a fortnight ago? Andris could not yet grasp why the wife had been the victim and not the husband, but then his blinkered view of what happened fifty-five years ago allowed only one scenario to flash up. Who knew what *she* had got to hide, what enemies *she* might have made over the years?

It was not until he reached the trees that he finally made a link between the woman and his father's murder. There was a chance, however unlikely, that Castille had been telling him the truth after all. He remembered the old man's confident manner, the adopted tone of a man who was on firm ground even if his memory was playing tricks on him. And the look on his face as he realised that a sort of bungled vengeance was on its way; a look of disbelief, of injustice that a thoroughly wrong conclusion had been drawn. He *was* in Africa, wasn't he? He *was* in Africa after all. In which case his wife could, Andris supposed, if she were capable, have acted in his place, and to more brutal effect. He didn't know enough about her to be sure of anything, but suddenly the pedantic redactions in Macduff's report made sense. *She* for *he*? And suddenly Erika appeared at the forefront of his mind. She knew about the report. She knew everything he knew, and maybe more. Almost certainly more. But where on earth would she have got hold of a firearm? He had to ring, just to be sure, just to hear her voice at the end of a telephone hundreds of miles away from the scene of the crime.

What a coincidence that she was in England. But a funeral in London was not a murder in Dorset, and there would be plenty of witnesses at the service, no doubt, who could verify her presence.

Andris opened up his phone again, rubbing his cheeks: he hadn't shaved today. He would try his mother's mobile one more time. No, what was the point? Leons had put his mind at rest and there was nothing more to be done. It was up to the police to solve a crime that was actually no concern of his at all. His focus had to shift, and rightly so, to helping more about the farm, to looking after his precious Polly, and to preparing for what in February next year would, all fingers crossed, be the happiest day of his life.

4

Just as her son and her husband were ending their telephone conversation, the one in the shade of the oaks in Pattercombe Wood, the other bathed in the glow of an outsized television screen in a chalet-style house in Mezaparks, an exhausted Erika Fleet was being helped down from the carriage of her train on to a busy platform at London Waterloo. She thanked the young black man who had taken her hand, watched as he strode off with his backpack and melted into the stream of passengers heading single-mindedly towards the exit, and allowed herself a smile. It had been a challenge to a woman of her age but she felt satisfied that she had accomplished her mission. One more night and she would be on her way home.

In comparison with the incidents of the previous twenty-four hours, the journey from Bournemouth had been uneventful, a lull which had afforded her time to relive in her mind's eye images of the immediate past. Haphazard yet vivid, they all re-formed, with the exception, already erased as far as possible, of the sight of the inert old woman in the splintered, bloodied armchair with her chest and face burst open.

*

The overweight man in a business suit was listening to something on his headphones with his eyes shut, tapping a knee with his fingers, keeping up the rhythm to a private mystery song. The train was not full, but for some reason he had chosen to sit next to her, only to put his briefcase on the rack above her and then ignore her. He had spent twenty minutes on a laptop computer reading e-mails and adjusting figures on a spreadsheet. Erika had taken sly glances at the screen: he was a technician in the solar energy industry. A young man in a uniform pushed a trolley along the aisle, and was interrupted to serve tea and snacks to impatient passengers who never had the right change. Erika was neither thirsty nor hungry; she was simply tired and felt grubby.

Growing weary of staring at her own reflection in the carriage window, she closed her eyes and began to scroll through the show. She saw instead a woman in a headscarf the colour of straw kneeling in the early evening shadows of a secluded corner of a cemetery in Highgate, scratching out a hole in a puzzle of tree roots with a brand new hand trowel. It is tiring work and she looks round nervously every few seconds, anxious not to be noticed. And when she finally finds what she is looking for, and wipes away the claggy earth from a flaking bundle of half-perished plastic, she stuffs it into a supermarket bag and sets about repairing the deep burrow she has made, refilling the soil and stones, stamping it down, covering the ground with a few twigs and a handful of fallen leaves.

She sees the same woman in a hotel bedroom an hour later, removing the damp outer shell of sticky plastic debris, then carefully unwrapping layers and layers of intact waterproof tape, still sound after half a century, until she is holding a greased revolver and a small sealed case of six bullets.

The same gun reappears in the next frame of Erika Fleet's video memory. Now the woman is standing on a long, narrow road bridge just a couple of miles from the spot where the weapon has been fired. It is the middle of the afternoon, the sun has never cleared the haze today but over to the east the cloud has thinned and a ghostly moon is already rising above the distant treetops. She looks up to watch a pack of surlier clouds crawling slowly across the sky directly over her head. The woman is waiting for her moment, her headscarf flapping lightly in the breeze, waiting for the passing traffic, thin though it is, to clear completely. A car, a filthy tractor, then a cyclist. Then, when her moment arrives, when no sound beyond the twittering birds reaches her ears, she aims the gun at the darkest, deepest point in the river below and flings it away, ten, twenty yards, out into the swirling brown water where it tears the surface with a splash and swiftly sinks to the silt below. And then, before she moves away from the bridge, she rummages in her bag for her reading glasses, takes out her phone, selects voice-recorder, and in a matter of seconds deletes all conversations from its memory.

Suddenly the woman is standing on the platform of a deserted railway station. She is clever enough to have chosen a day when the place is closed to visitors. She has crossed a boy on a bike as she followed the trailway to the station, but it appears she has the platform to herself. Erika Fleet sees the woman stepping into a small garden at the far side of the station buildings, watches her as she stands before a stone plinth, and, with the trembling fingertips of her outstretched right hand, touches as she reads the words inscribed on a burnished metal plaque. Then, after a full minute of reflection, she places a single blood-red rose at the base of the stone and seems to bow her head. But Erika does not see, at the woman's back, a mile or two away, high on the tussocky furrows of the whaleback hill, brushing lightly on the wind-whipped grasses, what she cannot see are the spirits of centuries long past, invisible witnesses to the familiar ritual of a grieving woman respecting the tomb of her fallen man.

A later frame casts her in near darkness. The woman is closed in a dank room, its old brick walls painted but flaking, the sound is of a dripping tap, the smell is of drains and of bleach. The toilet door on the platform is unlocked, she takes the chance to rinse her hands and arms of another woman's dried blood.

As Erika crosses the old redundant railway tracks to rejoin the trailway, it begins to rain: a light, warm drizzle. She is not alarmed, in fact she feels refreshed by the soft, wet touch on her face. She has no great distance to walk to her car, parked where the footpath crosses the road. She is walking slowly, feeling old, very old, picking her way unsteadily across the rough gravel in the fading light.

Her car can wait. She needs more time to calm her nerves. Before the image fades, Erika watches herself shuffle onwards to find a spot beneath a heavy brick railway arch, sheltered from the rain, out of the wind, where, in an act that could be mistaken for bravado, she lights a slim cigar, takes a deep, satisfying pull and gently blows a slow, soft plume of smoke up towards the curved, crusted ceiling above her head.

AUTHOR'S NOTE

The beautifully renovated station on the northern edge of the village of Shillingstone does, of course, exist, as do many of the locations featured in the story, but the characters are all fictitious, as are the events described in their imaginary lives.

I had driven through the village a hundred times before I found myself for the first time at the station after a meandering walk by the Stour one quiet Sunday morning. Before long I had become immersed in steam train-related nostalgia, and left with the flickers of an idea for the story. Many dramas must have played out there in the station's heyday and I needed to come up with just one on which to hang a fiction.

I wish to thank all those at the station who helped me with my research and in particular Derek Lester-Jones, who not only authenticated my vision of the Somerset & Dorset railway in the year 1960 but also broadened it.

I thank also my wife Heather for her encouragement and patience as I became more and more absorbed by the writing. And especially Warren Shore for his expert eye as an editor, his advice and his sense of humour. Thanks too are due to Chella Adgopul at Honeybee Books who skilfully led me along the twisty lanes of self-publishing.

As a tourist destination the county of Dorset has its fair share of attractions. I hope that this novel will encourage more and more visitors to discover and rediscover what is truly a most underrated place: accessible both by road and by trailway between Sturminster Newton and Blandford Forum (but sadly not yet by rail), the Shillingstone Railway Project offers history, romance and a spark to ignite anyone's imagination.

Brent Shore
July 2015

ABOUT THE AUTHOR

Brent Shore grew up in Hyde, a small town on the eastern edges of Manchester. He studied Modern Languages at the University of Nottingham, where he also trained as a teacher. His career took him firstly to North Yorkshire, then to Bermuda, and finally to the middle of Dorset where he has lived since 1991.

Since retiring from the classroom, he now channels much of his energy into writing fiction. *Shillingstone Station* is his first novel to be published.

Visit: www.brentshore.co.uk
Contact: stories@brentshore.co.uk